A MOUNTAIN OF EVIDENCE

A

MOUNTAIN

OF

EVIDENCE

AMY O. LEWIS

ARROW ROAD
PRESS

This is a work of fiction. Names, characters, organizations, places, events, and incidents are either products of the author's imagination or are used fictitiously.

Copyright © 2021 Amy O. Lewis

Published by Arrow Road Press, Denver, CO

Edited and designed by Girl Friday Productions
www.girlfridayproductions.com

Cover design: Emily Weigel
Project management: Alexander Rigby
Editorial: Tiffany Taing
Image credits: cover © Shutterstock/ArnaudS2;
Shutterstock/Stefan Haider

ISBN (paperback): 978-1-7372977-0-3
ISBN (ebook): 978-1-7372977-1-0

PROLOGUE

It was the last ordinary moment.

It hadn't occurred to her she would notice—or care—when the last ordinary moment spun itself out of the dark web that had led to today. Now that she had noticed, she did care.

She swiveled in her chair for a final view from her seventeenth-floor office window. A labyrinth of gray and black buildings cascaded toward the barely visible Lake Michigan in the distance. The sky was overcast, hardly surprising. The Chicago sun hadn't shone for a week.

She tucked the image of the cityscape away, wherever such things went. It would be there if she wanted it. None of these were thoughts she ought to be having. She was supposed to be focusing on an open spreadsheet cell on the laptop in front of her. It was yet to be filled in, but it never would be, not by her. Instead, the cursor was a metronome ticking off a finite series of rapidly dwindling beats.

She glanced at the door, still closed, and reached for a notepad and her phone. Using time she wasn't sure she had, she jotted down two numbers. One belonged to her therapist, whom she hadn't spoken to in months, the other to a Department of

Justice field agent. The DOJ guy wasn't listed by name. Anyone looking, and, of course, no one would look, would find his number attached to the name Julia, her sister-in-law.

She slipped the note with the numbers in a pocket a fraction of a moment before a knock sounded at the door.

The latch clicked. Light and air shifted as Betsy, her assistant, breezed in. "You're going to be late," Betsy announced in a summary, bossy tone.

By then, the woman's attention was where it was meant to be, riveted to the laptop. She looked up as though pulled there from a distant place. "What?"

"Your doctor's appointment. Are you going to keep it?"

The appointment was for an annual exam. Scheduled months ago, it was completely unnecessary, as she was twenty-nine, healthy, and in no need of medical advice or prescriptions.

"What? Yes. I don't know. The report isn't finished," she said in a voice edging toward panic. She glanced at the computer, stricken by the fear that she had already played it wrong. Betsy knew her as well as anyone did. Her assistant would hear any false note.

"Oh, come on. You know how hard those appointments are to get. If you cancel now, it will take six months to reschedule."

She did know. Which was why the appointment had emerged as the fulcrum of her plan. Everything revolved around it. Except for a case of raw nerves, the pieces were falling into place exactly as she had choreographed them. She pushed away from the desk, reaching, as she did so, for her purse in the bottom drawer.

Betsy watched, untroubled. Her wavy hair was bound in a clasp, her expression frank and unassuming. She didn't seem to think anything was out of the ordinary, and that was all that mattered.

"Speaking of appointments," Betsy said, "do you want me to call Diane and see if she can squeeze you in? You're two weeks overdue for a trim as it is."

The woman's hand shot to the offending strands dangling near her eyes. "No! I mean, yes, I do want a trim. Not this week. I have too much going on."

She should have answered yes. What difference did it make? "Yes" would have been the right answer.

She shuttered her mind against overthinking every single word that came out of her mouth. One more mistake and Betsy would know something was wrong. "How the hell can someone lose a trainload of coal?" the woman said, standing at her desk, pretending to be stuck on the spreadsheet.

Betsy lost patience. "I don't know. I'll call Carl again. If he hasn't found the shipment, we'll have to write it off. It'll show up eventually. You know that. When it does, we'll book the sale. I told you, I'll finish the report. You can review it when you get back."

"What time is it anyway?" She glanced at her watch and shrieked, gratifying the woman who had been trying to goad her into leaving for five minutes. "Call me," she said. "Call with any problems."

"Of course I'll call. It's what I do," Betsy said, arms crossed and a satisfied smile on her face.

Passing by her assistant, she thought to say something. Something simple, like: *Whatever happens, don't worry about me.* She owed Betsy that much. Obviously she couldn't say a word.

Beyond her office, the floor buzzed with the sound of low voices behind cubicle walls, her staff busy at work. Twenty junior- and senior-level accountants plus support personnel, all members of the Materials Management Accounting group, of which she was head, went about their daily routine while she blithely passed, palming her phone, striding toward the bank of elevators. At the end of the corridor, two colleagues stood huddled in a mini-conference, heads bent over a report. One man looked up and smiled as she approached. She smiled tightly in reply.

It was the moment she couldn't predict. Whether she would make it the length of the corridor, into an elevator. Or her boss, knowing what he couldn't possibly know—or so she promised herself—would intercept her, stopping her.

The elevators were in sight. She walked faster, heels clicking on the marble floor. A soft ping signaled the arrival of an elevator. The door whooshed open and a junior associate held it. "Going down?" he said. She nodded. "Early lunch?" he asked when they were inside.

"Doctor's appointment," she said, then added, "One I don't have time for." She studied a nonexistent message on her phone.

At ground level, she crossed the lobby. Flanked by a stream of people dressed impeccably in tailored suits and wool coats, she kept her eyes on the revolving door until she was through it, met on the other side by the brutal slap of a cold wind. Quickening her pace, she opened the back door of the first cab in line in the circular drive. She gave her doctor's address.

"Are you a baseball fan?" the middle-aged white driver asked, easing into the flow of traffic.

"What?"

A sports talk show was playing on the radio. Barely three weeks into the season and already two Cubs' starting pitchers were sidelined with injuries. "My father is," she said, lying through her teeth. Her father was dead. "I sometimes watch games with him."

Doing what she had promised herself not to do, she turned to look out the rear window. All she could see of the downtown skyscrapers were their massive shapes and the street lying in their shadows. No vehicle pulled out behind them. It was a small thing, possibly irrelevant.

At her destination, she paid the fare and strode toward the building. Halfway there, she raised her phone and peered at a blank screen, keenly aware of invisible eyes on her. Cameras were everywhere. There was no avoiding them. The best she could hope for was misdirection. Feigning distress, she called her gynecologist's office and, for the second-to-last time, gave her real name. "I'm sorry. Something urgent has come up. I won't be in for my appointment," she said. She listened to a barrage of complaints, and ended by saying, "I understand perfectly. I'll reschedule soon." Call terminated, she powered off the phone.

She tightened her coat around her shoulders and walked to the Lexus dealership two streets over where she had left her car that morning, pretending, to anyone who was watching, that it was in for service. She got in and drove away.

On the far side of town, she pulled into a Bank of America branch office. She didn't think she had been followed. Possibly Stephen no longer needed to have her tailed. Not if he had planted a tracking device on her car. Or in her cell phone. Or in some other place she would never imagine looking. It didn't matter about the cell phone. It wasn't going with her. As for any other tracking device, if it was there, they would find her. And kill her.

Inside, she requested access to her safe-deposit box. For several tense minutes, she paced with straightened shoulders. Finally a woman at a nearby desk ended a call and walked over. For the last time, she gave her real name. She signed for access and was escorted into the vault. "Do you need the privacy room?" the woman said.

"Yes. Briefly." She took the box from its slot.

In the sanctity of the adjacent windowless room, she raised the gunmetal-gray lid and stared at the two brown envelopes inside. They contained cash, a bit over $10,000.

You don't have to do this, a voice inside her head whispered.

It wasn't an argument she ought to be having.

Yes, I do, a stronger voice answered, knowing the truth.

Aware she was wasting time, she removed the envelopes. She opened her purse, took out her wallet, cell phone, and a large white envelope, which contained what she once had counted as her most valuable possessions—her birth certificate and passport. Also inside were her car title and a letter from her mother, plus several pieces of jewelry, also from her mother. She ticked each item off a mental list as she dropped it in the box.

It was harder to part with the cell phone. She held it for a moment, aching for a reason to keep it. There was none. It was a direct link to her should she ever use it. And if she never meant to use it—

She dropped the phone in the box.

Only two items remained, both easy to part with. One was a thumb drive, the other was a sheaf of computer printouts. Both were gifts from a dead man. She didn't expect either to prove the least bit useful. In truth, she didn't expect to lay hands on any of the items in the box ever again.

With the envelopes holding the cash safely stowed inside her purse, only one task remained. She left the privacy room. Outside, she stood before the door to the vault, waiting to return the box to its slot.

The woman who had let her in and promised to wait was nowhere to be seen. Standing there, stamping one foot, then the other, she felt the beginning of a scream in the back of her throat. Her hands were shaking. In another moment, her mask would shatter and she would show herself for who she was: a madwoman.

Finally, she saw the bank woman, who emerged from a back office and called sweetly, "I'll be right there."

"This box is rather heavy," she called back. "I've been waiting several minutes as it is," she added with authority when she saw another employee—a man dressed in a suit—emerge from the same back office. Either the appearance of the suit or the imperiousness of her voice convinced the woman to do her job.

Two minutes later, it was finished. She exited through thick plate-glass doors into a crisp April day, free, in a manner. Whatever the word had meant to her once, it would never mean the same thing again.

Driving, she joined the slow parade of traffic moving toward the interstate. If ever there had been a time for thinking, it wasn't now. That would come later. Assuming there was a later. Her eyes darted to the rearview mirror.

She forced herself to look ahead, past the gritty, end-of-winter hangover clinging to Chicago. She was about to trade that for California sunshine. Los Angeles, she thought. Or San Diego.

She accelerated onto the ramp leading to the interstate. Her breath caught in sudden fear at the clear proof of her intent.

Michael Leeds was dead. There was no changing that. Eventually they would blame her for his murder, and for other crimes not yet discovered. She hadn't killed him, but she might as well have. She hadn't done a single thing to save him.

CHAPTER 1

The first flakes of snow found her in the mountains of Colorado. They fell from a patchwork of gray clouds, dusting her windshield in a mosaic print until they were swept away by the swish of wiper blades. Slush had accumulated in spots along the edge of the road. The ground itself was clear except for white-tipped tall grass swaying in the breeze. Traffic was light—rather, nonexistent. She was on a two-lane road winding through an empty landscape, the last town so far behind her she couldn't remember its name, and the last city, well, that was easy. It was Colorado Springs.

That's where the trouble began.

She might have been a few ticks over the speed limit when a police car appeared out of nowhere on the interstate and sat on her bumper. She moved over one lane. The cop did the same. Though cars around her were going faster, the cop stuck with her. Her heart was beating much too fast when she set her turn signal for the next exit and moved into the off-ramp lane. The cop sped past. Coming off the exit, she found herself on a broad boulevard offering no shortage of places to turn around, and yet—she didn't turn around. Instead, she drove west. She drove west because she liked the road, because there were no cops, and because she felt safe.

Four hours later, no one needed to tell her she had made a terrible decision.

The road continued on, dropping into valleys and climbing onto plateaus. Pastureland, if it was even that, lay all around. She might have thought it pretty under other circumstances, but not today, not with periodic snow squalls turning the world blindingly white and making the pavement difficult to see.

A curve appeared in the distance. Rounding it, she descended a long, steep hill into fog. She was most of the way down when she glimpsed red lights flashing ahead. If she could have turned around, she would have.

A sign for a town called Cimarron emerged out of the swirling fog. It wasn't much of a town, not that she could see. Only a few buildings along the roadside.

A cop stood in the middle of the road emphatically raising and lowering his hands as she approached. Beyond him, she saw a pickup truck tilted on its side in a ditch. The cop threw up one hand, signaling for her to stop. She did. He walked over.

"Where're you headed, ma'am?" he said through her lowered window.

Mistrusting her voice, she shook her head and looked over her shoulder at the skeleton of a town called Cimarron. She didn't doubt for an instant he had registered her Illinois license plate. "The next town, I guess," she said, hating herself for sounding uncertain.

"Montrose. Good call. Roads are getting slick, as you can see." He waved at the truck. He tapped twice on the base of the open window. "Take care and drive safely."

She nodded and raised the window. She pressed the accelerator lightly, feeling the cop's eyes on her as she rounded the sharp curve that had bedeviled the truck's driver. It was a steep climb out of the valley. She gripped the steering wheel, grateful for tires that held traction. She was well past the summit before her heart returned to its normal steady beat.

Twenty minutes later, she passed a sign telling her she had reached Montrose city limits. She passed two motels lit with "No Vacancy" signs. At the third, she pulled in and cut the engine.

"Kim Jackson," she said to herself, dispelling the hush of silence.

The name meant nothing to her. Saying it out loud hadn't yet served to make it real. "Get used to it," she said as she pushed open the car door. It was her name now.

In the office, she paid cash for one night and took her bag to the second-floor room. Inside, she turned on lights and pulled the curtains tight. She resisted the temptation to throw off the bedcovers and lie down, settling instead for a padded chair. Weariness for having spent the past seven hours behind the wheel washed over her and, with it, the prickly pins-and-needles anxiety that was with her nearly all the time now. In the three days since she had left Chicago, nearly everything that could have gone wrong had gone wrong. Except for the main thing. She hadn't been found.

This time yesterday, in a dusty, blow-away motel on the western edge of Kansas, she had nearly botched her escape. In a room more decrepit than this one, she had sat on the edge of a bed, one hand on the telephone, the other holding a slip of paper with two phone numbers. She didn't know who she meant to call: her therapist or the DOJ field agent. Her mind was spinning fast, too fast. She should have known what that meant. She should have known she needed to do something to yank herself back from that particular abyss, but she didn't know anything, not until hours later when she surfaced from an altered state. A blackout, damn it. Call it what it was. She had lost four hours with no idea what she had done in the interim.

Except she had done something. She had left the room. Empty food cartons littered the scarred faux-wood table.

It wasn't until this morning that she knew for certain she hadn't called anyone. No additional phone charges appeared on her room bill. It was a relief. What wasn't: sometime between checking in and checking out, she had lost the slip of paper with the phone numbers.

Agitated by the memory, more by the fact that it was the middle of the afternoon and she had nothing to do, she stood up, parted the curtain, and looked out on a gravel-studded parking lot and adjacent restaurant. The bare branches of a tree obscured the sign for the business next door. Otherwise, all she could distinguish on the horizon was a thin gray line of asphalt and cars moving on the road. The snow had stopped. Rotten luck. She should have kept driving. She could have put another hundred miles between her and Chicago.

She dropped the curtain. A new argument kicked off in her head: Should she burn the money spent on this room and drive on? Why not? Her car had good tires. It was the middle of April. How much more snow was likely to fall?

Without a smartphone and access to the internet, there was no easy way to tell. She checked the road map of the western United States she relied on to get her from one interstate highway to another—or had, until a few hours ago. It was sixty-five miles north to the highway in Grand Junction, not a problem, except she didn't want to go there. It was much farther to get to any major highway to the south, hundreds of extra miles, too many to add up with a cursory glance. *Nice job,* she told herself, not meaning it. She had driven straight into the heart of nowhere.

She walked over to the sink and turned on the tap. She knew she was on the verge of making a truly bad decision, and it wasn't about the money. Needing to hold herself still, she cupped her hands beneath the faucet and splashed cold water on her face. Over and over, the water ran from her forehead to her chin, trickling onto her wrists and down her arms, drenching her sleeves.

Shirt soaked, she turned off the tap and reached for a towel. With a cloth pressed to her skin, she searched her reflection, aching to see a glimpse of the woman she had recently been: accounting director at a Fortune 500 company. Adept at juggling schedule, staff, and accounts worth millions. The glass showed her someone who needed a haircut. Damp, dark strands fell in front of her eyes. She pushed her fingers through the ends, chasing them to where they belonged but wouldn't stay. It was going to take months, perhaps a year, before her hair grew long enough to change her appearance.

Her face was small, heart-shaped, with fine features distinguished by a long, thin nose. Without it, she might have looked like anyone else. Not *anyone else*. Like any woman with short, dark hair and an attractive if not exceptionally pretty face.

Her eyes were her strongest feature, though not for a good reason. Dark circles intensified their smoky-blue, haunted look. She laughed. It occurred to her she didn't know who she was looking at. Kim Jackson, she supposed. A new woman emerging into the body another woman had inhabited for twenty-nine years.

For an instant, she wondered whether she could feel one soul departing while another arrived.

Then she thought it better not to tempt the madness.

Moving decisively, she changed her shirt. She put on a jacket and left the suffocating confines of the room. She needed supplies, food and gas for tomorrow, at least. She got back in her car and drove a mile to the center of town. Idling at an intersection, she turned right when the light changed and drove a few miles without finding anything more interesting than farm shops and a county airport. On the return trip, she topped off the gas tank and saw signs for a grocery store and city park. She drove a few blocks off the main road in search of the latter, in no hurry to return indoors.

She found the park without difficulty. There were two ball fields and a youth soccer field at the far end of the parking lot. She left her car and set off walking in the opposite direction. Before she had taken a dozen steps, she stopped. In the distance, a massive ridge of jagged spires soared toward the sky. Seeing the mountains, she didn't know how she could have missed them before now. The longer she stared, the more convinced she became that the rocky cathedral descended from clouds rather than sprang from the earth.

"The San Juans," a voice announced, coming from somewhere much too close.

She jumped. "I'm sorry," she said automatically to the man who was suddenly beside her.

"What you're looking at," he said. He was an older man. Grizzled white showed at his chin and beneath his cap. A beagle tugged impatiently at the end of a leash. "Those are the San Juan Mountains. Thirty-five miles from here. Incredible town there. Ouray. Ever been?"

She shook her head.

"I didn't think so." He nodded sagely. "You should go. What you'll see there, it'll blow your mind."

Feeling more comfortable, she smiled. "I expect I'll be driving through." Vaguely she recalled that Montrose served as a dead end. She could drive north or south out of town but not west. North, she had decided, was not an option.

"Not any time in the next few days, you won't," he said. To her questioning eyes, he flicked a gaze westward. "There's a storm moving in. The pass will be closed. All of the passes." He read her confusion for what it was and added, "Red Mountain Pass, that's the one out of Ouray. Come down off of it and you get Molas Pass, then Coal Bank Pass. If we get all the snow that's predicted, it may take three, four, days before roads are clear."

She didn't believe a word. Roads closed for days? She nearly laughed. "Then I suppose I might as well make myself comfortable here. Or save the sights for another trip and drive—north," she sputtered, memory failing on the name of any town to the north.

"That would be Delta," the man supplied. "Or Grand Junction. Depends on where you're going."

He didn't seem to expect an answer, so she gave none. Returning his attention to his dog, he nodded goodbye and walked on.

She finished her walk in the solitude she craved, pausing every few minutes to gaze at the distant mountains. They seemed something out of a storybook, a backdrop to castles and kingdoms that wars might be fought for. Their otherworldliness lifted her spirits.

But the skies were darkening. She left the park and hurried on to the grocery store. A tinkling overhead bell announced her entrance, followed immediately by a man bellowing, "Emily! Is that you?"

Alarmed beyond measure, she stopped. She hadn't moved when a man's head appeared over a low door five feet away. He grunted. "Sorry. My girl. She's late. Thought you were her." He withdrew into his office.

Apples and cheese, she thought, reminding herself why she had come in.

She chose an aisle and walked down it, peripherally registering the store's grungy feel. The floor was scuffed. Shelving and food cases were dated. Overhead fluorescent lights were functional, but, as with nearly everything else about the place, they were unattractive. The produce section was small, though the quality looked surprisingly good, as did the selection of poultry and meat. She suspected the store was privately owned, and that the owner was the sharp-tongued man who had mistaken her for his girl Emily.

She found what she wanted. At the checkout, she took her place in line. Emily, apparently, was supposed to be working the second cash register. A teenage girl, harried and slow, did her best to move customers along. The backup of four grew to six, then seven.

Finally, Kim reached the front. Minutes earlier, the gruff-voiced owner had taken over the second cash register, causing an audible sigh of relief to go up among the patrons. Kim offered a sympathetic smile when she handed a ten-dollar bill to the girl. "Rough afternoon?" she said.

"You wouldn't believe it. I'm going to kill her."

"Who? Emily?"

The girl's eyes shot up. "You know her?"

"No. I heard your boss complaining she was late."

The girl handed over the change and the bag of groceries. "She could have called."

On a stand near the exit, Kim found a rack of brochures and tourist information. She tucked several complimentary flyers into her grocery bag. She noticed a local paper and thought to buy a copy, but the checkout lines were still long. She returned to her car and her motel room, satisfied to go inside.

Snow began falling again before nightfall. Storm reports from the Weather Channel kept her entertained through the evening. Long before she turned off the TV, she knew she wasn't going anywhere in the morning. Relieved from the need to decide anything, she slept soundly.

—

Montrose, Colorado, population seventeen thousand, with double that number calling the surrounding area home, had experienced rapid growth over the past fifteen years. In the early decades of the new millennium, the town was still struggling to find a balance between continued growth and preserving an old and familiar way of life. As she paged through back copies of the local newspaper at the library the next morning, Kim discovered the pastoral setting immediately bordering the town was anything but. The area's farmland was for sale. With land vastly more valuable than its by-products would ever be, a generation of family farmers was selling out and effectively driving to outer space the price of rich farmland. Everyone, it seemed, wanted a tiny spot of the Uncompahgre Valley to call their own.

"Un-com-*pah*-gre." She practiced rolling the syllables over her tongue.

She read four stories detailing much the same message. Finally it registered. The reporters recounted the town's evolution as if it were nothing more than an expected change of season. Which left her wondering whether it was really happening so painlessly.

Not that she cared. It wasn't her town.

Eight inches of snow had fallen overnight. More was predicted for later in the day. Kim had awoken to a winter wonderland purely delightful except for the fact that she wasn't properly outfitted for the conditions. By stepping carefully in imprints made by others, she had avoided getting her feet soaked. Her black jeans were satisfactory, but her sweatshirt, worn over an oxford dress shirt, barely kept out the chill. She had packed poorly; that much had been brought home to her in three days.

In her apartment in Chicago, with its polished wood floors and gleaming stainless-steel appliances, a winter parka and other jackets in a variety of weights and lengths hung in a closet, surrounded by blouses and slacks, sweaters, and a hamper full of shirts, socks, and underwear awaiting laundry. She had left the apartment untouched. She hadn't wanted anyone entering to be able to decipher, by appearance alone, the reason for its occupant's disappearance. She had packed enough to get by, assuming, incorrectly, that she would want lightweight things.

It was the explanation for the wardrobe she didn't possess. What she couldn't explain were the four business suits, dry-cleaned and encased in zippered plastic bags, carefully folded and stowed in the trunk of her car.

She wanted to believe she would wear them again one day. But, really? Wasn't that a pipe dream?

She stood up to return the newspaper to the rack.

The library was preternaturally quiet today. Kim suspected the deserted atmosphere had something to do with the weather. Earlier this morning, too restless to stay in her motel room, she had come to the library to pass the time. So far, she had read the *Wall Street Journal*, the *Denver Post*, and three recent editions of the *Montrose Daily Press*. Ready for something different, she found a paperback in a cart.

"Those are giveaways," a dark-haired librarian said, finding her standing there. "Feel free to take one home. Bring it back, or bring another in its place. Or don't," she said, smiling whimsically.

The smile was contagious. "Thank you," Kim said.

"Just passing through, or are you visiting in the area?" the librarian said.

"Passing through," Kim replied, not even wondering what gave her away. "Although staying until roads open to the south. I didn't expect this storm."

"No one did. It blew up from the Gulf of California and headed due north without missing a beat. Course a springtime storm around here isn't unusual. By the way, my name's Lois Hays. Welcome to Montrose."

"Kim Jackson," Kim said, clasping the woman's outstretched hand. Sudden searing at the back of her throat sent a flush to her face. To date, she had written her new name on three banal motel registration cards. This marked the first time she had used the name to introduce herself to another person.

Summoned by a ringing phone, Lois turned away. "Well, enjoy your stay. And please, help yourself to the books."

Kim returned to where she had been sitting and sank into an orange-cushioned chair. Staring into a shadowy space where gray carpet met the base of a metal bookshelf, she felt something slipping inside. It ought to have been a warning, but she didn't react until a distant noise startled her. She moved to a different chair, one near a window flooded with light. Gazing outward, her vision was filled with flashes of a past she was loath to call her own.

Kim Jackson. The only Kim Jackson she had ever known, or more accurately *known of*, was dead. She died seventeen years ago at the age of fourteen after suffering massive head trauma in an accident. Their mothers had been friends and colleagues in the Economics Department at the University of Chicago. After her own mother's death six years ago, Kim began visiting Muriel Jackson, the original Kim's mother. It was a way for them to share memories of a woman they both had loved.

More than a year ago, Kim had stopped by one day to find Muriel rummaging through insurance papers and medical bills, trying to understand a bill for a recent hospital stay. The charge indicated on the stub was enormous. Muriel had been frantic with worry at what she might have to pay. "Please, can you help me?" she had pleaded.

Kim had followed Muriel to a tall file cabinet containing the entire history of her health care, including insurance claims filed and bills paid. She chanced upon one folder simply labeled: "Kim." Curiosity piqued, she opened it and discovered a death certificate. The folder also held school report cards and a child's drawings. In a separate envelope, she spied two other documents, a birth certificate and a social security card, for which the deceased Kim Jackson would never have use.

That day, secure in her own life and identity, never dreaming the day would come when she would think of the envelope again, she had replaced the papers and hurried on to the relevant insurance files. One year later, she had remembered the pair of documents, and a plan had taken shape around them. To her shame, and with a fervent prayer that Muriel would never discover their absence, Kim had stolen the birth certificate and social security card with the thought of using them to create a new identity.

"Kim. Excuse me, Kim."

She glanced up. The dark-haired librarian stood a few paces away.

"I'm sorry, Kim. I hate to disturb you. But this weather is beginning to take a turn for the worse. I wondered whether you might want to get back to wherever you're staying before the roads get slick."

She glanced out the window into cloud-covered skies. Thickly falling flakes obscured the view. She had no idea how long she had been sitting there. "Yes, thank you. I should go."

If Lois Hays thought to speak again, she didn't. She merely smiled as Kim eased past her, book in hand.

The book proved to be a godsend. Back at the motel, through the remainder of the stormy day, she read. Late that night, she turned the last page. Ignoring her grumbling stomach, she turned off the bedside lamp and went to sleep.

—

Kim awoke the next day to a world turned a fresh shade of white. Resigned to keeping the motel room for yet another night, she paid on her way to breakfast at the restaurant next door. Awaiting her meal, she read about the storm's impact in the morning paper. The mountains to the south had been hammered by heavy snow. Roads remained closed and would likely stay so for the next two days. Reading this, she remembered the gentleman at the park and his prediction.

Near the bottom on the front page, she read a disturbingly brief article. "Local Girl Missing," the headline announced. Emily Riley, an eighteen-year-old senior at Montrose High School, had been reported missing by her mother.

Emily. Kim remembered the absent checkout clerk at the grocery store and wondered if it was the same girl.

She finished her breakfast in a somber mood. When she left the restaurant, she went back to her motel room, picked up her car keys, and drove into town. On Main Street, mounds of snow backed up by plows occupied fixed intervals along the roadside. She found a parking spot, then went for a walk in the crisp air, glad the ground remained frozen. Her feet would stay dry, even if they were cold.

She had much to think about.

When she left Chicago, she had had a plan. Move to Southern California, either Los Angeles or San Diego, she hadn't decided. Cities meant anonymity. California cities did, anyway. She didn't expect her new life to be happy. Since she hadn't left a happy life behind, she hadn't imagined this would be anything she would miss.

She had envisioned renting a shabby apartment in an ugly tenement building. Her new job, in all likelihood, would be menial. A few days ago, living in Chicago, all she had dreamed of was living somewhere she felt safe. Now, it seemed, she wanted more.

Forty minutes later, thoroughly chilled, and with damp feet despite her best effort to keep them dry, she went to a coffee shop. Over a cup of coffee and a pastry fresh from the oven, she considered her situation. She had made a clean break. Stephen Bender, her former boss, did not know where she was. If he did, she would already be dead.

But he was searching for her. She knew that too.

She couldn't predict how he—or, more likely, his agent— might find her. Stephen had a job to do. He couldn't leave his prestigious position as subsidiary director for Blackwell Industries to go on a protracted hunt for a wayward employee— not even one who knew of his crimes. Stephen would send someone. The man in the pale-blue Ford, she thought. The man who had shadowed her for the past month, ever since every brick in her world had shattered.

How would he find her?

The question hung in the air.

She went back to what she knew. She had the documents needed to acquire a new identity. She had enough money to live on for a while. How long would depend on where she chose to live and how quickly she found a job. At that thought, she glanced out the steamed windows of the coffee shop and knew that the cost of living in Montrose, Colorado, had to be inordinately less than in any California city.

She wanted to stay here. Since waking this morning, the feeling had stuck with her. Her strongest objection, initially, was that the decision flew in the face of her plan, which was a joke. Staying safe mattered. Where she lived didn't. Her parents were dead. The reminder rose out of a tangle of emotion, nothing she needed to be thinking about now, yet there it was. She had one brother who would miss her as little as she would miss him. Or, to put it bluntly, not at all. Her last serious relationship had ended more than a year ago. She had no close friends. What she had—or *had* had—was her job. She might have laughed at how well that had worked out, except it wasn't funny.

She forced thoughts of the past aside.

Her car was a problem. The Lexus was registered in her real name, the sole link to her past. It mattered, but it was too large of a problem to worry about now. More pressing was her need to get a driver's license. It might prove to be tricky, but it was doable. She needed to pass a state driving test. She had Kim Jackson's original birth certificate, social security card, and a photo ID from a Chicago community college where she had enrolled in Kim's name solely to acquire the ID. She had become her. Until the IRS sent a representative to inquire how a girl dead seventeen years suddenly became a tax-paying wage earner, she didn't think her false identity was likely to be discovered.

She finished her coffee. Outside, she walked to the grocery store where she had shopped two days ago, possibly down one employee. She forced herself past the grim reminder of a high school girl gone missing. "Emily Riley spoke to friends of her desire to leave Montrose," the article had said, planting the suggestion that the young woman had left town of her own accord.

Kim Jackson intended to inquire whether the grocery store owner currently had any job openings. If the missing Emily had worked at his store, he might be looking to replace her. Kim planned to try and get that job. At least until Emily Riley returned and took it back.

CHAPTER 2

Kim paused before reading the chapter's final words aloud: "'No, Sam, return to the kitchen: I am not in the least afraid.' Nor was I; but I was a good deal interested and excited."

When she finished, Kim looked over to see a contented expression on the face of the elderly woman sitting upright in the chair near the window. With snow-white hair and eyes as blue as the day's brilliant sky, a permanent smile seemed etched upon Christine Gregory's face. "That's it. The end of chapter eighteen. We're halfway through the novel," Kim said, slipping the worn copy of *Jane Eyre* in her jacket pocket.

"Are you off to softball practice today?" the woman said.

"Yes. Don't be alarmed if I have a black eye the next time you see me. My fielding skills aren't what they used to be."

Christine's smile grew full. "I had quite a throwing arm when I was young. My targets were the rampant bunnies breaching the garden chicken wire and destroying our badly needed crops."

"You never pelted any directly, I hope."

"Of course not. My aim was true."

After leaving Christine, Kim hurried down the corridor, worried she would be late for practice. Near the main entrance, she saw three women huddled close together, talking excitedly. She slowed as she drew near. "What's going on?" she asked Justine, the receptionist. The other two were nursing aides. Kim had met all three women when she'd begun volunteering at Pine Village Convalescent Home weeks ago.

"Emily Riley's body was found this afternoon. She was murdered," Justine said.

"Oh!"

"I knew it. Since the day she went missing, I knew she was dead," Justine said.

Weeks had passed since the eighteen-year-old had been the focus of local conversation. With no updates about her, the consensus grew that she had left home on her own, probably on the arm of a new boyfriend.

"How? Where?" Kim said.

"No word on that yet."

With an air of self-importance, Justine repeated what she had heard from her husband: that a body had been found, it was almost definitely Emily Riley, and she almost definitely had been murdered. Kim nodded, shocked by the news, while at the same time thinking that the information was a far cry from the summary conclusion first reported. "I have to get going," she said. "I can't believe this."

Justine nodded grimly. "Oh, Helene's coming in. She called a little while ago to ask if you were here. I think she wants to talk to you."

"I have softball practice. I'm going to be late as it is," Kim said, backing away from the trio of women. "Tell Helene I'll see her next time."

Conflicting emotions gripped her as she left the building. Waves of shock rolled over her. Emily Riley was dead.

Murdered. Perhaps had been dead since the first moment anyone noticed she was missing. Outside, she hurried to unlock her bicycle. She threaded the plastic-encased chain through the spokes and stowed it inside the canvas bag clipped to the rear rack. She pedaled away quickly. Her rush to leave seemed pathetic in light of the news of Emily's death. But she did not want to see Helene Strickland.

A week ago, Helene, a part-time office assistant at Pine Village, had done Kim an enormous favor. She drove her to the local office of the Colorado Department of Motor Vehicles and allowed her to use her car to take the state driver's test. Helene had an unassuming and naïve manner that made her an easy mark for the string of lies Kim needed to tell to get what she wanted: a car and someone to drive her to the testing office. Helene hadn't questioned her story of having lived previously in a large city where she had relied on public transportation. She hadn't asked how or when Kim had learned to drive. She hadn't inquired about what had brought her to Montrose or even how she had arrived in town. All she knew was that Kim rode a bicycle to the nursing home where she had been volunteering for several weeks.

Kim passed the test. Unbeknownst to her, she left the DMV office indebted to a stranger to whom she had become a fast friend. Since then, Helene, unhappily married and the terrified mother of two teens, had turned to her as a newfound confidante. Kim avoided her whenever possible.

Softball practice hadn't started when she reached the ball field. Lois Hays, the Montrose town librarian and team captain, stood at the center of a circle of women near the dugout. When Kim approached, Jackie, a teammate, stepped aside and whispered to her, "Emily Riley's body was found this afternoon."

"I heard."

"I'm telling you, I just heard," Lois said to the group. "I was on the phone with Daniel the second before I drove over here.

The story is some tourist found her body off of Red Mountain. The idiot, I think he's British, was climbing down from the overlook and caught a glimpse of her below. Hell of a place to dump a body. It's a wonder the guy didn't trip and fall to his death too."

"Who's Daniel?" Kim asked Jackie.

"Her kid brother. He's a detective."

The circle around Lois swelled with new arrivals, then broke apart as one woman after another heard the news for the first time or added bits of information to the pot. Kim hung on the edge of the group, listening to voices that had become familiar in the short time she had lived in Montrose. Playing softball hadn't been on her list of priorities when she decided to stay in the town. Nor had volunteering at a nursing home. She had underestimated how hard it would be to fill the hours when she wasn't working, a need that had ultimately led her to Pine Village and, separately, to accept Lois Hays's repeated invitation to join the team.

The latter hadn't come without complications. At Pine Village, the staff was happy enough to see her come and go. Not so, her softball teammates. It wasn't enough for them that she had played softball in high school and brought rusty, if improving, skills to the game. To her horror, they wanted to get to know her. They asked seemingly innocuous questions, like: What brought you to Montrose? What kind of work do you do? Where does your family live? She had stumbled in the beginning. She hadn't prepared a past history to share, and, of course, there was no possibility of lifting bits and pieces of her real life to the surface. She couldn't begin to explain why a former high-level corporate accountant would choose to work as a checkout clerk in a grocery store. Unexpectedly, her reticence became its own answer. Whispers circulated among her teammates. Someone decided she had left an abusive relationship. She heard the theory from a woman who assured her she was better off without the bastard. Kim was happy enough to let the explanation stand. In its own way, it was close enough to the truth.

Lois called for the group to start warming up. After that, it was business as usual for the next hour as women rotated through drills and took batting practice. When practice ended, several announced they were going to the Den, a popular locals' bar. Kim declined the invitation to join them.

"Everything okay?" Lois asked as she hefted a canvas bag loaded with gear onto a shoulder and started walking toward her truck.

Kim fell in step alongside her. "Yes. Aside from the day's startling news."

"I hear you. Emily's murder is going to be hard on a lot of people in this town. Locals don't generally make a habit of getting themselves killed."

Kim managed a small laugh. "Where is Red Mountain?"

Lois pointed at the mountains visible through the new growth of trees at the edge of the ball field. "South, thirty-five miles. It rises above the town of Ouray."

Kim followed her gaze to the rocky formation she still thought of as a cathedral descending from the sky. "The San Juans," she said, remembering the first time she had stood in this park, and the white-haired gentleman who had spoken to her. She hadn't seen him since.

"That's right. You sure you don't feel like going to the Den?" Lois said, looking at her more closely. "I'm only planning to stay for one beer myself."

Kim managed not to squirm under the gaze of the one woman who had been looking closely at her for weeks. She thought about going home to an empty house and the room she was now renting month to month. Then she thought about a dead teenager whose job she had taken. Suddenly she wanted to be anywhere except alone.

"On second thought, I think I will."

CHAPTER 3

With his stocky build and dark hair showing signs of going gray, John Trimble was a man well past his youth. But it was his square jaw and plain, black-framed glasses that cemented his look as an old-timey shopkeeper. Which left Kim all the more surprised to hear John shout, "Christ, Mickey, it's all the same effing day to me. How the hell am I supposed to remember one blasted day from another?" A Janis Joplin quote was the last thing she expected to hear from her curmudgeonly boss.

Montrose Police Officer Mickey Burke spoke placidly. "All I'm asking is for you to try and remember. The last time you saw Emily."

Kim slouched against the checkout counter, momentarily idle. The conversation going on behind John's closed door was audible without any clandestine effort on her part to listen in. John's "office" was a five-by-seven cubicle, enclosed on all sides, open above the door. In it, he had stuffed a desk and swivel chair; shelves were built above the desk, and a row of grimy file cabinets lined the wall behind. It was all he could do to lever himself into the space and close the door. Kim couldn't begin to picture two men inside.

After a pregnant pause, John said, "All right. I know from the paper the date Emily disappeared. April twenty-first. I know she missed her shift somewhere right around then. Probably the same day." The sound of shuffling papers interrupted his speech, punctuated by a dull thud, as though he'd struck a page with one thick finger. "Right. She was supposed to work the twenty-first. Which means the last time I saw her, though understand I'm not going to swear to it 'cause I sure as hell can't remember, would have been the twentieth. The day before."

A middle-aged woman began unloading groceries onto the belt. Kim smiled at one of her regulars.

Mickey Burke sounded tense. "Then try this one on. Can you tell me exactly where you last saw Emily?"

"Hell, yeah, that's easy. It was here in the store. The only place I ever saw her. Talk to Ashley, Mick. She's the one who knew Emily best."

"Thought I might do that," came the reply. Kim wondered whether she imagined hearing sarcasm in the even-tempered policeman's voice. "Is she working today?"

The door flew open and John's face appeared in the space. "Ashley working today?" he yelled.

"At two o'clock," Kim replied.

"She'll be here at two," John repeated.

"Listen, John, we've got a bad situation," the officer continued. "You saw Emily most every day, maybe more often than anyone else in town. You've got to think about this. At the end, the last couple times you saw her, did she seem worried or something, different in any way?"

"Nah. I told you. Nothing different except for the one day she didn't show."

Kim rang up her customer. Mornings were typically slow, and this one was no different. Her customer no sooner had left than Kim sensed movement inside the office. The door opened and Mickey Burke emerged.

"Morning, Kim. How's it going?"

"Fine, Mickey. How are you?"

He rolled his eyes. Handsome now, still in his twenties, Mickey didn't have the sort of good looks destined to last. She guessed his long jawline would grow slack with age, and if he didn't take pains to stay fit, his trim build would balloon into a bulkier body. He had been in the store enough times over the last few weeks for her to feel comfortable in his presence. She had never suspected his apparently casual visits were tied to Emily's disappearance. He said, "Frustrated, that's how I am. Long as I'm here, mind if I ask you a couple of questions?"

She glanced at the aisles to see if any customers were about to bear down on her. "You're not going to get me in trouble, are you?"

"No chance of that. Did you know Emily Riley?"

"I never met her. I didn't start here until after she went missing."

"I thought that was right." Even Mickey seemed to feel he was grasping at straws when he said, "Since you've been working here, ever notice anything strange, out of the ordinary? Anyone asking about Emily?"

"No. Ashley Crane talked about her a lot, especially in the beginning. She hasn't said much lately."

The morning paper had reported that Emily Riley's naked body was found two hundred feet below an overlook off of Red Mountain Pass. Speculation was that she had been there since her disappearance. Between the recent melt-off and the foolish exploits of a British tourist who had nearly tumbled over the rocky cliff, her body was spotted. A further search was being undertaken in the area for clothing and other forensic evidence.

The police officer had few additional questions. When two customers came into her lane, Mickey left, saying, "I'll be back later to talk to Ashley. If you happen to think of anything, let me know."

Kim nodded and went to work.

She had been employed at the store since her first week in Montrose. Getting the job had proved easy, despite not having credentials. In the interview, John Trimble had been wary of her lack of experience handling cash and processing credit cards. Ultimately he was swayed by her maturity and air of confidence. In the short time she had been at the store, her schedule had grown from twelve hours to twenty-five. Little as she liked working here, and however much she chafed at the lowly position, she had sworn to make the best of it.

"All right, enough dillydallying, Kim Jackson. Are you here to ring up my groceries or shall I do it myself?"

Kim, caught daydreaming, smiled at one of the few customers who knew her name. She reached for the first item on the conveyor belt. "Hello, Dottie. I can't imagine how I missed seeing you come in."

The retired high school principal would have been hard to miss under any circumstances, even if she were a stranger. With her alabaster-white skin and white hair, she appeared almost wholly lacking in skin pigmentation, though she was not albino. The white hair was attributable to age. Kim pegged Dottie Goddard somewhere in her seventies. Her black-framed eyeglasses contrasted sharply against both her skin and hair color. Her shirt, bright turquoise, was an explosion of color. The last time Kim had seen Dottie, she was wearing hot pink.

"I've bought a mess of swordfish, as you can see for yourself. Woke up this morning and thought, the hell with mercury poisoning, I want swordfish."

Kim smiled as she ran the butcher's packet across the scanner.

"Why haven't you been back to see me? Did I scare you off?"

Kim's smile broadened. "Just got busy. Besides, I—" She started to make an excuse. "I just didn't get back."

"Good girl. Tell me the truth, that's all I ask."

While Kim turned her attention to bagging groceries, Dottie said, "What I want to know is have you started on that thing you and I talked about last time? Oh shoot, I can tell by looking that you haven't. Maybe you will now."

Kim smiled uncomfortably. "They've found Emily's body. Surely the police will discover who killed her."

"Maybe. And maybe not. My money's on the maybe not. So I take it your interest in investigative work was a passing fancy? I didn't think so at the time."

"It was a book signing, Dottie. It was wonderful entertainment for one evening."

Two weeks ago, Kim had wandered into the adult education wing of the local community center seeking information about classes and activities. While there, she had met Dottie, a volunteer at the center, and learned of an upcoming book signing by a professor of criminology from a nearby college, which she attended a few days later. The man's words had swept her away from that harshly lit room, away from the town where she had made a new home. They took her into a realm where truth, however deeply buried, was chiseled out of its hiding place by persons possessed of the skills and perseverance not to give up on their search. The professor gave her, for just one night, hope. She didn't know how long she had sat in her chair afterward, lost in thought. Long enough to pique Dottie's interest. Long enough to have the straight-shooting woman pose an absurd proposition: You're interested in solving crimes? Why don't you figure out what happened to the girl?

"Hell, Kim Jackson, it's just a thought," Dottie Goddard had said that day.

Kim added the final item to the bag. "I'm out of my depth," she said, not sure how many questions she was answering.

"Huh," Dottie grunted. "Ask me, it's the local police who are out of their depth. Listen, Kim, screw that. Just say you'll come and talk to me sometime. These idiots I have to deal with, the ones who only want bridge tournaments and bus tours to casinos, they make me crazy. I curl up and die inside if I don't get real conversation now and then." Dottie took her change and headed for the exit.

"I will," Kim called to her back.

"Is she gone?" a woman said softly, pushing a cart into the lane.

Kim turned. "Who—Dottie?"

The woman nodded. "I had her in school when she was still teaching. I'm friends with her daughter. I don't know if it's because I never did finish reading *Bleak House* or if it's because I'm friends with her daughter, but Dottie always wants to read me the riot act on something. Do you know how long a book *Bleak House* is?"

Kim smiled.

"Her nickname is Dottie God, did you know?"

Kim laughed. "Who gave her that?"

"I think she did."

By midafternoon, Kim was counting the hours until quitting time. At exactly one minute to two, Ashley Crane arrived. The slender brunette picked up her cash drawer, then took an extra five minutes before opening her lane. Kim wondered why she was at work at all. Surely the discovery of the murdered body of her best friend would justify her absence.

"Saint John gave me yesterday off," Ashley muttered when she and Kim had a chance to talk. "He said I can have the day of her funeral off. And that's it."

"When is Emily's funeral?"

"Who knows? I stopped by Deena's house last night just 'cause I thought I should. But, of course, she was a total wreck, blubberin' and everything as if she really cared Emily was dead."

"Deena?"

"Emily's mother."

Their conversation was interrupted by the need to get back to work. Fifteen minutes later, Officer Burke came in. The policeman spoke to the store owner briefly before escorting Ashley outside for questioning. They were only gone a few minutes. Kim didn't have a chance to talk to her coworker for the next hour. She wouldn't have bothered then, except the teen looked like she was ready to explode.

"What did Mickey say to you?" Kim said during the first momentary lull.

"The police in this town are so stupid! He asked the same questions I've been asked a million times already." Ashley huffed in annoyance. "He wanted to know if I saw Emily the day she disappeared. Okay, that's fair. I didn't. Last time I saw her was the day before, when we finished here. She wanted to get something to eat. I had to go straight home and study. I had a history test coming up. If I failed the test, I failed the class. If I failed the class, I was not going to graduate. End of story." Ashley frowned, as if suddenly aware of the last time she'd seen Emily. Kim wondered whether it pained her to know she had refused the last thing Emily had asked.

Kim read too much into the silence. In the next instant, Ashley resumed her tirade. "So Mickey wants to know about Emily's boyfriend. Excuse me, *boyfriends*. It's like everyone knows she broke up with Mike way back and she'd been dating different guys ever since. Like that has anything to do with why she got herself killed. I can't believe it."

Ashley continued her litany of high school grievances until a customer came into her lane. Kim didn't get another chance to talk to her. Just before she was getting ready to leave, she noticed Ashley gesticulating wildly to a teenage boy standing outside the store.

"I told him not to come here," Ashley complained about the young man, her boyfriend. Tears streaked her face. "I knew I'd start bawling if I saw him."

"Take a break," Kim said. "Go talk to him. Things are quiet here."

Ashley declined the offer. Then, a second later, she put a "Closed" sign on her register. "Maybe I'll do that."

Kim waited ten minutes after Ashley returned before she closed her lane and took the money drawer to the office.

John squinted at her and the clock. "You were supposed to be outta here twenty minutes ago."

"A tiny stampede at the end," she lied.

"I'm clocking you out at five anyway. Your call you wanted to stay, not mine."

CHAPTER 4

The neighborhood northeast of JT's grocery store was an unpretentious mix of small- to medium-size homes, most of wood-frame construction, some brick. Trees lined the streets, providing much-needed shade, especially in the late afternoon under a strong Colorado sun. It was a family neighborhood. Walking the streets to and from work, Kim heard mothers calling to children and kids shouting to each other. She saw older men and women tending flower beds and lawns. To her surprise, she noticed more than a few handsomely refurbished homes with upscale cars parked out front. There were enough BMWs and Land Rovers in the neighborhood to allow her Lexus to blend in. But of all car makes and models, one brand, in particular, stood out as the most popular vehicle in Montrose, and that was a Subaru.

Which partly explained her failure to notice the dark-blue Outback parked at her house, which wasn't precisely her house, when she walked up to the front door and let herself in. Sounds of jazz blared from the rear of the house. An unmistakable aroma of Italian tomato sauce wafted from the kitchen.

"Hello," she called out as she closed the door with a loud bang.

"Hey, I'm in the kitchen. I've made enough to feed an army. You haven't eaten yet, have you?" Andrea, her roommate, said.

"No. What are you making?" Kim's voice came out much too loudly. Andrea chose that moment to lower the volume of the music.

"Spaghetti. Wine's open." Andrea pointed at a liter of red on the counter. A telltale line halfway down the bottle marked the volume remaining. By the faint slurring of her housemate's words, Kim assumed Andrea had imbibed a fair amount already.

"Thanks. Give me a minute."

Kim went to her bedroom to change clothes. Ordinarily she took a shower the second she walked in the house after work, eager to wash off the day's accumulation of grit and something less tangible—her feeling of repugnance for her job. Tonight she settled for scrubbing her face and running a comb through her hair. She needed a haircut. People were always telling her that, often adding they knew a stylist who would do a nice job for her, but that wasn't going to happen. The strands weren't long enough to tie back and were too short to stay put behind her ears. A headband did the trick, but she hated its look more than its feel—as if she were a teenager still waiting to grow up.

A clattering sound from the kitchen reminded her she wasn't alone in the house. She didn't know Andrea well, nor did she feel the slightest interest in getting to know her. Andrea spent few nights here. Her job as a park ranger frequently kept her away from the house she was renting. Still, it was her house. Kim didn't quibble with her luck in having found a room in it.

But luck hadn't led her to Andrea Sampson.

Lois Hays had.

Already, it seemed a lifetime ago that Kim visited the Montrose library on a near-daily basis, spending every spare moment, of which she had many, in the building's hushed interior. From the beginning, Lois had emerged as a solid presence in her life. The librarian quickly learned Kim's preferences in fiction, and regularly engaged her in conversation about the books she read.

From there, they moved on to other subjects, including Kim's revised intention to stay in Montrose. The turning point in their fledgling friendship came one week after she decided to stay. By then, Kim had exchanged the luxury of a private motel room for a single room in a rooming house. The price was right, but her housemates were not a good fit. One other woman lived there. Kim had no idea what she did for a living, or if she even worked. She rarely left her room, and while at home, had the television on constantly. Kim, one door down, could hear its dull reverberation through the walls.

Two men also took lodging in the house, but her only problem was with Tyler Haas, the first-floor tenant. Tyler was a well-built man in his thirties. He had dark hair reaching his neck, a dark mustache, and black eyes. They weren't really black. Kim knew that. By their piercing quality, she thought them so. She would have been content to be ignored by him, as she was by the other tenants, but that didn't happen. When Tyler was friendly initially, she was friendly, if guarded, in return. Quickly she sensed his cold arrogance and became frightened of him. Plus, no one she spoke to, including her landlady, knew a thing about him other than that he had been living at the house for two months. Kim began to wonder whether he had spent time in prison. If he had been arrogant and dull-witted, she might have been less afraid, but Tyler was very bright. Very aware. He took immediate notice of her car and began baiting her about it. It was much too nice for a checkout clerk to own.

A Lexus—where did she get it? Did she steal it? He winked, as if he, too, knew something about stolen cars.

At the library soon afterward, Lois found Kim pacing, agitated after her most recent encounter with Tyler. Lois asked what was wrong. Kim told her, emphasizing what was frightening about Tyler, omitting mention of his digs about her car. While talking, she had wondered whether she would come to her senses and recognize an obvious overreaction to a non-existent threat. Lois hadn't seen it that way. The librarian had listened sympathetically, then made a phone call and returned with a triumphant smile. One of the women on the softball team had a spare room she was willing to rent, if Kim was interested. Kim had taken her up on the offer on the spot.

Having stalled long enough, Kim returned to the kitchen.

"The sauce smells great. What kind of tomatoes are these?" she said, reaching for an empty can with a yellow-and-red label.

"San Marzano. Imported from Italy. Makes all the difference. Hey, I went by the softball field but nobody was there. Was practice canceled?"

"Practice was yesterday." Kim poured a glass of wine and watched Andrea grate Parmesan cheese.

Andrea Sampson was an assistant district attorney from Pueblo, Colorado, presently on sabbatical from her professional life. Her current job was at the Black Canyon of the Gunnison, a national park ten miles east of Montrose. The pertinent detail about Andrea's employment was that lodging came with the job. Most nights she stayed at the canyon.

Andrea, in her thirties, was an attractive woman, approximately Kim's height of five six, with straight brown hair and an opinion on most everything. Kim had heard the bare-bones story of the courtroom disaster that had led Andrea to take a leave of absence from her job. Andrea was the lead prosecutor in the trial of Aleksander Voigt, a man alleged to have killed an elderly couple. Eyewitness testimony from a neighbor should have been sufficient to convict him, but the neighbor recanted on the witness stand, and the man, who had taunted Andrea throughout the trial, walked away, free.

The neighbor woman was murdered that same night—poor thanks, everyone in Pueblo agreed, for having given the man his freedom. He hadn't been seen since despite a massive manhunt launched to find him.

"What the hell's that?" Kim said. Her gaze froze on an object lying on the table. Adjacent to one of the place settings was a gun.

"This?" Andrea walked over and picked it up, giggling. "This is a Glock 19. Nine millimeter, striker-fired, five-point-five-pound trigger pull. Exceptionally reliable." She picked it up as though to demonstrate something.

"Put that thing away!" Kim sputtered furiously.

A slightly maniacal gleam lit Andrea's eyes. For the second time, Kim wondered how much her roommate had had to drink. A drunk with a gun, she thought, flabbergasted at the precipitous turn the evening had taken.

"I forgot it was still out." Andrea moved the gun to her bedroom.

Kim took a long swallow of wine.

When Andrea returned, she said, "So, you never said. Was softball practice canceled today? I went over to the field but no one was there."

Kim repeated her previous answer. "Practice was yesterday."

"Oh, Lois must have switched days. I'm surprised she didn't call me." Kim had no chance to correct her roommate's misunderstanding. In the same breath, Andrea said, "Don't you love our team's name—the Brazen Hussies? Thank God some people in this town have a sense of humor."

Andrea gave the marinara sauce a quick stir. After dipping a spoon in and tasting, she declared dinner ready. Kim served herself a plate of spaghetti. Andrea topped off both wineglasses and sat down.

"Mmm, this is delicious," Kim said after her first bite.

"Spaghetti sauce is easy. I'll teach you to make it sometime. Are you still working at JT's?"

"Yes."

"I don't know how you can stand that place. I've been in a couple of times. It feels filthy to me."

"It's not—"

"Hey, I know. Maybe you can get hired at Safeway. That would be a promotion, wouldn't it?" She giggled again.

This time Kim distinctly heard her roommate's slurred speech. She felt a rise of heat but stopped herself from snapping back. She didn't know Andrea. To date, they had seen each other at several softball practices and spent a total of three nights under the same roof. The longest conversation they had had concerned the terms of their living arrangement. She was still fuming when her temper got the best of her.

"So what's the future hold for you? Do you aspire to become a career counselor when you stop being a park ranger?" she asked.

Andrea took no notice of the jab. "Hell no. All I'm saying is, I'd hate to see you bagging groceries when you're sixty." She twirled spaghetti on her fork and took a long time chewing and swallowing. "I heard they found that girl. Damn shame."

"It's all anyone's been talking about," Kim said, glad to change the subject.

"They're never going to catch her killer. Not unless there's solid forensic evidence. Which there won't be." Andrea finished her wine, stumbling slightly when she pushed her chair back to get a refill. "Too much time has passed," she said when she sat down. "If the police had a suspect, we would have heard about him."

"How do you know they don't?"

Andrea smiled. "I have my contacts. Anyway, as I was saying, they might as well dump this one in the cold-case file. That's where it'll end up 'ventually."

Dottie Goddard had said much the same thing earlier that day. Kim wondered why she minded more hearing the judgment from Andrea.

"What would you do?" she said, suddenly interested in her roommate's opinion. "If you were hired to investigate this crime?"

Andrea gave an indifferent lift of her shoulders. "I'd dig as deep as I could to find the evidence. Trouble is, you know it's not going to be there. Have you ever seen a canyon filled with spring runoff? I'm surprised that girl's body wasn't washed clean away."

"What about her life," Kim pressed. "Where would you look, if you were looking at her life? For a clue someone missed. About who she was spending time with? Or something she cared about?"

Andrea looked indignant. "What do you think? That there's some easy answer for why she was killed?"

"And you think the answer isn't easy?"

"All I'm saying is no one's ever going to know it."

Kim finished her spaghetti and took another serving of salad. Andrea helped herself to more bread. Nearly a full minute of silence passed.

"Do you miss it?" Kim said.

"Miss what?"

"Being a prosecutor?"

"Shit, no. Besides, I'll go back someday. What I'm doing now's only temporary."

It was a pure disconnect. Kim laughed to herself, knowing Andrea hadn't heard it. Then she had to wonder if her erstwhile roommate's entire life had become a disconnect. If true, it was one thing they had in common.

"Why do you have a gun?" she said.

Andrea grinned sloppily. "A girl can't be too careful."

Kim went to the sink to fill a water glass. Standing there, she watched the spaghetti sauce burbling on the stove. Small spoons flecked with green flakes were scattered across the counter. Two bowls, one rimmed with red sauce, the other with grated cheese, were in the sink. At the far end of the kitchen, a collection of pricey gadgets shared space on a wooden cart. Kim knew their names—food processor, mixer, blender, spice grinder—but that was the extent of her familiarity. Cooking was at rock bottom of things she liked to do.

"I'm curious," she said. She turned around and leaned against the counter. "Did you ever try a case where a defendant claimed the evidence against him was fabricated?"

Andrea made a scornful sound. "Defendants always scream they're innocent."

"Don't you think some are?"

"None I ever prosecuted."

Kim smiled. For one fleeting instant, she felt as if she was in a boardroom asking questions she already knew the answers to of subordinates who were sweating to get it right. She had forgotten the feeling of power.

"Fingerprint evidence, for example," she said. "Did you ever have a case where a defendant said fingerprint evidence against him was a sham?"

Andrea tried to focus. "Sham? What do you mean by sham?"

"Exactly that. A fabrication. That fingerprints found on a presumed murder weapon were placed there some other way than during the execution of a crime."

Andrea struggled to follow. Her eyes rolled unsteadily. She gave up on eye contact and reached for her wineglass. "Nah, there was never anything like that. That stuff you see on TV is bogus. Cases tell whole stories. Sure, some are stronger than others. And some juries are a hell of a lot better than others. But a case never turns on one damn thing." She paused to drink her wine. Her eyes were laughing when she looked over. "Are you thinking you want to be a lawyer when you grow up? You have to go to college first, you know."

Kim also laughed. She almost said: *You asshole. I have an MBA, I'm a licensed CPA, and you may have seen your share of shit, but I've seen mine too.*

"I'm just curious about the system," she said instead.

"You want to know about the system? Here's what I can tell you. No one's life ever gets better by messin' with the system."

"No one?"

"No one. Anyone shows up there, it's 'cause something bad already happened."

CHAPTER 5

A memorial service for Emily Riley was scheduled for Saturday morning. That week, Kim heard of little else from customers passing through her checkout lane at JT's. By the end of the week, she thought she understood why. She was standing in the exact spot where her regulars were accustomed to seeing Emily. Her presence was a constant reminder of Emily's absence, and of a fate no one had wished for her.

Saturday morning, she awoke with no thoughts of attending the service. She drank coffee and ate a small bite of breakfast while the minutes dragged. A haunted feeling stuck to her. There was no earthly reason why she should want to attend the service, yet the fact was she did. She waited until the last possible minute before caving in. She changed into reasonably nice clothes and left the house to walk the six blocks to the Presbyterian church. Moments after settling into a rear pew, she was joined by a softball teammate.

"Hi, mind if I sit with you?" Jackie Melnick said.

Kim slid over.

"Did you know Emily?" Jackie said.

"No. I feel like I did. I've heard a lot about her from every-one who works at JT's."

"I had her in class. I think I've told you that," Jackie said.

Kim nodded. Since becoming teammates, she had had sev-eral conversations with the petite, soft-spoken English teacher, enough to sense Jackie wanted to be her friend. It wasn't what she wanted. She also knew Jackie was leaving Montrose at the end of the school year to go on an extended camping trip in the Sierras with her sister. Between now and then, Kim hoped to keep their relationship cordial, and uncomplicated.

"I wonder if he's here," Jackie said, peering at the crowd.

"Who?"

"Emily's killer."

Kim searched the profiles of the men seated in front of her. The church was packed. It could be anyone, she thought, figur-ing, as Jackie did, that the killer was male.

The church went quiet when the pastor emerged from a side door. A young life cut short, the preacher intoned gravely. Two minutes later, he was still speaking in dull platitudes. Kim expected him to do better on behalf of those gathered. Her mind wandered.

"Damn her, anyway," Ashley Crane had said weeks ago.

Kim, working in the checkout lane one over, had asked her coworker what was wrong.

Ashley proceeded to share her theory that Emily had up and left. She said Emily couldn't wait to get out of Montrose. Probably she had gone off with some guy. Either that or she had hitched a ride to Grand Junction. Grand Junction, the closest thing to a major city on Colorado's western slope, served alter-nately as a source of scorn to Montrose residents and as a hal-lowed point of departure. If you could get to Grand Junction, you could get anywhere, or so Ashley believed.

Except Emily hadn't made it to Grand Junction, or to any-where else. She was dead. Two weeks after turning eighteen,

Emily had been strangled and tossed naked over the side of a rocky cliff.

That was the gist of the newspaper reports. The sexual element of the crime was suggested in every account Kim had read so far, though there was no evidence the high school senior was raped. At least there was no forensic evidence left on a body exposed to the elements for three weeks. The circumstances clearly pointed to a male killer. Unless, Kim speculated, a clever female had murdered Emily.

She tuned in and out while the pastor rambled on. Ten minutes later, he led the congregation in prayer before inviting friends and family to speak on Emily's behalf. The first woman to do so was a neighbor who had known Emily since she was a child. The second was a teacher.

Then Ashley Crane took the pulpit.

By now, there were few dry eyes in the church. As Ashley opened her remarks, the atmosphere shifted from one of fragile restraint to unchecked grief. Kim was staggered by the power of Ashley's speech. Emily came alive for the first time as a strong, intelligent woman whose life was filled with poetry and dreams. Ashley painted Emily as someone who longed for horizons beyond the mountain-capped vistas of Montrose. "Don't get me wrong," Ashley said, midway through the eulogy. "Emily could be a real pain in the ass too. We all knew that about her." The words shocked her listeners into titters of laughter, but it broke the mood, and suddenly Kim felt Emily, a girl whom she had never met, present.

When the service ended, the crowd rose. Emily's mother made her way out of the church, escorted by a man with shaggy hair who looked uncomfortable in an ill-fitting suit. A small boy with wispy brown hair held her hand. Ashley, on the arm of her boyfriend, followed the family. Behind them, a larger crowd swarmed toward the door. Kim and Jackie slipped into the crush of people and were delivered into extraordinary sunshine. The brightness seemed offensive to the backdrop of grief. It heightened Kim's feeling of discomfort.

"I need to get going," she said.

"I thought I'd wait and say hello to Lois," Jackie said. "I saw her sitting several rows ahead of us with her boys."

"I'm due at Pine Village," Kim said, anxious to leave. "I'll see you tonight at the game."

She darted past strangers until she found a clear path on the sidewalk. After that, she walked more slowly. Though she succeeded in putting distance between herself and the crowd, she couldn't escape the lingering sense of grief.

She wondered what she had expected.

Or why she had gone in the first place.

Saturday wasn't one of the days she ordinarily volunteered at Pine Village. Having intimated she had a commitment there, she let momentum carry her home, where she changed clothes, then turned around and headed out the door. She unlocked her bicycle and started off on the three-mile ride. The bicycle had become her main source of transportation since she had purchased it at a garage sale several weeks ago. In the beginning, it was a means to an end—namely, avoiding driving her car. Lately, she had come to enjoy cycling for itself.

Almost overnight, it seemed flowers had bloomed in the neighborhood between her home and the residential facility. Red and yellow tulips lined porch walls and walkways. Irises were growing taller every day, some beginning to blossom in shades of violet and white. Farther out of town, the formerly brown fields sprouted green tufts along neat rows of tilled earth.

Fifteen minutes later, she walked into Christine Gregory's room. "Hello," she said, greeting her friend with all the warmth she had grown to feel in their brief acquaintance.

"Kim, what a surprise! I didn't expect you today."

"Haven't caught you at a bad time, have I?" Kim winked. "No boyfriend planning to sneak in your window?"

"Pshaw. In my dreams. In my dreams when I was your age, anyway."

Kim crossed the small space and took her usual chair near the window, longing to open it against the overheated interior. One look at the light sweater around Christine's shoulders and she knew better than to tease her friend about the benefits of fresh air.

She opened her copy of *Jane Eyre*. After reading one chapter, she paused to get the glass of water she normally kept within reach. Beyond the partly open room door, she heard shuffling. Puzzled, she went to check. A woman in a wheelchair lurked at the door. She looked up, startled, and moved swiftly away. She disappeared into the room next door with all the speed of a mouse darting for its hidey-hole. "Wait," Kim called to no avail.

Perplexed, she returned inside. "I think the woman who lives next door was listening in."

"Oh, that's Lucy. She's daft. Pay her no mind. Chapter twenty, then," Christine said, eyes bright with anticipation.

Kim read two more chapters before stopping for the day. On her way out, she scanned the corridor, hoping for a second glimpse of the woman next door. There was no sign of her.

That evening, she arrived at the ball field amid a cloud of dust kicked up by cars and trucks driven by teammates. No one was late, but that didn't stop Lois from barking orders. "We've got first warm-ups. Let's get moving," she shouted.

Despite occasional bursts of sparkling play, the Hussies lost. Afterward a plan was formed to reconvene at the Den. By the time Kim arrived at the locals' bar, the group had commandeered two tables in a back corner. Two pitchers of beer were half empty, and a plate of nachos was being demolished. She sat down at the first open seat and was immediately joined by Jackie Melnick.

Talk of the game rapidly gave way to talk of other things. Someone commented on what a beautiful day it was. Kim didn't know when exactly the conversation turned to Emily Riley's memorial service. The previous boisterousness ebbed, replaced by a hushed tone. One woman's words seemed to capture the mood. "I went to the service today, and I have to admit, it hit me hard."

In a flurry of murmurs, the others concurred. When someone mentioned Emily's mother, Kim spoke up. "I don't know the family's situation. I saw Emily's mother with a younger child today. Much younger than Emily."

Lois said, "That's Dustin. He's Emily's half brother. Her father left her and her mom eight or nine years ago. Deena—Emily's mom—took up with a motorcycle guy named Craig Warren and they had Dustin. Craig rode out of town a couple of years ago on his Harley to no one's great surprise. Except maybe Deena's."

Kim laughed, not amused but shocked. In the world where she had grown up, fathers hadn't walked out on families. Yet it had happened twice to Deena and Emily.

"Now she's running with that jerk Clark Adams. Did you see him today?" someone said.

Soon the talk turned darker. The women speculated on the identity of Emily's killer.

"I know a lot of people think he must be someone local, but I just can't buy that," Lois said. The ferocity in her tone took Kim by surprise. "My older boy was a year behind her in school, but he played ball with the guys in that crowd Emily ran with. He said she became a different person after she and Mike Lasko broke up a year or so back. Said she started going out with a lot of different guys, some of them older. Her reputation, well." Lois shrugged.

"I heard she'd been dating much older guys too," another teammate said. "Learned that from her mother, I guess."

Lois seemed flustered by the avenue she had opened and promptly tried to soft-pedal the prejudicial tone. "She was young. She didn't know any better. And she sure didn't have anyone looking out for her. All I'm saying is she probably made a mistake about someone."

Kim noticed Jackie brushing tears away. "Sorry," the schoolteacher said softly. "I've been tearing up all day. It's such a waste. For Emily—for any girl—to die like that! Especially Emily." She lowered her head, obviously struggling with emotion. Kim handed her a fresh napkin. With a firm press of the tissue to her eyes, Jackie said, "The smart kids at school always know what they have to do to get good grades. Emily was smart in a different way. Not that she didn't get good grades. She did, at least for a while. She was first in her class until junior year."

"I didn't know that," Kim said.

Other conversations were going on around them. At the moment, no one was listening in on theirs.

"Something happened," Jackie said angrily, though still speaking softly. "Emily changed. From one day to the next, it was as though she became a different person. Her grades tanked. I have no idea why. I tried talking to her but she wouldn't talk to me."

Kim was intrigued. Had she and Jackie been alone, she would have begged the teacher to go on. Instead, she reflected on the photograph of Emily she saw at the memorial service this morning. In the enlargement of her senior picture, Emily appeared as a fair-skinned young woman with long blond hair. She was smiling for the camera, seemingly unafraid of what it captured of her. The look of self-possession magnified her appeal. It gave her an air of spontaneity, as if she were ready for whatever came next.

She left the women debating the questions to go to the restroom. Passing through the bar, still troubled by her thoughts, she didn't see the man sitting there, or his arm when it shot out to grab her.

"Hey there, sweet thing. I've been looking for you." Tyler Haas leered at her from the barstool.

Kim wrenched free. She felt no inclination to retort that Tyler knew exactly where to find her, that he already had found her several times when she was working at JT's. The man sitting next to him looked over. There was something familiar about him. It was Clark Adams, she realized. The man she had seen this morning walking alongside Emily Riley's mother.

Tyler laughed dangerously. "Took me a while, but I also found that nice car of yours. Oh yeah, parked out there on that side street. What—you thought I wouldn't find it?"

She started to walk away.

"Now here's something funny," Tyler said, raising his voice insinuatingly. "I've got a buddy who's a real smart guy. He can find out anything on that damn computer of his. I mentioned that fine car of yours, and he said, 'Hell, let's do ourselves a little checking.' And do you know what I found out?" Mocking her, he spoke in exaggerated seriousness.

Kim stared at him, furious.

"What I found out is that car doesn't even belong to you. I knew it. Lord bless me, but I knew it. That car belongs to some other woman."

"Shut up, Tyler." Her words scorched the air.

His dark eyes gleamed in triumph. He pointed, bringing one finger close to her chest. "You and I need to talk. So how 'bout we make ourselves a little date?"

"Everything okay, Kim?"

Kim spun around to see Jackie standing there. She had no idea how long the schoolteacher had been there or how much she had overheard. "Yes. Everything's fine," she said.

She passed Tyler without another word.

CHAPTER 6

She would have killed him if he had said her name. Her real name. Not the one she had been using for the last month. She wouldn't have killed him there, in the bar. She would have waited and killed him later. After she hunted Tyler Haas down in some dark alley, lowlife that he was.

Alone at home in a darkened house, Kim sat at an open bedroom window. Her car was a problem. She knew that. Weeks ago, she had considered driving to Grand Junction and stealing a set of license plates: two, front and back, as required by Colorado law. The blatant illegality of the act stopped her. She didn't know how many laws she had broken so far. She had presented Kim Jackson's social security number when she was hired at JT's. She had received a driver's license using the identity of a dead girl. Still, there was a limit to what she was willing to do, however ludicrous her belated show of conscience.

Now she was thinking of murder. In her present frame of mind, the line between being falsely accused of murder and actually committing one seemed negligible.

Andrea came in sometime after midnight. Kim heard her moving about the house, from the kitchen to her bedroom to the bathroom. Water ran in the shower for several minutes, then stopped. Soon afterward, the house fell quiet. Eventually Kim slept for a few hours. She awoke at first light, dressed, and slipped out of the house.

At a shop on Main Street, she bought coffee and the morning paper. She took her purchases to an outside table, heedless of the cool air. Ignoring the front section, she flipped through to the classified ads, looking for garage space to rent. After Tyler Haas's digs last night, she knew she had to move her car.

The answer was no, nothing available. Not unless she was willing to rent a house to go with it, and that was out of the question. Not on her salary.

While still in the classifieds, she skimmed through job openings. Some of the big retailers in town were hiring. The postings were for customer service agents and warehouse assistants, causing her to wonder when "checkout clerk" and "stock boy" had been replaced by loftier titles. There were ads for cooks, waitresses, and dishwashers. Kim read one for a bookkeeper. She laughed when she came to the requirement: "Must be fluent using a computer!"

She was refolding the paper when she noticed the front-page story about Emily Riley's memorial service. There was a photo of Deena, Dustin, and Clark Adams, all three with heads lowered emerging from the church. According to the story, more than two hundred people had attended yesterday's service. The report said police were pursuing dozens of leads, and were confident they would catch the murdered teen's killer.

Kim left the paper in a recycle bin. She hadn't found what she went looking for, but she had found something better.

Andrea still wasn't up when Kim let herself in through the front door. Moving quietly, she searched a kitchen drawer for a tape measure, bungee cords, and rope. She came up empty. There were probably other places she could look, but she didn't want to wake Andrea. There was an easier way to get what she wanted. She took her keys and wallet and drove to the Safeway grocery store on the south side of town. There, she purchased what she needed along with a heavy-duty Master Lock. She left the new purchases in the car, the car in the parking lot, and walked home.

There was no point in taking chances. Not now.

The early-morning chill had burned off ahead of another gorgeous springtime day. A light breeze blew, setting tree branches swaying and newly burst leaves into a frolicking dance. Flowers bloomed everywhere, in boxes attached to houses and along neatly tended paths. At home, Kim didn't bother going inside. She took her bicycle from where she kept it around back, mounted it, and rode back to the Safeway. Once there, she opened the car's trunk and put the bicycle inside, lowering the lid over the protruding handlebars, then securing it, best she could, to a latch beneath the bumper using the cords she had purchased.

She drove south. Her destination was a self-storage facility located on the main highway out of town. She'd seen an ad for the place in the morning paper, and she was kicking herself. A self-storage unit was the obvious solution. She should have thought of it before now.

As she drove, she reveled in the Lexus's smooth power and in the allure of the mountains cresting along the horizon. The same celestial spires that had been calling to her since the day she arrived in Montrose were still there, beckoning. She blew past the self-storage facility. With a tank full of gas and the knowledge that this was likely her last time driving anywhere for days or weeks or, possibly, months, she drove on for the pure pleasure of driving.

Beyond the city limits, she passed signs pointing to subdivisions built somewhere off to the right. After that, there weren't any more signs. She was cruising through a broad landscape, an expansive sweep of pastures and farmland. The mountains, no closer, cut a jagged swath across the sky.

She passed a turnoff for a town she had never heard of called Ridgway and saw a sign for a different town she had heard of: Telluride. People she used to know took skiing vacations there. By now, she knew where she was going. Ouray lay less than ten miles ahead.

The formerly open vista shrank with each passing mile. She drove past a sunlit meadow dotted with wooden houses and barns, cows in pasture, and horses in corrals. To her left, the view was walled-in by shadows. Peering more closely, she saw the source of the shadows in the tall trees growing close to the road. The dark shape of a hillside rose behind them.

The road narrowed. Abruptly, it wound around a sharp bend before straightening and starting to rise, a climb that took her up a steep pitch and brought her face to face with the granite spires she had seen from a distance. The view looming in front of her was of the steepest, rockiest mountains she had ever seen. Mountains that didn't seem possible, yet were there, exponentially gaining stature with each patch of pavement she put behind her.

Spying a free parking space, she nosed into it.

Something had changed in her since this morning. Maybe it was driving the Lexus. More likely it was having solved the problem of how to keep the car safe. She walked, and she thought, and when all she wanted to do was gaze at the mountains, she bought a cup of coffee and sat outside to drink it.

Her old life was lost to her. It wasn't something she allowed herself to think about often. Stephen Bender—her former boss—had framed her for a pair of crimes he had committed: for the corporate fraud Michael Leeds had stumbled on, and for Michael's murder. Nobody—other than Stephen and his cronies, whoever they were—knew about the fraud. Michael's shooting death on a Saturday night outside a popular Chicago sports bar was a sad statistic in a city that had far too many unsolved homicides. Stephen had evidence linking her to both crimes. He had her forged signature on documents Michael had found that exposed the fraud. Her fingerprints were on the gun used to kill Michael. Stephen would only release that evidence if he had to.

She exhaled quietly, wondering whether she had made a mistake by running away rather than taking her chances with the justice system. Michael had left her with the proof he had uncovered. Stephen had assured her that there was no proof. It already had been erased from the database. She had believed her ex-boss.

She asked the questions for the first time: What would it take to bring Stephen Bender down? What would it take to go back to Chicago and fight for the truth? How much would she be willing to risk for the right to take back her name?

All the good things, her therapist used to say to her when she was in a dark place, before she knew darker places existed. Think of all the good things you've ever seen, or known, or done. Think of the smile on the face of someone you love. Think of simple joy and complicated dreams.

Taking Stephen down was a complicated dream.

To achieve that particular dream meant knowing what questions to ask and where to look for the answers. It meant becoming invisible and remaining that way until she was certain she had solid proof of his guilt. There were other threads that would require untangling, other complications beginning with the identity of his partners and accepting the reality that there was no one, absolutely no one, from her past whom she could trust.

She realized her dream meant acquiring skills she had never imagined needing. Investigative skills.

"Hell, Kim Jackson," she heard Dottie Goddard say. "It's just a thought."

She stood up, shook off the mental cobwebs, and threw away the coffee cup.

She got in the car and drove up a road that grew steeper as she went. Past the last house in a block of neatly kept Victorian houses, she rounded a bend that led to a hairpin turn. From there, the road wound a serpentine path, rising and curving back on itself until the town of Ouray lay far below. Two hairpin turns later, she lost sight of the town altogether. The side of the mountain dropped off precipitously. Ahead, a deep canyon split the earth, dwarfed by the pitch of towering rock above.

She turned in at a pull-off on the right, parked the Lexus, and got out. She might have stood there staring at the magnificent peaks rising thousands of feet above, except sprays of flowers strewn on a rock wall told her she had come to the right place.

It was the overlook where, somewhere far below, Emily Riley's body had lain. For weeks, while people's lives went on. Or, in Kim's case, while she created a new one. Out of the vacuum Emily left behind.

She didn't owe the dead Emily anything.

Finding Emily's killer wasn't the reason she wanted to become an investigator.

But it gave her a place to start.

CHAPTER 7

First thing on Monday morning, Kim went to the Montrose Community Center. Despite the early hour, she found Dottie Goddard in a meeting. The former high school principal waved from her office, at the same time excusing herself from her companions to come to the door. "Kim, good to see you. Something I can help you with?"

"I thought I'd stop by to visit, but you're busy. I'll come back."

"Now just hold on. Something brought you here. What is it?"

Kim had planned to work her question into a casual conversation. However uncomfortable she felt blurting it out, Dottie gave her no choice. "I've forgotten the last name of the man who did the book signing last month. I thought I'd look for his book at the library."

"Oh good! You are getting started," Dottie said, which was exactly what Kim didn't want to hear. "His name is Dr. Abraham Craft. He teaches at Western Colorado University. I have a copy of his book here." Dottie, wearing a blazing-yellow jacket over a black T-shirt, went to a bookcase and took a paperback from a shelf. Handing it over, she winked. "Come back and tell me what you find." She turned away, giving Kim no chance to say another word.

Book in hand, Kim went to the library. She still had questions, among them where Western Colorado University was located. The answer was Gunnison, sixty-five miles east of Montrose. Perusing a *Rand McNally Road Atlas*, she found Gunnison on the Colorado map, and thought she must have driven through the town on the day she drove into a snowstorm and landed in Montrose. She couldn't recall the place.

So much for her brilliant idea of taking classes at the university, she thought. The university was much too far of a commute. Not to mention she had no interest in driving anywhere. Studying the map, she found highway US 550, the road that linked Montrose to Ouray. Her car had a new home inside a self-storage unit somewhere along that stretch of highway. She had rented the space yesterday and ridden her bicycle home, relieved, at last, to know that her car was safe from Tyler Haas's prying eyes.

US 550 interested her. Using her finger, she traced it beyond Ouray to the top of Red Mountain and down the other side to a town called Silverton. It was the sole road out of Silverton, traversing a couple of passes before reaching Durango, a major crossroads of two US highways in southwest Colorado.

Satisfied with her geography lesson, she put away the map.

By then, one of the internet computers was free. She sat down and embarked on a search of Dr. Abraham Craft. Craft, by his photo, was a distinguished-looking African American man in his fifties with a neatly trimmed beard and piercing, intelligent eyes. An acclaimed criminologist, he was chairman of the university's criminology department and a highly sought-after consultant to the CBI—the Colorado Bureau of Investigation. He was also the author of several articles and two books, *The ABCs of Solving Crime* and *The Science of Crime*, an anthology of case studies. She checked the front of the former, confirmed that his initials were in fact "ABC," and decided that the man didn't want for a healthy ego.

Dr. Craft was a proponent of the "murder board," a view of the "crime at a glance," as he referred to it. Kim skimmed the lengthy article in which he articulated the benefits, obvious and otherwise, of assembling details of a case in one place. He had much to say on the subject of an investigator becoming prejudiced by early assumptions and overlooking the presence of outliers—the pieces of the puzzle that didn't fit.

Kim decided to give his methodology a shot. She opened a notebook to a fresh page and started with a list. In one column, she wrote what she knew about Emily Riley, every single fact, whether gleaned from newspaper accounts or from other people. In a second column, she meant to note possible actions to take to verify the truth of what she had written. Long before she finished, she admitted it was a false start. She was logging a compendium of what everyone knew, or thought they knew, about Emily Riley.

Twirling the pen in her hand, she reread the list, bothered by a feeling that something was missing. No one had ever said whether Emily planned to attend college. She jotted the question down as something to ask Ashley Crane. Then it hit her. Nowhere on the list was there any mention of Emily's poetry and dreams. She wondered whether Emily had kept a journal. It was another question for Ashley.

Encouraged, she started from the top of her list, reading slowly and trying to see beyond what was there to what wasn't. Satisfied she'd done enough musing for now, she headed home feeling hopeful about her start.

—

At Pine Village later that morning, Kim made a new friend. She arrived at Christine's room at her usual time. After reading only a few pages, she stood up, and continuing to talk with Christine about nothing in particular, walked to the door. Without giving any sign of what she meant to do, she burst into the hallway, startling, as she had expected, the woman huddled in a wheelchair.

"Hello. My name is Kim Jackson, and I would be delighted to have you join us," she said, offering her hand. The other woman just stared.

"Kim! What in the world are you doing?" Christine called.

The brown-eyed woman in the wheelchair didn't break eye contact. When she tried to speak, her voice caught, as if rusty with use. "Lucy," she managed. "My name is Lucy Wentworth."

"I'm very pleased to meet you, Lucy. And I would love to have your company while I read."

Lucy looked uncertainly toward the room, or perhaps toward its occupant. Desire overcame her reticence. "I would like that. If it's okay with—" She nodded beyond the wall toward Christine's resounding voice.

"Kim, really, is there something you require?"

"Come on." Kim signaled for Lucy to follow. Entering the room, she said, "Christine, guess what? We have someone who wants to join us."

"Who is it?"

"It's Lucy, your next-door neighbor." As she crossed the room, Kim kept her body between the two women, thereby preventing Lucy from seeing the daggers shot at her by Christine. She took her chair, opened the book, and resumed reading. One paragraph into the chapter, she stopped. "We're reading *Jane Eyre*," she said to Lucy. "We're on chapter twenty-six. It's the day of Jane's wedding to Mr. Rochester." Lucy nodded eagerly.

Occasionally while reading, Kim dared to glance at Christine, who by small degrees began to look less put out. Lucy had parked her chair several feet back. Her expression was rapt. A tiny smile knitted itself into her features. Otherwise, she didn't move.

Foolishly pleased by the attention of these women, Kim stayed longer than usual. When she finished, Lucy's eyes shot open. Beaming, she said, "Thank you," and deftly wheeled away.

"I'll be back soon," Kim said to the retreating figure. Less heartily, she turned to Christine. "She's been listening at the door. Today and the last time I was here, at least. Is there any harm in having her join us?"

Christine gave a small, hopeless gesture. "Only that she can be so—unpredictable." The word, Kim suspected, was not first on her lips. "Naturally, she behaved quite civilized today."

"I'm sorry I invited her without discussing it with you." Kim's eyes softened. "If it matters, I'll undo what I have done."

"And do what? Banish Lucy to the doorway? Then I'm sure you'll feel obligated to read to her privately, and how dull will that be for you, covering the same material twice?" Christine began harshly, but ended in clear jest. "I have no complaint, as long as she comports herself in a civil manner."

"Thank you, Christine."

On her way out, Kim stopped at the office where she found a fresh spray of flowers on the desk and the receptionist typing at a computer, oblivious to her presence. "Hello, Justine," she said.

"Hi, Kim," the younger woman said.

"I was wondering if you could tell me something about one of the residents. Lucy Wentworth. I caught her listening at the door today while I was reading to Christine."

Justine broke out laughing. "Lucy! Do you mean to tell me it's taken you this long to catch her? She's been there practically since the first day you started visiting Christine."

"Why didn't somebody tell me? There was no reason she had to sit in the hall."

"It's what she wanted. Some of the nurses tried to encourage her to go in, but she always ran away. Wheeled away. She's quick in that chair."

"As of today, she's officially a member of our reading club."

"How is Christine coping with that?"

"So-so. She says it's fine as long as Lucy behaves. Any idea what that means?"

"Oh yes. Lucy's only been here a few weeks. She's having a tough time adjusting. Crying fits, mainly. Loud enough to disturb the other residents. Let's face it, not many of these folks are happy about being here. The ones who do best come to terms with it. They get angry when someone else makes a fuss. But Lucy is a character. For the first two weeks, she was up every night trying to slip away. Early on, she got as far as one of the side doors, which, thankfully, was locked. Afterward the night staff kept closer tabs on her. Seems like she's been doing better lately."

Kim smiled at her new friend's spunk. "What's wrong with her?"

"She injured her hip and shoulder in a fall down the stairs at her house. Maybe had a concussion too. She spent time in the hospital and at rehab. As you've seen, she gets around pretty well now, but somewhere along the way, her mind started to go. She has fits of dementia. Other times, she seems as sane as you or me."

"How old is she? Oh, you probably can't tell me."

"Not officially." Justine typed something at the keyboard. A second later, she said, "Huh. She's only in her midseventies. I'd have guessed she was a good bit older."

Kim agreed. "Does Lucy have family in the area? Isn't it possible she could live with a son or daughter?"

"She has both. Scott, her son, lives in town. I'm surprised you haven't seen him around. Tall, good-looking guy. Very conscientious about visiting his mother. Her daughter lives in

Denver. To answer your question, Lucy's prognosis isn't great. Because of the mental stuff. Scott and her doctor figure she's better off getting settled here while she can still recognize her surroundings. Then, later, when she can't, maybe some things will be familiar."

And possibly comforting at that, Kim thought, thanking Justine.

Subdued by what she had learned, Kim hurried on to work. By the time she arrived at the grocery store, she was thinking less of Lucy Wentworth and more about the questions she had for Ashley Crane. She had rehearsed an opening and prioritized her queries, knowing she would only get to a few, at most. But by early evening, when her shift was nearly over, she hadn't had a single opportunity to speak to Ashley in relative privacy. Unwilling to leave it for another day, after clocking out, she volunteered to bag groceries for her coworker. Predictably, the high school senior gave her a disparaging look. "Knock yourself out," she said.

Kim waited until several of their regular customers had passed through the lane. "I went to the memorial service on Saturday," she said. "I wanted to tell you how much I liked what you said about Emily. It seemed like you were the only one who spoke who really knew her."

Ashley gave a "whatever" shrug and handed over a carton of eggs to bag.

Undeterred, Kim said, "I liked what you said about her life being full of poetry and dreams. Did Emily keep a journal?"

"Yeah, she was always writing stuff down. It made me crazy. Like, why was I hanging out with her if she wasn't even paying attention?"

"Nobody ever said. Was she planning to go to college?"

Kim expected her coworker to drip sarcasm, asking: *What difference could that possibly make now?*

Ashley surprised her. She said, "She was. She definitely was. Right up until the day Deena stole her money."

The groceries for the order were rung up. Ashley took four twenties from the man standing in the lane and gave change while Kim added the last bag to the cart.

"What money?" Kim asked when the man walked away.

CHAPTER 8

The money that wasn't there.

The money, Ashley Crane explained in a withering tone, as though she had told this story one too many times, that Emily's biological father gave her from an inheritance he received from some dead California relative. He showed up out of the blue one day from wherever he lived in Utah or Idaho, took Emily to lunch, gave her a check, and left again on the same fickle wind he'd blown in on.

Ashley roughly pushed four tall boxes of cereal to the end of the lane for Kim to bag.

It took another two customers for Kim to be sure she had heard the whole story. Details emerged in emotional bursts, usually anger. By the end, there was unmistakable pain in Ashley's voice. "Why are we even talking about this?" she demanded as she handed over a jar of imported jam that required a price check. Kim didn't answer. She went to the appropriate aisle and returned with the information.

Kim left the store soon afterward. She walked home, retelling herself the story she had heard, wanting to keep the details fresh. At home, she wrote it down. A little over a year ago, during the middle of her junior year—when Emily still gave a shit about her grades, according to Ashley—Emily's father paid an unexpected visit and left her with an even more unexpected gift: a check for $8,000. Ashley wavered on the details of whether the money was truly a gift or if it was actually Emily's share of the dead California relative's estate. "Whatever, it was a ton of money," Ashley had said, adding, "Yeah, Emily planned to go to college."

Until Deena took the money and spent it on a car.

After that, Emily didn't give a shit about anything.

In Ashley's words.

Kim reread what she'd written, searching her memory for anything she may have left out. She wanted to tell Jackie Melnick what she had learned. She wanted to ask the schoolteacher whether there wouldn't have been other ways for Emily to find the money to attend college. Scholarships, perhaps. Or loans. There had to have been some way for Emily to go to college.

Kim mulled over the question of whether anyone involved in the official investigation into Emily's murder knew about the money her father had given her and how her mother had spent it. The longer she thought about it, the more convinced she became that however great a tragedy losing the money was for Emily, it probably hadn't played a part in her murder.

She put away the notebook.

At Pine Village the next morning, she read to Christine and Lucy for a solid forty-five minutes. They were coming to the end of *Jane Eyre*. Though it was a cruel place to stop, Kim knew too much of the story remained for her to finish it today.

"Really, this has been wonderful of you," Christine exclaimed. "I feel as though I've lived these last few weeks in nineteenth-century England. I dare say, for all Jane's troubles, it's been a delightful adventure."

Lucy, who spoke rarely, nodded vigorously.

A few minutes later, Kim accompanied Lucy to her room. Outside the door, Lucy dug in her sweater pocket. She came out with a slip of paper. "Please, might this be our next book? I don't recall his first name," she said, handing it over.

Kim took the paper and read four neatly printed words: "*Howards End*. Mr. Forster."

"It's E. M. Forster," she said. Until then, she hadn't considered whether there would be a next book.

"E. M. Yes, of course. That would be Edward Morgan. Thank you. It means so much." Smiling, Lucy wheeled into her room.

Kim returned to share news of the request with Christine.

"She's better today," Christine said. "She had a bad afternoon yesterday. Twice, I saw her hunched over asleep. To see her that way—" She waved her hand, either in sadness or disapproval, Kim didn't know which.

"I'm sorry to hear that."

"I don't think she cares for—" The white-haired woman didn't finish.

"You don't think Lucy cares for whom?"

A battle waged in Christine's eyes. "It's not for me to say."

While Kim debated whether to press her elderly friend, Christine spoke acerbically. "Her son. I don't think she cares for her son. There, I've said it. Perhaps I shouldn't have. But if I'm not to speak up for her, who will? In any case, she was perking up today. As you were reading, it was as though a light came on in her eyes."

Kim smiled wanly.

"Blast it all if you don't believe me," Christine said. "I know what I'm talking about."

Kim laughed. She was about to say something when a sound from the hall caused them both to turn toward the door.

"Oh good. You are here today," Helene Strickland said from the entryway. She looked at Kim without sparing a word for Christine.

Kim coolly said hello.

"Promise me you'll stop at the desk on your way out. I have to talk to you," Helene said.

"All right. I'll see you then," Kim said, decisively turning her back.

For more than a week, she had avoided seeing Helene—the woman who had done her the favor of driving her to the local DMV office and allowing Kim to use her car for the state driver's test. Today there was no escaping her. When Kim reached the front entrance, Helene was standing at the reception desk, a veritable sentry guarding against her escape. "Let's go to the dining room," she said peremptorily. "I'm overdue for my break as it is."

Helene had a premature matronly appearance. Only thirty-seven, her brown hair showed tinges of gray. She wore it straight and short, its bowl-like shape conforming to the contours of her head. It was a becoming style, and she was an appealing woman—until she began talking. The moment they were seated in the dining room, she complained about her son and daughter. They were refusing to sign up to attend summer church camp. Barely listening, Kim tried to break away only to suffer Helene's accusations that she had been avoiding her. "I've invited you for dinner twice," Helene said sharply. "Is there any reason we can't set a time now?"

"I'm never quite sure what my schedule's going to be at JT's," Kim said, her familiar excuse sounding weak. "There's been a lot going on around Emily Riley's death. She used to work there."

Helene shook her head. "That girl. I've heard quite enough about Emily Riley, thank you very much."

Kim heard something ugly in Helene's tone. She glanced away, not wanting to dignify the remark with a response.

Beyond the window, flowers moved in the breeze. The sky was a cloudless cerulean blue. Kim would have given a great deal to be out there, not stuck in here.

Helene's shrill voice drew her back to the present. "May God forgive me for speaking ill of the dead, but I am fed up with all the boo-hooing going on in this town over that girl's death. I won't say she got what was coming. I will say she was playing with fire by letting sex be her calling card to any man who showed a flicker of interest. You can't tease and tempt men and run from one to another without somebody taking notice and getting angry."

"That's not what Emily did!"

As if she hadn't heard, Helene said, "And if there's one good thing that comes out of her sorry life, maybe she will serve as an example to other girls of what's in store for them if they drop their drawers thinking that's the way to be popular. There was a name for it once, and it was called whoring. Calling it sleeping around or anything you like doesn't change what it is or make it morally acceptable."

Kim's jaw dropped. Helene had glanced away while delivering her speech. She looked back now, indifferent to the stunned expression on Kim's face. She merely sniffed, as if to accent her piece.

Kim pushed back her chair. She stared hard, trying to command her anger. In an icy voice, she said, "A person is not the sum total of the one thing you know about her." A second wave of anger swelled on the heels of the first. "Emily didn't deserve to be murdered, no matter how she chose to live. Your words are unspeakably cruel. Goodbye, Helene."

Kim stood up and walked away, half expecting to hear the repentant cry of an abandoned woman. It didn't come. Stony-eyed, she walked the length of the corridor. Even knowing there was nothing Helene could do or say to ensnare her again in guilty friendship, she didn't feel consoled. Anger hardened within her. She felt the probing tentacles of a question: Was Helene alone in the community in her opinion about Emily?

"Miss Jackson. It is Miss Jackson, isn't it?" a man said.

The name didn't register. Kim didn't stop until the man caught up with her, urgently repeating her name. She looked at him. "Yes? What is it?"

He broke into a broad smile. "Obviously I've caught you at a bad time. I apologize. I only wanted to introduce myself. I'm Scott Wentworth. Lucy's son."

The spell gripping Kim broke when she heard Lucy's name. She smiled at the man out of fondness for his mother. "Kim Jackson," she said, offering her hand. "I'm sorry. I had something on my mind just now."

"You don't say." Scott raised one eyebrow sardonically. "I had hoped we might go for a cup of coffee. But I gather this isn't the time."

"No."

"Perhaps another day, then." Without giving her time to respond, he said, "Thank you for the time you've spent with my mother. She's grateful, as am I."

"Your mother is quite wonderful, Mr. Wentworth. I'm sorry, I have to be going."

"It's Scott," he called as she walked away. "Call me Scott."

She turned, repeated her goodbye, and kept walking.

—

It was the end of an era hardly worth noting.

Outside, refreshed by the clear country air, Kim allowed herself one grateful moment of knowing she was finished with Helene Strickland. She felt pity for the small woman and her small life. Briefly, she wrestled with the question of whether she had behaved badly toward her. Friendships weren't a score-card. She couldn't say whether they had come out even in their dealings with one another.

Dissatisfied with her train of thought, she unlocked her bicycle, stowed the chain and *Jane Eyre* in the canvas bag, and rode home.

She made a grilled cheese sandwich and ate it, hardly tasting it.

Her words to Helene sprang to mind again: "A person is not the sum total of the one thing you know about her." It was as if they were emblazoned on a pop-up placard in a carnival ride, rising and lowering at odd intervals, almost ominously. There was little doubt that Emily Riley had been reduced by the citizens of Montrose into a one-dimensional girl more deserving of contempt than compassion.

Kim wondered whether she, too, had been written off by the people who had known her in Chicago. It was no secret that some had thought her a mental case. She cut off the thought. For once, this wasn't about her.

She pushed away the plate. She gripped her hands around her water glass.

Her plan was absurd. She knew that. Logic had abandoned her, washed its hands, said good riddance. She stood up and left the house. She rode her bike to JT's, where she made a sin-gle purchase, then rode to the home Emily Riley had shared with her mother and Dustin, her five-year-old half brother.

Kim didn't know Deena Warren. All she knew about her she had learned through other people. Ashley Crane, in partic-ular, consistently painted Deena in a poor light. So it was with little faith that Kim took herself to the woman's home.

When she arrived in the neighborhood, she didn't go immediately to the front door. She rode by the house, taking stock of what she saw. Set back on a large lot, the small wood-frame house was in obvious need of repair. A fresh coat of paint would have made a good start. Shingles flapping on the roof hinted at a more serious problem. By contrast, a row of yellow tulips along the front wall lightened the sense of shabbiness. Kim leaned her bicycle against the house and knocked on the door.

"Hello, Mrs. Warren," she said when the door swung wide. "My name is Kim Jackson. You don't know me. I haven't lived in Montrose long. I came here today because of Emily and to say how terribly sorry I am for your loss." She held out a box holding a cake.

"Deena," the other woman said. "Please, call me Deena. Nobody ever calls me Mrs. Warren. I hardly recognize the name. Come on in. Kim, did you say?"

"Yes."

"Excuse the mess," Deena said, holding open the door. "I'm always picking up after my son, but I never can keep up." She cleared a space on the sofa. Kim sat down. "This is very kind of you. I had so many people come by right after—well. Everyone was so nice and brought us so much food, I thought the refrigerator was going to burst."

A wispy-haired boy emerged from a back room to stand in the doorway. He looked young, and wary.

"Hey, Dustin, come on out and meet Kim. She was a friend of Emily's," Deena said.

Kim started to correct her. Then she didn't.

"Excuse me one minute while I slice him a piece of that cake," Deena said.

Deena had no doubt once been a fine-looking woman. In her early forties now with fair skin and faded-blond hair, she had good bone structure and beautiful blue eyes. Women like Deena reminded Kim of what she wasn't: a naturally beautiful woman. Kim considered herself conventionally attractive. Until recently, she had looked and dressed the part of a corporate accountant, and had liked that self-image. Deena Warren was something else. Kim thought Deena was a woman who could transform her appearance in an instant into something stunning. At the moment, she didn't look as if she cared to try.

"All right, then," Deena said, returning to the living room, having left her son at the dining room table. "This is so awfully kind of you," she repeated.

Kim felt uncomfortable with what she had come here to ask. She told herself it would either work or it wouldn't and, either way, there would be no long-term consequences. She said, "I've never lost anyone in my life as close as a daughter, so I won't even pretend to know what you and Dustin are going through. I do know that life gets back to normal a whole lot quicker for other folks than it ever does for the one who was closest to the person who died."

"You've got that right. I won't say I blame anyone, though. Like you say, it's just how it is. It sure doesn't help that the police have gotten exactly nowhere in pinning down who killed Emily."

Kim winced at the woman's casual language. "I didn't know Emily very well. Our paths more or less crossed only once. I feel like I have gotten to know her from talking to people down at the grocery store. I work at JT's—"

"Oh, that's where I've seen you," Deena interrupted. "And that's how you knew Emily."

Kim ran with the lie. "Yes. Anyway, I've been toying with the idea of writing an article about Emily. I do a bit of free-lance writing, and I was thinking about trying to come up with something that would remind people in town of who Emily was, something to keep her story fresh when, otherwise, well, people are moving on. If I did manage to write anything, I'd want you to check it over first to make sure it says what you want. With time passing, I'm afraid folks are getting a chance to remember certain things about Emily, maybe some things about her wild side, and they're forgetting other things. Like how she was so smart."

"Oh Lord, I'd give my right arm to have people remember that! I won't pretend she didn't have her wild streak. I sure had mine when I was her age."

Treading lightly, Kim said, "Several people, including one of Emily's teachers, have mentioned what a terrific writer she was. Especially with her poetry. Now, I may be way over a line here, and if I am, I apologize in advance. I wonder whether you have any of Emily's notebooks. If you do, would you consider allowing me to read them? I'd like to be able to include some things she wrote in my article." Kim held her breath. She waited for emotion to flash in the other woman's eyes, probably fury, and an order to leave the house.

"Oh hell, I don't mind," Deena said. "The cops have been through her stuff. I tried to look at it, thinking I owed her that much, but, well. There's only so much time in the day." She stood up. "Hold on one sec."

Kim drew a quiet breath of relief. She looked at the little boy kneeling on a dining room chair, angling a hunk of cake into his mouth. "Hey, Dustin," she said. "Is the cake good?"

"Yes. But chocolate is my favorite."

Score one for Dustin, Kim thought. She'd brought vanilla. She ought to have known better.

Deena returned with a pile of notebooks. "The police were all over her room when she first went missing. They left these. I guess you'll be able to tell which ones are schoolbooks and which are her own."

Kim couldn't believe her good fortune. Neither was she inclined to give Deena a chance to reconsider. She reached for the stack. "I promise I'll take good care of them. And I'll get them back to you within a few days."

"You say you work down at JT's? So I can find you there if the cops come back needing them?"

"Yes. But, let me write down my address for you."

"Oh no, don't go to the trouble. If you're bringing them back that soon, I can't think why I'd need them before then."

Kim moved toward the door. "Thank you, Deena. It's been nice visiting with you and Dustin." Lowering her voice, she added, "Next time I come by, I'll bring him a chocolate cake."

Deena smiled. "Oh, you don't have to do that." In the same breath, she said, "Of course, he does love his chocolate."

CHAPTER 9

Kim rushed home with her windfall of material. Anxious as she was to begin reading, she held off. There was a softball game that night; she had to leave soon. Using what little time she had, she satisfied herself with thumbing through the notebooks and ordering them chronologically, the best she could tell from dates scrawled intermittently throughout. At first glance, it was obvious the books contained both personal writings and class notes.

Andrea drove up as Kim was preparing to leave. Rushing toward the front door, Andrea said, "Put your bike away. I'll give you a lift to the game. Give me a second to change clothes."

With cloudy skies threatening rain, Kim was happy to accept the offer. On the short drive, Andrea complained of being late due to a situation that had unfolded that afternoon at the national park. A young couple had returned from a three-day backpacking trip to find their car stolen. "It wasn't even a great car. A ten-year-old Honda. Trouble was it had all their stuff in it," she said as she turned onto the dirt road and bumped over ruts. "Hey, I wanted to ask. Do you feel like cooking dinner together on Friday night?"

"I can't cook."

"Great! I'll teach you," Andrea said as she pulled to a stop in the parking lot.

The Hussies hadn't won a game yet this season. The opening of tonight's contest repeated a familiar pattern. The team scored a couple of runs early on, only to lose the lead when their opponents piled on six runs in one inning. Late in the game, the team was down by two when Kim came to bat. Both batters ahead of her had reached base. Before she stepped up to the plate, Lois took her aside. "Look for something inside," the team captain whispered. "Get a good look at it and whale away."

Kim took the first pitch for ball one. The second came in low for a called strike. Nervously, she twisted the bat. When the pitcher released the ball, Kim clenched her grip. She thought the ball was coming straight at her. But she held her ground and swung. The ball sailed off her bat, over the first basewoman's head, and kissed the grass near the line. She sprinted toward first base.

Both runners ahead of her scored. Two batters later, she crossed home plate on the strength of another teammate's double. The Hussies had eked out their first win of the year.

"You've got that natural inside-out swing," Lois said jubilantly. "I knew if she gave you an inside pitch, we were golden."

There was no question of not going out to celebrate. At the Den, beer and food appeared on the tables. Lois led them through a more-hilarious-than-usual postgame analysis.

"What's new with you?" Jackie Melnick asked Kim when talk had moved on from the game.

Remembering how her day had started, Kim laughed. "I blew someone off today."

"What?"

"Who?" Linda Perez, another teammate, said.

"A guy named Scott Wentworth. I met him out at Pine Village. His mother is one of the women I read to."

"Oh, Scott," Linda said offhandedly. "Whatever you did, I'm sure he deserved it."

"What do you mean?" Kim said.

Instead of answering, Linda leaned forward and called to Lois. "You're not going to believe who Kim met today. Scott Wentworth."

"Lord have mercy," Lois said. She pushed her chair back and dragged it several places down. Once she was resettled across the table from Kim, she said, "What in the world are you doing messing around with Scott Wentworth?"

"I'm not messing around with him," Kim said, trying not to grin. "I only said I met him. I read to his mother at Pine Village."

Lois said, "Did he flirt with you? Never mind. I already know the answer."

"No, he didn't flirt with me. I blew him off. What's the deal with Scott Wentworth?"

"You don't know the story about the Wentworths?" Lois said.

"No."

"Then make yourself comfortable, darlin', because I have a story to tell you."

Lois reached for the pitcher of beer. She topped off her own glass and several others before she began.

"Sam Wentworth's legacy should have guaranteed the financial security of several generations of Montrose families. Instead, under the incompetent management of his only son, it dried up within a decade of his death. Sam Wentworth, now there was an entrepreneur worthy of the name," Lois said, pointing with her beer. "Decades ago, Sam started a distribution company. It's hardly front-page stuff now, but forty years ago, Montrose wasn't seeing the kind of traffic we see today.

Sam started out with a market and a gas station. When he ran into problems getting the quality of goods he wanted to sell, he spun out in a wider direction. He started running trucks between here and Grand Junction and, soon after that, on to Denver. He brought in a regular supply of merchandise folks quickly grew partial to having. Food, primarily, at least in the beginning. We didn't have any chain stores then, and sometimes the best we could get were the cast-off products from Grand Junction."

"Okay," Kim said. "So Sam Wentworth ran a fleet of trucks."

"It was more than that. Eventually he had a complete distribution network in place. Warehouses, auto maintenance guys, fueling stations. It was a mini-empire, to tell you the truth, and no one minded a bit because the guy running it was as clean as a freshly starched shirt. Linda, you tell her what happened."

Linda Perez said, "Sam keeled over from a heart attack one day some fifteen years ago. According to his secretary, he was at his desk popping Tums tablets like they were Life Savers. She got held up on the phone with one of their Denver suppliers. When she got on the intercom to Sam with a question, he didn't answer. He was dead when she found him. Heart attack. By then, Scott had been working at his father's business for a couple of years. He took over. Scott always was too big for his britches. He was determined to do things his own way. A few years into the job, and without letting anyone know what he was up to, he took money out of the business to play the stock market. Seems he had different ideas about how to make money. It wasn't sexy or challenging enough for him to go on running the company the way his father had."

"What did he do?" Kim said.

"He started some investors' fund," Lois said. "The idiot got his seed money in the form of a loan, collateralized with the company fleet." The team captain laughed unhappily. "His timing was terrible. The market crashed. The bankers foreclosed in a heartbeat. A business that had been worth maybe two million was sold off for a fraction of that. Lucy got whatever was left."

Kim said, "That's terrible. But all of that happened a long time ago. Why is everyone still angry at Scott?"

Lois said, "Sam's company, Western Slope Distributing, was the second-largest employer in Montrose when Scott lost control of it. The bankers holding the note sold it to a competitor who replaced local staff with their own people. A lot of fathers, husbands, and brothers lost good-paying jobs, not to mention their pensions. You bet there are a lot of hard feelings toward Scott Wentworth."

Kim knew she was waging a losing battle convincing her teammates that she had nothing to do with Scott. Similarly, she knew she would have to think about what she had heard. She smiled ruefully and opened another door. "What's Scott doing to make a living now?"

Linda said, "He's got a couple of those quick oil lube places. One here and another in Delta. I don't know a soul who takes their car there, but somebody must. He's stayed in that line of business since."

"And built a brand-new house a few years back," another teammate offered.

"Where did he get the money for start-up?" Kim said.

"His mother," Linda said. "I guess it must have come from his mother."

"Hey, did you hear his wife filed for divorce?" someone else said.

"About time," Lois declared. "How long's Charlene been gone?"

"Christmas. Right after. She yanked those kids out of school and got them enrolled in California. I still get emails from her now and then. Her son and my Robbie were tight."

Linda cast a teasing look at Kim. "Sounds like the man's about to be single again, if you're interested."

Kim laughed.

"Do not even suggest that," Lois said. "If Scott Wentworth were the last man on earth, I wouldn't give him the time of day. He may look like one of the dashing heroes out of those romance novels you read, Kim, but trust me, he is not one of the good guys. Besides, he's got to be, what? Ten or twelve years older than you?"

Laughing, Kim said, "I never said I was interested in Scott. I only said I met him. I had no idea what kind of hornet's nest I was going to stir up."

A flurry of other stories followed. Virtually everyone at the table had something to say about Scott Wentworth. Except Jackie. Several times, she and Kim exchanged smiles.

"Welcome to small-town America," Jackie whispered as the conversation wore on. "If you sneeze on the north end of town, someone from the south side is bound to say, 'Bless you.' There's no escaping it."

"If I didn't know that before, I know it now."

"Love it or hate it, but that's the way it is."

CHAPTER 10

Andrea was out of the house early the next morning. Kim heard her moving from her bedroom to the bathroom to the kitchen but waited to get up until she heard the front door close and a car driving away. She found the bathroom warm and steamy from the recently used shower. There was enough coffee left in the pot for one cup. Kim poured it, pleasantly surprised by the lingering trace of her roommate's presence.

She was happier to have the house to herself. She drank the coffee and made a second pot. While it was brewing, she collected Emily Riley's notebooks and sat down to read.

In the opening pages of the first notebook, she found math problems. After that came notes taken for a civics class. By the occasional dates jotted down in the top right corner, Kim knew Emily took this class her sophomore year. Skimming details devoted to the Constitution and democracy, her eyes glazed over. She began to fear she was wasting her time.

Midway through the notebook, something in Emily's writing changed. In her unfocused state, Kim initially missed it and had to flip back several pages. Reading more closely, she began to find something brave in the passages. It seemed Emily was trying to anchor her life through her writing. She wrote in great detail, prompting Kim to wonder whether she was practicing writing advice someone gave her: evoke the details. Kim came to a personal sketch of a woman, almost certainly a teacher.

> *Her voice is strong. Her eyes looking down*
> *upon us are sharp, but I wonder if they are so*
> *sharp when she looks at herself. She wears a*
> *navy-blue blazer, plain skirts, plain slacks, has*
> *she ever noticed patterns and prints in fabric?*
> *No hair out of place, her face carefully made*
> *up, she walks with purpose, she drives a Chevy.*
> *If I close my eyes and listen to her voice, I hear*
> *something wise. When I open my eyes, I see*
> *a woman who would tell us what we need to*
> *know to live but has no clue what it means to*
> *be alive.*

Kim suspected she could stroll through the halls of Montrose High and easily identify the woman Emily described. Then she wondered whether she already knew her. She wondered whether Emily wrote this passage about Jackie Melnick.

Halfway through the second notebook, Kim came to Emily's first mention of family. She wrote in short bursts of affection and resentment about her then three-year-old brother. Early on, there wasn't a single reference to Deena. Much later—Kim was into the third notebook by now—Emily lost the discipline of prose and gave herself over to raw emotion. She wrote heatedly: "Screw her. Screw her. Screw her and that goddamned car and that goddamned kid and every lousy, stupid, goddamned thing she's done to ruin my life."

Kim stared at the thick black marks. She wondered whether Emily wrote these words the day Deena drove up in a new car. Had she perhaps been waiting at the door of their paint-chipped house and asked, unassumingly, *Whoa, Mom, where'd you get the new wheels?* And how would Deena have answered? Had she looked Emily straight in the eye? Or blinked rapidly and looked anywhere but at her talented daughter? *I took the money your dad gave us,* she might have said, sucking it up and putting it out there. *Now don't look at me that way. Somebody's gotta hold this family together, and it sure isn't going to be you or Dustin. Emily! Get back here, Emily! Listen to me!*

"He didn't give that money to *us,*" Emily may have screamed, watching her dreams shatter. "It was my money! He gave that money to me."

Kim blinked rapidly. She pulled herself out of the fantasy. Emily wouldn't have written these words that day. She most likely wrote them much later, when her pain had been blunted by bitterness.

Sloppy scrawls in the pages afterward denoted changes in her life. "Prom with M. Dumped M. I'm out of the game. A can say what she wants, I'm not listening."

"M"—Ashley had said Emily's longtime boyfriend was someone named Mike. "A" had to be Ashley.

Emily wrote of taking a job at Taco Bell that summer. In the first few entries, she tried to mimic the style of her earlier writing, evoking details of situations that struck her, sometimes involving customers, sometimes writing character sketches of coworkers. She couldn't sustain the positive energy. One paragraph broke off midsentence in brute anger. "I want money. Screw this other shit. I just want money."

The teenager suffered unwanted attention from her manager, a twenty-three-year-old man with a steady girlfriend and plans to marry. She wrote of tolerating his teasing while rebuffing his stronger advances. She reminded him some of his behavior verged on sexual harassment. He retaliated by reducing her hours. "I swear I should just quit. I would except I just spent four hundred bucks on a new phone," she wrote.

Kim wondered what had happened to that phone. She hadn't read any mention of it in news articles.

She deciphered the cryptic numbers Emily occasionally jotted down and guessed that despite splurging on a new phone, the girl banked something close to $1,000 from her paychecks.

Interwoven between passages of anger at her mother and frustration at the hours she had to babysit her brother, Emily kept a list of books she wanted to read. On it was *Educated* by Tara Westover. Kim silently cheered, and wondered if Emily ever got around to reading it. She suspected the teen would have found the memoir inspiring.

Late in the summer, Emily quit her job after an old friend came into Taco Bell one night, and the scene that ensued. In her own words: "I quit! Caleb—he goes by 'Cal' now—came in, and I was so happy to see him, I practically leapt over the counter. Not really. But I did run around to the front and hug him. G was so mad, his face was so red! He told me to quit flirting with customers. Caleb—I mean, Cal—cocked his head the funny way he does and said, 'You really put up with this guy's shit?' And I thought no. No, I don't!"

For many pages afterward, Emily wrote almost exclusively about Cal. Kim pieced their history together. Cal was a childhood friend, two years older than Emily, who had lived a few doors down. Cal had had a rough home life. The police were often at his house responding to "domestic incidents" between his parents. When Cal was sixteen, his older brother was arrested for dealing drugs. A few months later, Cal was arrested and charged with meth possession. He'd avoided a juvie record, but had been sent by the court to live with his grandparents out of state. Emily hadn't seen him since he left Montrose three years ago.

Now nineteen, Cal had been discharged from the army due to a previously undiagnosed medical condition. "He won't tell me what. Everyone in town thinks he was dishonorably discharged. Small-town bigots," Emily wrote.

The two began spending time together. Ashley didn't approve. Emily didn't care. Kim assumed Emily and Cal were lovers until she came upon the passage: "Everyone always wants something from me. Everyone always expects either that I *am* a certain way or that I should be that way. Cal doesn't. We play a game when we're together in public, pretending to be crazy about each other. And we are, in a way. Definitely. But it's not romantic. It's more like we're soul mates."

Emily wrote of the things she and Cal talked about. She said he spoke often of one of his buddies in the army, a guy he kept in touch with. Cal said his buddy once told him being in the army was the safest place he could be. He said this guy was saving every penny for the day he got out of the service. He had a plan for getting on with his life that didn't include going back to where he'd started out. "But to do that, you gotta have money." Cal's words. Emily's writing. She had underlined every word in the sentence.

Kim stood up, poured herself another cup of coffee, and took a short break while she drank it. When she resumed reading, she was unsurprised to come upon a question posed by Emily within a few pages. "Is Cal gay? I hope he knows I wouldn't care."

It wasn't anything Emily would need to wonder about for long. Shortly afterward, Cal left town. In the middle of a September night, he left an envelope taped to her front door with a note inside. "Life's complicated. Love you." Rumors of drug peddling followed him out of town. All this, according to Emily's scribbles.

Kim's shoulders tensed. She drew a deep breath. She sensed that whatever came next for Emily, it wasn't going to be good.

It wasn't.

Initially, it appeared Emily tried to be stoic. Her first comment had a faintly cavalier ring to it: "He said he might not stick around long. I guess I should have listened." Whatever she wrote next was gone. The pages had been ripped out of the spiral notebook. Only white tattered edges clung to the ring, indicating an absence. Kim was taken aback by the first entry on the next full page. "I HATE MY LIFE!" There followed a diatribe about a failed pre-calc exam and being turned down for a job at McDonald's.

Kim's eyes began to glaze over while she read dark lyrics lifted from Billie Eilish songs and something about caged rats in a song by someone named Karen O. Her interest was waning when she spotted a reference to a visit to an Edward Jones brokerage office. Reminding herself Emily was full of surprises, Kim stood up and took another short break. When she returned to the kitchen table, she double-checked entries and estimated Emily's visit to the brokerage office came in late October.

It quickly became apparent that the teenager wanted to learn how to play the stock market. She went to the office in the afternoon when it was typically quiet. Of the four people she described meeting there, one stood out. He was an associate in his early thirties whose first name began with the letter *B*. By Emily's second or third visit, he was quick to meet her in the nicely appointed outer room, furnished with a TV broadcasting a financial news program. Copies of *Forbes*, *Barron's*, the *Wall Street Journal*, and other newspapers were arranged on a coffee table. Emily confided to B that she had a bit of money to invest. "Gotta have money," she scrawled in her notebook. She drew the figures: "$1,000 $\rightarrow$ $8,000." It was an easy leap for Kim to imagine the girl was still trying to recoup the money given to her by her bio-dad, which her mother had spent.

Emily summarized the investment lessons B gave her in a list. At a minimum, she needed to learn about P/E ratios. Better yet, she should learn to read a company's annual report. Before investing in a stock, she should know the company's earnings, current and forecasted. Also, their expenses. And debt. "Just tell me the FCCCCKKNG secret!" she wrote.

Kim flipped the page and came across a string of smiley faces. There was no further mention of visits to the brokerage office. The last time Emily referred to B, she said, "What a dork."

Kim had no idea what had happened.

She skimmed through the notebook, assessing how much remained. There were another twenty pages or so. Having come this far, she persuaded herself to read on.

By December of her senior year, Emily had one clear goal: to leave Montrose. It was as if she woke up one morning and knew a better life awaited her beyond the confines of her hometown. Reading between the lines, Kim sensed the girl's deep-seated fear that she wouldn't be able to escape. She wrote poems about it. Several were quite extraordinary. Kim wondered what Jackie, who taught English, might say about them. Perhaps she would find out. Kim intended to make copies of at least two poems.

Otherwise, the writings were scattered—scathing blasts of emotion that ineffectually hid Emily's underlying pain. Nor had she lost her obsession with money. In dark letters, Emily scrawled in one corner: "Clark Kent, super money man. Where the hell does he get his money?"

Clark was the name of Deena's on-again, off-again boyfriend, according to Kim's softball teammates. She recalled seeing him escorting Deena from church at Emily's memorial service. And again that same night, sitting next to Tyler Haas in a bar.

She pondered the association. With nowhere to go with it, she read on.

In the winter, something changed for Emily. Tired, and skimming quickly, Kim nearly missed it. She backed up several pages to read more closely. On the surface, it didn't seem terribly interesting. Emily was taking a photography course. The wonder was that she had reconnected with something and was no longer merely passing time until she meant to escape. Every word she wrote testified to that. Long paragraphs were dedicated to describing a new world as seen through the lens of a camera. There were notes about filters and apertures and shutter speeds. Emily was doing photography the old-fashioned way, with a 35 millimeter camera and a variety of lens sizes. And she loved it.

In addition, she had a new lover. Kim flipped back through the pages, trying to find a date that marked the start of the relationship. She couldn't find any time references to nail down when Emily had written these pages. Then she found mention of a Saint Paddy's Day toast with a man she called "Mr. Money Bags." Kim began to feel disconcerted, sensing a euphoric tone in the writing, and also Emily's smugness. She wondered whether Emily had had an affair with the man named B, from Edward Jones, and possibly resumed it. Her instincts told her no, but she quickly admitted she had next to no insight into what Emily might have been up to or with whom.

The writing was about photography; the doodles on the side of the pages were a string of dollar signs. There were no initials to give even the faintest clue as to the new lover's identity. Near the end of the notebook, Kim came upon another poem. It held a place of honor on the lower half of a page, carefully printed in lowercase, in the style of E. E. Cummings. Kim read it once, stopped, then read it again. It threw her. She read it a third time, convinced by the time she finished that Emily had written this poem about a different man in her life.

phantom lover, you are not mine,
i through you, you through me, our
    dreaming desires wander separately,
    ascending;
but for a moment's touch, and
a moment's glance into the steely gray
    glint of your eyes descending,
i doubt you are real.

Haunted by the words, Kim couldn't fathom what Emily was trying to tell her. She did not for one instant think these heartfelt words were written for someone nicknamed "Mr. Money Bags." Which led her to the fascinating conclusion that Emily had had more than one lover toward the end of her life.

CHAPTER 11

A day passed while Emily Riley's notebooks remained on top of the dresser in Kim's bedroom. Inertia and a vague sense of having missed something kept her from returning them to Emily's mother. She had made notes and copied a few poems. Having no excuse to delay returning them, she loaded the four notebooks along with a crisp new copy of *Howards End* in her backpack before leaving for Pine Village.

"By request," she announced to Christine and Lucy, "we have a new book to read."

Sheer delight shone in Lucy's eyes. "You found it."

"I found it," Kim said, lightly thumping the book against her hand. "I haven't read this novel. I have no idea what to expect."

"Then you don't know about the goblins?" Lucy said in surprise.

Kim said she did not.

"Beethoven's Fifth Symphony and the goblins. Chapter five. I have never loved anything in literature as much as I love that. Beethoven tells us bravely that the goblins are there. He banishes them, but tells us they may come back. And that is why he can be trusted." She ended with a knowing nod, as if she, too, endorsed this truth.

"How many times have you read *Howards End*?" Christine said. Her voice was full of incredulity, though Kim suspected her shock was at the slew of sentences Lucy had strung together.

"Oh, not so many. Perhaps four."

"Goodness! And that's not so many?"

"No. There were always so many other things to read."

To Kim's amazement, Lucy answered each question Christine proceeded to ask. She told of having had three years of college "back East" where she had concentrated her studies in English. After coming West with her husband, she'd taught the subject in school.

"We were fortunate. Money wasn't our problem," Lucy said. "Well, I say that, but let me add that Sam did have periods of worry with his business, as anyone does. I taught because I loved it."

Kim smiled.

"Did you settle immediately in Montrose?" Christine said.

"No. Grand Junction was our first destination. We lived there for five years. It was a bit of a gamble coming to Montrose, but Sam showed spunk and made a go of it. Best decision of our lives," she said softly.

Kim stayed longer than usual. When the time came to leave, she stood and, with a promise to return soon, left her two friends sitting together. Lost in her thoughts, she was nearly at the front entrance before she realized where she was. With a start, she spied the man standing at the counter. Scott Wentworth smiled broadly.

"Kim, hello. What perfect timing."

"Perfect timing, my foot," Justine said from behind the counter. "He's been waiting for you for fifteen minutes."

Kim smiled from one to the other, unsure how to reply.

"Ignore her," Scott said. "She's irritated because she's stuck behind that desk. While you and I are free to go wherever we please. Including for ice cream, if we'd like." He stepped back as though a decision were made, intending to usher her forward. It was a completely theatrical gesture.

"I'll see you in a few days," Kim said over her shoulder to Justine, of no mind to go for ice cream or anywhere with Scott Wentworth. She had to go to work, and had an errand to run beforehand.

Once they were outside, she said, "Scott, wait. It's nice to see you again. Actually, I want to apologize for the way I behaved the other day. I was distracted. I'd had an unpleasant conversation with someone, and when you saw me, I was—"

"Hopping mad," he finished.

She laughed. "Yes."

"Good. You can tell me about it over ice cream. It sounds like a good story."

"Thank you, but no. I can't go for ice cream with you."

"Why not? Have you already had ice cream today?"

The boyish look of expectation on his face exasperated her as much as it amused her. Scott was a tall, good-looking guy in his midforties. When she saw him several days ago, he was wearing a suit. Today he wore a polo shirt tucked into chinos. On a Chicago street, he would have been indistinguishable from hundreds of other men. In the hinterlands of Montrose, he stood out.

"No. But I do have an errand to run."

"Perfect. You can do it later."

"Where is this ice-cream shop?" she said skeptically.

"It's right up the road," he said, pointing north, the opposite direction Kim traveled between Pine Village and home. "A half mile, tops. I stop there nearly every day to pick up a milkshake for my mother. What good luck I forgot to stop today."

Kim wondered how much luck had to do with it. By Justine's comments, she gathered Scott knew she was at Pine Village and had been waiting for her. Despite herself, she felt flattered. She glanced at her watch and realized she had time enough to spare before she was due at work, assuming she postponed returning Emily Riley's notebooks until later in the day.

She and Scott had another minor scuffle when she insisted on riding her bicycle to the shop. Scott wanted to drive her there. This time, she held her ground and cycled the distance, which was not quite as short as promised, and met Scott in the parking lot. As they walked toward the window to order, she said, "Your mother was in good spirits this morning. She's been doing better lately. You must be pleased."

"Yes and no," he said with a distinct air of hesitation. "Of course, I'm always pleased when she's better. But I have the doctor's word that she's at the upper limit of how well she'll ever be. I'm trying not to have expectations for her."

"I'm sorry, Scott. I didn't know that. This must be terribly hard on you."

"It is. It's nothing I ever wanted for her."

They waited in line behind a woman and two small boys. When it was their turn, Scott said, "My treat. Order anything you fancy."

"Thanks, Scott, but I'll be happy to pay for my own ice cream."

He turned a frown on her. "Hasn't anyone told you this is still the Old West where a few of us male chauvinist types insist on doing right by our lady friends? Besides, and more importantly, I want to thank you for all you've done for Mom."

They ordered. He paid.

"Come on, let's walk for a bit," he said. He touched her arm lightly and led her around to the back of the ice-cream stand. A path led through a thicket of trees. On the far side,

they emerged onto a trimmed lawn furnished with three pic-
nic tables, currently vacant. They chose one and sat down.

He said, "Now, this is my idea of a good way to start a day,
eating ice cream with an attractive, beguiling young woman
on a beautiful summer morning."

Kim flashed him a warning look.

"Sorry," he said. "Safe subjects. How long have you been
living in Montrose? And what brought you here?"

Kim concentrated on eating her ice cream. When no better
answer came to her, she said, "I've been here for a few months.
I was planning on driving to the West Coast, but I got caught
by a snowstorm. My plans changed so I decided to stay for a
while."

"So you do have a car. Good. I was beginning to worry
about you. It's positively un-American not to own a car."

"Had a car. I loaned mine to a friend in Denver." The lie slid
easily from her lips.

"Must be a good friend. That's a generous thing to do."

Kim changed the subject. "I can't tell you how much I've
enjoyed the time I've spent with your mother. Are you as pas-
sionate about books as she is?"

"No. I'm sorry to say, Mom has all the literary genes in our
family."

"Do you have brothers and sisters?"

"One sister. Eliza lives in Denver. Mom and I don't see her
much. A year ago, she went to work for a start-up. I gather the
business shows great promise, but it's at a cost to her. Sixty
hours per week is her minimum."

"Is she married?"

"Divorced. No kids. So, families," Scott said. "Tell me about
yours."

Kim laughed uneasily. She bought a moment pretending
to sculpt her ice cream into a manageable shape. After an
instant's reflection, she decided to tell the truth. "I have one

brother. Both my parents are dead. My mother died a while ago. I lost my father last year."

"Wow," Scott said. "And your brother?"

"We're not close. He's older than I am. We didn't grow up together."

Scott's handsome face squinted in a look of concern. "So you're basically alone?"

Kim shrugged off the suggestion. "It's not that bad. I have aunts and uncles. And cousins."

"Friends? Boyfriends? Come on," he said, laughing now.

"Oh well, yes. Boyfriends, past tense, anyway."

Scott spent a moment eating his ice cream. "It sounds to me like you're on a grand adventure, traveling the highways and byways of America."

Kim's first thought was to correct his impression. When she couldn't think of any easy way to do so, she agreed. "Yes, that's about it. It is an adventure. I'm drifting—no, I'm not drifting as much as I'm, oh, I don't know. This will sound silly."

"Say it anyway."

"Call it a journey of self-discovery. I'm trying to find out what I really want to do with my life."

"Lucky you. Brave you. I wish I'd had the nerve to do something like that." He stood up and went to throw away his blue plastic ice-cream dish. When he returned, he said, "So when you're not gallivanting all across America, what kind of work do you do?"

The question paralyzed her. For the first time since leaving Chicago, Kim wanted to tell someone the truth—that she was a professional accountant. She wanted Scott to know she had her MBA and was a licensed CPA. She caught herself before blurting out the truth. "I've worked in business. Inventory management, customer service, a little bit of a lot of things."

He nodded. In that instant, she knew he assumed her position had been low.

"And you?" she said.

"I own a couple of quick lube franchises." Scott nervously glanced at his watch. "Kim, I need to get going. But I wanted to ask you something. Are you seeing anyone? Now hold on," he rushed to add. "I'm married, yes. Separated and about to be divorced is the absolute truth. I'm not—"

"You're not what?"

His smile was wan. He seemed at a loss. "I'd like to have dinner with you sometime. That's all."

She stood up. Her answer was no. She had to tell him no, absolutely not, under no circumstances would she have dinner with him, and it wasn't because he was married and on his way to getting a divorce. "Maybe," she said.

"Maybe?"

"Let me think about it."

"At least that's not an outright refusal."

"As if that would have stopped you from asking again anyway," she said.

"Uh-oh. You already know me too well," he said, flashing a grin that captivated and disarmed her.

"Somehow I doubt that."

—

The afternoon shift at JT's was hectic. An unrelenting flow of unfamiliar faces—summer residents, Ashley complained—kept the checkout lanes full. Kim was minutes away from ending her shift when she heard the crash of glass breaking in her lane.

"Jamie!" a harried young mother exclaimed. "I told you not to touch that."

Kim leaned forward to see liquid pooling around large chunks of glass and a pick-up-sticks arrangement of dill pickle spears splayed in the center of the mess. She hurriedly thrust a

"Closed" sign on her conveyor belt and rushed to where mother and son stood staring shame-faced at the floor. "Stand back," she said. "This will only take a minute. You didn't get cut, did you?" she asked the little boy, who shook his head fiercely. Not taking his word for it, she inspected his bare legs and his feet inside flip-flops. Ashley's call for assistance from one of the stock boys went unanswered, so it was left to Kim to get a pail and mop and clean the floor. The woman and boy were gone by the time she finished.

She opened her lane and handled a few more customers before putting up the "Closed" sign to end her day. She turned her cash drawer over to John and was halfway to the door before she remembered the cupcakes. Hardly in the mood any longer to do anything but go home, she marched to where the boxed cakes were displayed and took a six-pack of chocolate cupcakes from the shelf.

"Can we switch shifts next Tuesday?" Ashley said when Kim went through her lane to pay for them. "I'm supposed to work at eight. I wanted to ask you earlier, but I never had a chance."

"I volunteer on Tuesday mornings," Kim said. Something made her add, "I can probably rearrange my schedule." Of course, she could. Christine and Lucy wouldn't care.

Atypically urgent, Ashley said, "Thanks. I have an interview. I just found out." She lowered her voice. "Please don't tell anyone."

The news that her coworker—barely a week out of high school—had snared an interview for a better job did nothing to improve Kim's mood. After leaving the store, she pedaled the mile across town to the house teetering on the edge of disrepair, anxious to dispense with Emily Riley's journals and her obligation to return them. There was no response to her knock. She tried again.

"Yes," Emily's mother said coldly when she answered the door.

"Hello, Deena," Kim said.

Deena looked at her blankly.

Kim reintroduced herself. "I stopped by the other day. You were kind enough to let me borrow Emily's notebooks. I'm here to return them. Also, I brought these cupcakes for Dustin." Kim ended brightly, hoping to defuse the other woman's sour attitude.

"Oh. You're that reporter who's doing a story on Emily."

"I'm a freelance writer. I'm not a reporter with the paper in town."

Deena seemed neither to understand nor care about the distinction. Sensing she was about to have the door slammed in her face, Kim rushed to say, "I'd like to ask you one more question."

"What?"

"In her notes, Emily wrote about a photography project. It seemed to be something she was interested in. I wondered whether you have it."

She doubted Deena would allow her to look at it even if she did have it. But Emily's mother gave another answer. "Hell, I forgot about that. It's not here. It must still be at school. I should go and get it."

Kim doubted that Deena, given her lack of interest in her daughter's writing, cared much about her photography. Sensing the woman had reengaged, she pressed her advantage. "Emily obviously loved photography. Do you know what her project was?"

"What? You think she talked to me? Well, she didn't. All I know is that girl was running around in the dead of night with a camera. Beats the hell out of me what she was doing." She stepped back and started to close the door.

"Is everything okay?" Kim said, wondering at Deena's detachment. A few days ago, they had had a perfectly cordial conversation.

"Is everything okay?" Deena returned mockingly. "Well, now let me think about that. The bill collectors are banging on my door, my daughter's dead, my little boy split open his head and needed eight stitches, and to top it all off, the police are snooping around looking for my old man. Other than that, everything is just fine, thank you very much."

"I'm sorry for your trouble," Kim said. "I'll try to bring Dustin a chocolate cake now and then."

Deena took the cupcakes and closed the door.

CHAPTER 12

Emily Riley's notebooks were a complete dead end. *Almost* a complete dead end, Kim amended, musing over the possibility that she had missed something in the journals. Not that it mattered now. The books were back in Deena Warren's possession, and all Kim had from the stash were copies of a few pages she had wanted to keep for reasons that now escaped her.

It wasn't Emily's writings that she couldn't stop thinking about after she left Deena's house. It was a photography project. Emily had written passionately about photography. Kim wondered whether the high school senior had left visual evidence of her lover, or lovers—or, failing that, whether another clue existed in a photograph that pointed to the reason for the teen's murder.

Frank Tattinger, Montrose High School photography instructor, was probably only in his thirties, though thinning hair and wire-rimmed glasses long out of style made him look older. He seemed to be doing three things at once while Kim explained why she was in his classroom the next morning. No students were present. Classes had ended for the year. When she finished, Tattinger gestured toward a large walk-in closet

at the rear of the room and assured her that Emily's photo project was "back there somewhere." He was on his way to a final
staff meeting for the year and didn't have time to look for it
now. They made plans to meet the following Monday morning
when he'd be back in the classroom doing inventory. Kim, disappointed, reluctantly turned to leave. At the door, she paused
and asked, "Has anyone else been here asking to see Emily's
work?"

The man's jaw jutted forward. He shook his head. "No.
Can't think why they would have been."

Dinner with Andrea was on tap for that night. Kim couldn't
remember explicitly having agreed to the social engagement,
not that it mattered. It was on her calendar now. After leaving the high school, she went directly to work, arriving early
enough to do the shopping, per Andrea's instructions. She
took her time selecting ingredients for poached salmon with
dill sauce, new potatoes, and fresh asparagus. Kim disliked
grocery shopping nearly as much as she disliked cooking. By
the time she finished, paid, and deposited the bags in a store-
room refrigerator at JT's, she was relieved to have the odious
task behind her. She hoped Andrea would be good to her word
and split the bill.

Early that evening, she arrived home to see the dark-blue
Subaru parked outside the house and the front door open. She
walked in to find her roommate celebrating happy hour. Cubes
of ice were melting in a tumbler on the coffee table. An open
bottle of Jack Daniel's stood on the kitchen counter. "Help
yourself," Andrea said from the living room couch.

Kim needn't have wondered what they would talk about
that evening. When Andrea roused herself to begin dinner
preparations, the conversation didn't stray far from the cooking lesson the ex-prosecutor had promised. She was insistent
on the importance of knife skills and repeatedly demonstrated
her chopping techniques on the fresh dill and potatoes. "Buy a

bag of carrots," she advised. "They're cheap and good to practice on."

Kim avoided the whiskey but availed herself of the chilled
wine in the refrigerator. It was both a relief, and not, when
at the end of the meal—which came together as delicious as
advertised—Andrea left the kitchen cleanup to her. Andrea
withdrew behind her closed bedroom door and didn't emerge
for the rest of the night.

It was far too early for Kim to do the same. Of no mind to
stay indoors, she took Dr. Abraham Craft's book *The Science
of Crime* to the front porch. She skimmed the chapter she had
read days ago on the importance of maintaining a "murder
board" in an investigation. She meant to read on, but in the
dwindling light and with a niggling sense of a job left unfinished, she opened her notebook and wrote down the facts she
had gleaned about Emily Riley's life as revealed by the young
woman herself in her journals. She expected the results to be
an unilluminating restatement of "what everybody knew" with
the mildly surprising revelation that Emily had been seeing
two men in the weeks before she was murdered. But there was
more.

Kim started over, composing the board in the manner
advocated by Dr. Craft, taking her time and thinking carefully
about each piece. The money bothered her. When she died,
Emily presumably had at least $1,000 in a bank account. If
the money wasn't still there, when had Emily withdrawn the
funds?

Kim lingered outside until the last of the day's light had
faded, pondering questions she hoped soon to answer.

—

On Monday morning, she was at Montrose High School before
nine. She made her way to the photography classroom, where

she found Frank Tattinger dressed casually in shorts, sandals, and a T-shirt.

"Good morning," he said. "I have my hands full taking inventory. But I did find Emily's project. I put it on the desk up front. Have a seat and take a look. I'll be there in a minute."

"Thank you."

Kim sat down and opened the thick binder. The first page was a single white sheet with Emily's name and the date, April 11. Kim started to turn the page. Then she did a quick calculation. April 11 was a Monday. Exactly ten days later, Emily had disappeared. Kim hesitated. When Emily assembled this album, she had no way of anticipating the devastating events about to befall her.

She turned to the first photo. It was a black-and-white image of a street intersection. Immediately, Kim recognized the major crossroads in town: the intersection of Townsend and Main, US Highways 550 and 50. Her initial impulse was to dismiss it, but something stopped her. The composition became interesting by its lines: the buildings framed on either side of the intersection, streetlights on the corners, and the cars caught midstream in the road while others pointed perpendicular, stopped at the traffic light.

After a minute, she turned the page. On the left, smaller photos were arranged. Each one was a Montrose storefront. JT's was represented, as was the Laundromat and coffee shop Kim frequented. By the fourth page, Kim had distinguished a pattern to the work. Emily had interwoven images of the old with the new to produce a collage reflecting the town's evolving state. She went back to the first photo and saw Emily's theme symbolically announced: it was a town at its crossroads.

"Several of those are professional-quality shots," Tattinger said, coming up behind her. "I told her so. Never had a kid take to the camera the way Emily did. Damn shame what happened to her."

Kim felt a flare of anger, hearing something glib in the photography teacher's remark. Unsure how to respond, she ignored him and flipped to the next page. Emily's subject changed. Here, her photos captured a stand of trees and, separately, a thicket of grass with a small stream in the background. Turning the page, Kim nearly laughed out loud when she saw the sprite-like boy peeking out from behind a tree. It was Dustin. His face was lit with pure joy. Other photos of him followed, taken in different settings, but the identical quality of innocence and joy shone in the boy's face.

"Deena would love these," Kim said. The moment she said the words, she felt a flash of betrayal. She knew why. Deena would love these photos for how they captured Dustin, not because Emily had taken them.

"It's always an interesting relationship between photographer and model," Tattinger said. "I believe the boy is Emily's brother."

"Yes."

"It's easy to see they had great feeling for each other."

Kim nodded. She moved quickly through the remainder of the pages. When she finished, she felt disappointed. Just as with the notebooks, there were no clues here. There were no shots of any men, no lover, friend, or stranger. Closing the album, she started to thank the photography instructor for his time, but then she remembered something. "Now that's strange," she said.

"What is?"

"When I was talking to Emily's mother the other day, she said Emily went out at night with a camera. Even in the dead of winter. I don't remember seeing any nighttime shots here."

"No, she didn't use any of those. Hold on a sec. I forgot about the others." Tattinger went to the storage area and returned with a box. "There may be something here. I do remember her taking those pictures, as she had to make special arrangements to keep the camera overnight." He sorted through the contents of the box, which contained brown envelopes with student names printed on top. Halfway through, he found Emily's. "These were other photos she took. Some were for assignments, some she just took, who knows why. Help yourself. I need to get back to work, but give a holler if you have any questions."

Kim took the envelope. She removed a thick pile of photos of various shapes and sizes, all black and white. Many were of the same style and subject matter as those selected for inclusion in the project. Others differed. There were several portraits, some staged, some candid. On a mission, Kim flipped through quickly, looking for night shots. She came to the first and squinted, puzzled. It was another storefront. Dave's Auto Body. The name was written in script on the white-washed building facade, but there was nothing remarkable about the place. She moved through the dwindling collection.

When she came to the next photo of Dave's place, there was more to inspect. A flatbed tow truck was in front of the building, a broken-down car on its bed. There was a man in the open doorway of the garage, his face averted and unrecognizable. All of the remaining photos were similar shots of cars or trucks on flatbeds going into, or possibly coming out of, the auto body shop. Several showed the figure of a man, but as with the first, the person was unidentifiable. They were the only nighttime photos in the mix.

"Do you have any idea why Emily took these?" Kim asked the photography instructor the next time he paused from his work.

"No. We didn't cover night photography in the class. That was something she took up on her own."

Studying the last photo, Kim said, "So that means, what? She needed to use different film speed?"

"Yes. Also, she wanted to practice using a telephoto lens. I believe all of those shots were taken with a telephoto."

"Huh."

"Weird, I agree."

"She never said what this was about?"

"No. I thought she might be trying to show a contrast, blue-collar guys versus white-collar guys, something like that. I saw the theme in another photo." He went through the pile looking for one in particular. "Here it is. She was definitely trying to capture something about a white-collar guy."

The photo was the front of the Edward Jones office. Flipping through quickly the first time, Kim had missed it. Studying it now, she saw two suits standing on the sidewalk, sunglasses on and coffee mugs in their hands. Was one of them Mr. Money Bags? Maybe. More likely one of them had a first name that began with the letter *B*, she thought, recalling what she had read in the journals. She checked her watch. "What's going to happen to these photos?" she said, knowing she had to leave soon for work.

"I suppose they should go to Emily's mother. The project, anyway."

"These too?" Kim asked, indicating the pile of prints.

"Ordinarily, I'd throw everything away. It's what I do this time every year, toss out material nobody bothers to pick up."

"Would you mind if I keep these?" Kim pointed at the prints.

Frank Tattinger frowned. "Makes no difference to me. But if Emily's mother wants them—"

"I'll clear it with her. I promise."

"Fine. Take them. In fact, if you know the family and you're going to see her anyway, why don't you take this too?" He picked up the photo binder.

Kim reluctantly took it. It would mean another trip to Deena's. She wasn't sure how she would explain why she had the binder, unless she embellished her cover story of wanting to write about Emily. On the whole, it seemed a small enough favor to perform in exchange for Tattinger's trust in letting her walk away with Emily's collected work.

CHAPTER 13

Kim's best-laid plans for delivering Emily's photography project to Deena Warren posthaste faded for lack of any reasonably good explanation for how she came into possession of the work. She took the binder and envelope home, where they occupied the same spot on the bedroom dresser that Emily's notebooks had a week ago. Deena wasn't looking for the photos. No one was. A short article in the newspaper furthered Kim's reluctance to see Deena anytime soon. The police were looking for Clark Adams. Anyone with information on his whereabouts was asked to contact a detective by the name of Dan Czernak.

However brief the article, it had an impact. At JT's, Kim heard expressions of relief from customers who were glad the police were finally looking at Adams as a "person of interest." It seemed not to matter that the article hadn't used those words. For some townspeople, Adams was as good as guilty of Emily's murder—with Deena Warren bearing some responsibility. After all, she had brought Adams into the family home. Given the prevailing wind of public opinion, Kim felt in no hurry to return to Deena's door.

On Tuesday, she was at the store when it opened. Ordinarily she worked afternoons on Tuesday, but she and Ashley had swapped shifts. Then John Trimble complicated her morning by announcing the hire of a new checkout clerk, his wife's niece. He wanted Kim to train her.

Edie, the niece, wasn't due in until midmorning, which was just as well, as the store stayed busy for the first half hour after opening. The early crush of shoppers finally ebbed long enough for Kim to take advantage of the lull and reach for the water bottle she kept on a shelf below the cash register. She stood up to see a tall, young man entering the store. It was Jeff Nelson, Ashley's boyfriend. Jeff did a quick tour of the aisles before returning to the front.

"Is Ashley here?" he said.

"No," Kim said.

"I thought she was working this morning."

"Normally she does open on Tuesdays, Jeff, but we switched shifts."

By his sweat-stained T-shirt, Jeff looked like he'd just been at the gym or finished a run. From Ashley, Kim knew Jeff had won a football scholarship to Western Colorado University over in Gunnison. Where Dr. Abraham Craft taught, she thought, apropos of nothing.

Obviously Ashley hadn't told him about her interview.

"Do you know what time she's coming in?" he said.

"She should be here at noon. Let me double-check on that." Kim kept one eye on her lane and walked over to the closed office door. "Is Ashley coming in at noon?" she called to John.

"Yeah. You need anything?"

"No. I just wondered."

When she looked back, Jeff's face was without emotion. "I guess you heard," she said.

He nodded. In the same instant, he lowered his gaze, breaking eye contact.

Something resonated. Kim backed away from the instant knowledge, uncertain and, more than that, afraid. Not of Jeff. Rather, of what she had seen. It was a characteristic gesture of his, abruptly lowering his eyes. Seeing it now, she recalled noticing it previously in the handful of times she had spoken to him. To anyone else, he might look like an awkward teenage boy, unhappy not knowing the whereabouts of his girlfriend.

A customer pulled into her lane. Kim went back to work, disturbed. Unbidden, a phrase popped to mind: "the steely gray glint of your eyes descending." It was the line from Emily Riley's poem. The phrase described with uncanny accuracy the look she'd seen a moment ago on Jeff's face. It was nothing she would have been able to name, but maybe Emily had. And perhaps in doing so had named her phantom lover.

Except that wasn't possible. Jeff was devoted to Ashley. Everyone knew that. Kim knew it, and she had only known Ashley Crane for two months.

The next hour passed in a blur. Kim made small talk with the customers she knew and was extra pleasant to those she didn't. All the while, her brain refused to quit. It operated on a separate wavelength, leaping to its own miserable conclusions.

Ashley breezed in at noon. When Kim asked about the interview, Ashley didn't share much other than to say it went fine. Kim told her Jeff had been in. Ashley sighed in a long-suffering way. Sensing an opening, Kim said, "How long have you and Jeff been seeing each other?"

"Three years. Since tenth grade."

"He's totally nuts about you. Anyone can see that."

"Yeah. He is."

Her voice was flat. Uninterested. Bored, possibly. Kim took advantage, and asked, "Does it ever start to feel like too much pressure?"

Ashley's reply came fast. "It was way too much pressure, especially in the beginning! Jeff made up his mind he wanted to marry me the first week we started going out. I straightened him out on that real fast."

"Good for you." Kim glanced down the aisle looking for any customers about to bear down on them. One woman with a heaping cart was still inspecting a sale display of juice drinks. Still pretending this was just girl talk, Kim said, "And you two have been going steady ever since? Three solid years?"

"Yeah." Ashley studied one fingernail with great interest. "Except for five weeks and two days. Jeff swears those don't count."

"No kidding? When was that?"

"Last winter. I broke up with him a week after Valentine's Day. Isn't that horrible? He'd just showered me with all these presents and was so intense. And there I was about to flunk out of my senior year. I blew up. I told him I couldn't see him anymore. I was a witch, but I had to be. I'm sorry, but I never would have graduated if we hadn't broken up." Ashley flung her hair back in a wave of frustration.

Kim began ringing up her next customer. She could do the math. Jeff and Ashley hadn't been seeing each other in the weeks leading up to Emily's disappearance. She stopped there. This wasn't the time or place to take it any further.

Besides, she knew the thoughts would return later.

They did. At home that night, she reread the poem she had copied from Emily's notebooks. "Phantom lover, you are not mine." The words seemed transparently obvious now. "I through you, you through me, our dreaming desires wander separately, ascending."

She couldn't be sure what the words meant. She couldn't be absolutely sure Emily wrote the poem about Jeff Nelson. But if she had? Emily hadn't been blind. She would have known Jeff wanted Ashley, not her. But what had she wanted? Someone to hold her? Maybe it was that simple. Maybe Jeff had sheltered her from loneliness in those final months when she was resigned to staying in Montrose.

If Kim's theory was correct.

Sorely troubled, she turned to the second poem she'd copied from Emily's notebooks. It had preceded the phantom lover poem, suggesting it was written first. Reading it, Kim felt the depth of Emily's ache for a different life.

> I am coming home, to a place I cannot
>   name or point to
> on any map,
> I must travel great distances,
> wrestle down the demons who would
>   bind me,
> and I shall;
>
> at journey's end I will arrive in this place I
>   cannot name,
> or even imagine beyond the certainty of
>   this truth:
> I will know it when I am there.
>
> I am coming home, to a place in this
>   world where eyes and lips
> do not lie,
> where deceit claims no power,
> where I will inhale deeply of air that
>   strengthens me to live
> as I am.

She blinked back tears. Emily hadn't named the poem. Kim had titled it "Homecoming." She acknowledged the poem might as well have been written for her.

She knew she couldn't blame herself for having been sucked into the web of Emily Riley's life. Coincidences bound them, the coincidence of arrival and departure, at least. She had taken Emily's job. She had traced the sad saga of Emily's life, her final weeks, anyway. She had dug deeper into the young woman's life than any stranger perhaps had a right to, purely for her own reasons.

But Emily was dead and Kim was alive, at least for now. And Jeff quite possibly had been Emily's lover, but that didn't mean he was her killer. But if he had been her lover, he certainly needed to be considered a suspect.

CHAPTER 14

Andrea came in late that night. Startled by clattering at the front door, Kim was out of bed and standing in the hallway when her housemate came in. "Sorry. Didn't mean to wake you," Andrea said.

Kim searched her memory, wondering whether she had forgotten a game. She said, "That's fine. I was awake reading."

"I met up with a few of the gals at the Den. I would've called you but had no way to get a hold of you." Andrea closed and locked the door. "That's the one thing I don't get about you. How can you not have a phone?" She walked unsteadily into the house.

"It's an experiment. It's my version of living off the grid."

"Ha! That's a good one." Andrea passed by and went straight to her bedroom.

She was gone before Kim was up the next morning. She left a pot of coffee and a note on the kitchen table. "Dinner Saturday? I have another recipe I want to teach you. A."

Kim didn't mind the prospect of another dinner, little as she bought into the notion that Andrea was doing her a favor. Andrea enjoyed cooking. Perhaps not quite as much as she enjoyed drinking while cooking, which Kim suspected was the real point. At their last game, she had overheard Andrea telling a teammate one of the downsides of living at the park was having a teetotaler boss.

With the house to herself, Kim opened the envelope holding Emily Riley's photos and dumped the loose pile on the table. Purely as an exercise, she separated the photos. Those with people went in one stack, those of town or country scenes in another. She set the second group aside. She subdivided the pictures of people further. Some shots obviously were staged; others were taken of men and women unaware they were being photographed. Earlier, Kim had thought she saw several portrait-like photos of different women, but when she looked more closely, she found the subject in each was the same: a young woman approximately Emily's age. In one photo, the girl held a camera to her eye. Possibly she had snapped a photo of Emily at the same moment this one was taken of her. Kim kept this shot separate. She wished she had asked Frank Tattinger the student's name.

She continued to sift through the pile until she came to the two men standing outside the Edward Jones office. One, she believed, had a first name that began with the letter *B*. Had Emily christened him "Mr. Money Bags"?

She sipped her coffee. Darker thoughts inexorably took shape. They drew her back to a gray-eyed teen named Jeff Nelson.

Kim drew a deep breath and reminded herself she could be wrong—very likely *was* wrong about Jeff being the subject of Emily's poem. Emily could have written those words about anyone. Jeff and Ashley had broken up. So what? In all likelihood, Jeff had spent those weeks walking around with a hangdog look, never sparing a second glance at another girl. He'd probably spent the entire time waiting for Ashley to take him back.

The police had had access to the notebooks. They had interviewed everyone in Emily's circle of friends. They could have discovered this same set of curious facts. Except— something told her they hadn't. Emily's cleverness was her undoing. She had hidden the details of her life too well in the final weeks of her life.

Kim satisfied herself with adding a few notes to her murder board before putting it and the packet of photos away. She meant to keep the collection of loose photos, at least for now. Her only defense in doing so was the conviction that Deena didn't know about them and wouldn't want them, regardless. Deena might not want the photography project either, but she was going to get it. Soon.

At the end of her morning shift at JT's, Kim bundled the binder in brown wrapping paper and, expense be damned, sent it anonymously through the mail. The deed absolved her from another visit to Deena and an almost-certainly-futile effort to explain how she had come by the project. Deena likely would assume it was sent by someone at the school. If she assumed anything.

Late that afternoon, Kim returned to town after spending an hour at Pine Village with Christine and Lucy. Restless, she walked the streets Emily had once walked. She paused at the corner of the town's major crossroads, Townsend and Main, wondering which direction Emily would have gone had she realized her goal of leaving Montrose—north to Interstate 70, east to Colorado Springs, or south to Durango? Had Emily despised rural life? Had she loved the mountains? Where would her dreams have taken her?

Kim walked on, only mildly surprised when she found herself on the same block as the Montrose Community Center. She went in.

"Kim! It's great to see you," Dottie Goddard said. "What have you been doing with yourself lately? Still volunteering out at Pine Village?"

"Hi, Dottie. It's nice to see you too," Kim said to the white-haired woman dressed in a lime-green T-shirt. The blazing color looked perfectly natural on the woman with the curiously unnatural white hair and skin. "Yes, I'm still reading to my friends Lucy and Christine."

"Wonderful. You were reading *Jane Eyre*, as I recall. You must have finished that book by now. What have you followed with?"

"*Howards End*. It was Lucy's request."

"Ah," Dottie exclaimed. "England's fate. The struggle between the old and the new, the landed gentry and the rising industrial class, the 'new money' and the rights forthwith to buy in, so those kinds of people always think."

Kim's smile gave way to an easy laugh. "You've lost me. I thought it was a love story."

"Oh, it is. It's the greatest of love stories. It's a sweeping love story of the best and most profound affections individuals can share with one another, and then it goes far, far beyond, telling the ragged tale of being in love with life itself."

"I can see I must give it a closer read," Kim said, warmed to the core.

"But you didn't come here to discuss books with me, now, did you? Though, if you did, I'd be thrilled."

Kim sat down on the plastic chair adjacent to Dottie's desk. The desk was covered with scattered papers, though she suspected Dottie could put her finger on any single item in an instant. "I was out for a walk when I thought of stopping by to say hello," she said, hedging. "But it's true. I do have some things on my mind."

Dottie dropped her pen and sat back with a clear air of expectation. "Great. Let's hear it."

Kim knew that Dottie had started her career as a teacher and ended it after twenty years as a high school principal. Fleetingly, she felt as if she had been called into the principal's office to explain herself against some ignoble infraction. She fought the urge to fidget. "I've been doing a bit of snooping around," she said, uncomfortable with the word. "I, uh, don't see myself as a detective. Not in the least. There were just some things—"

"Say the words, girl. You've been snooping. You've already told me that. What have you found?"

Kim managed a smile. "It's about Emily Riley's murder. I never could stop thinking about it." She drew a deep breath. "Ashley Crane—Emily's best friend—told me that Emily kept journals. I figured the police had looked at them, and they had. But I decided to try and read them. I wanted to see if I could find anything. So, I approached Emily's mother about them. I expected her to say no, flat out, when I asked."

"But she didn't."

"No. She gave me four of Emily's notebooks."

"And?"

Kim squirmed. The single-word question felt almost like a physical jab. "Well, there wasn't a lot there. As I said, the police had been through the notebooks. I did find interesting entries written late last winter suggesting that Emily had at least one lover then. By her various descriptions, I thought she was probably seeing two men."

"Huh. If true, seems like something someone else would have known, or could have learned if they'd put their heads to it. I take it she didn't come right out and name names?"

"Nothing so simple."

"But you think you know who she was seeing?"

"No, I—she didn't leave much to go on," Kim sputtered, taken aback.

Their eyes locked briefly. The intensity in Dottie's seemed sufficient to burn the truth straight out of her.

"I have an idea," Kim conceded. "Nothing more concrete than that."

"Who is it?"

"I can't say." She shook her head. "I don't know nearly enough to say."

"Then how are you going to get the rest of it, further proof?"

"I'm not!" Kim exclaimed in protest.

"The hell you're not."

For a second time, their eyes locked. Kim had come here looking for encouragement. Now that she was here, she regretted having exposed her fledgling theory.

She blinked and started to stand.

Dottie spoke imperiously. "Are you so damn sure the girl was killed by a lover?" she demanded, stopping Kim in her tracks.

"No. When I hear people talking about Emily, it's as if all they can say is what poor judgment she used around men. I don't have any idea who killed her, or why. What I do think is that if she was seeing someone, he should be identified, and questioned. Both men, if I'm right that she was seeing two people."

"No argument there," Dottie said. "So what are you going to do?"

"I guess I could talk to some of her friends," Kim said, mollified, thinking of the smiling girl in Emily's photos whose name she still didn't know. "Someone probably knew if she had a new love interest. Girls that age usually don't keep those kinds of secrets."

"Sounds like a good place to start."

CHAPTER 15

Midmorning on Saturday, Kim took her copy of *Howards End* and headed to Pine Village. Though summer officially was still several weeks away, the splendor of the season announced itself in the glow of light and the fresh bloom of flowers, shrubs, and trees. Already in early June, there had been a few days of scorching heat, but today was not going to be one of them. Nor did the clear sky suggest even a hint of rain.

She left her bicycle locked in its usual spot, chained to a post near the entrance. As she walked toward the door, Scott Wentworth passed her on his way out of the building. "Scott, hello," she said warmly.

He nodded curtly and continued on without a word.

Stung, Kim watched him walk away. Belatedly, her thoughts turned to Lucy. She rushed inside. In the lobby, she came upon two men and a woman standing together, talking. One man was Lucy's doctor, Richard Maron. Kim had met him on past visits to Lucy. The other man was approximately the doctor's age, midfifties. The woman was younger.

Kim slipped around the trio and stopped at the reception desk. "Hey, Justine, I just saw Scott Wentworth leaving. He looked upset. Is Lucy okay?"

"She's fine." The young woman's eyes flashed suggestively toward the group. "I'll tell you what's going on in a sec."

The two men shook hands. When Dr. Maron glanced over and saw Kim, his expression brightened. "Oh, there you are," he said. "I have someone who wants to meet you. Sara Shaffer, please meet Kim—ah, pardon me. I've forgotten your last name."

"Jackson." Kim offered her hand to the other woman.

The woman smiled. "It's nice to meet you, Kim. I've heard a great deal about you recently."

The doctor touched Sara Shaffer on the arm and begged her to excuse him.

"Thank you again, Richard," she said.

After he walked off, Sara said, "I imagine you're here to see Lucy. I wonder if you have a few minutes to spare."

"Certainly," Kim said.

They walked to a corner of the reception area, passing two elderly men in wheelchairs.

Sara said, "I'm Lucy's nearest neighbor. My grandmother was her friend for thirty years. With my work schedule such as it is, I'm only able to visit Lucy in the evenings. That's when I've heard about you. I find it terribly odd, but I'm all but persuaded you've done for Lucy what none of the rest of us has been able to do."

"I'm sorry," Kim said, not understanding.

"You read to her. That seems to be the thing."

"I'm pleased to have been any help to Lucy, but I honestly don't know what you're talking about," Kim said.

"It's brought her back, somehow. That's really all I can say. In the last several weeks, she's started talking at length again.

About literature, to be sure, which she's always loved. And other subjects as well."

Kim still didn't see the connection. "Christine and I have noticed a few changes too. Christine Gregory," she added. "Lucy's neighbor. I read to both of them. May I ask you a question?"

"Please do."

"I passed Scott Wentworth on my way in a few minutes ago. He seemed—well, furious," she said, uncomfortable at digging into what was none of her business.

Sara laughed. "I'm sure he was. We had a meeting this morning. Scott; myself; Lucy's attorney; and, of course, her doctor. At issue was Lucy's competency."

"Oh."

"There's a rather long story involved. I hope you'll forgive my bluntness, but the fact is that Scott had hoped to have Lucy declared mentally incompetent. There are significant legal implications involved in such an action. A few weeks ago, it seemed a sure bet Richard would do so. Lucy's improvement since then has changed everything. This morning, Richard refused Scott's request. And that is precisely why he is furious."

"I'm surprised. I would think Scott would be glad for his mother."

Sara Shaffer raised one eyebrow.

Kim said, "In any case, I suspect Lucy's improvement has far less to do with listening to me read *Howards End* than it does from a natural progression of healing."

"I disagree."

A moment passed in which Kim made a quick assessment of the woman standing opposite her. "Capable" was the word that came to mind.

Sara glanced at her watch and sighed. "The last thing I want is to keep you from your time with Lucy. And yet I would like to continue this conversation. It's easy to see why Lucy has grown so fond of you. Is there a chance you're free for lunch? I have errands to run and could meet you somewhere in, say, ninety minutes or an hour. Or perhaps you'd just as soon not."

Kim felt thrown, both by the compliment and by Sara's thinly veiled distrust of Scott. She said, "No, I'd love to have lunch with you. But I don't want you to think I'm intruding on Lucy's business."

"Lucy needs allies," Sara said matter-of-factly. "And I suppose I do too. Do you know Flynn's Restaurant?"

Kim didn't.

"It's five miles north on the left side of the road. You can't miss it. Shall we plan to meet there in, say—what is it?" she asked when she saw Kim's expression of dismay.

"I rode my bicycle here today. In general, I try to avoid the big roads as much as I can. Highway 50 is one I especially try to avoid."

"Then let's make it simple. Why don't I meet you back here and I'll drive."

They settled on a plan to meet in an hour. Kim felt deeply mystified by the encounter as she walked through the hall. She had no idea how Lucy would be that day. But Lucy was fine, as was Christine. She read three chapters before the hour was nearly up. After seeing Lucy back to her room, she said, "I met a neighbor of yours today, Sara Shaffer."

"Oh, I'm so glad," Lucy said. "Sara is a dear. Perhaps you and she will become friends. Do you ride?"

"Pardon me?"

"Horses. I was wondering whether you ride. Sara is a great horsewoman. She instructs."

Troubled by the slew of apparent non sequiturs, Kim said, "I haven't been on a horse since I was at camp. Many years ago," she added emphatically.

"Oh well, don't worry. Sara will know if you're fit for the task. She's had several students come away with blue ribbons at the more prestigious shows." Despite her engagement in the conversation, Lucy seemed tired. Not sleepy, as she had numerous times in the past. Simply wrung out. She slumped a bit and said, "I feel as if I should rest. That fool doctor and his battery of tests."

Her curiosity piqued, Kim asked, "What tests?"

"First thing this morning, math problems and the like. Name the day. Name the president. Idiotic questions. I can't imagine what he was thinking, testing me on such simple subjects."

Kim smiled. She left Lucy's room with a promise to return soon.

She stopped back to see Christine before leaving. They talked for several minutes about Christine's family and her plans to visit with her friend Grace that afternoon. Christine said, "I told Grace about the wonderful books you've been reading. She said that gave her an idea about loading my phone with audiobooks. I had no idea what she was talking about. Have you ever heard of such a thing?"

"Yes, I have. That sounds like a wonderful idea."

"Well, it won't be the same as listening to you read. But I don't like to disappoint Grace. Before long, who knows? Maybe I'll take to reading myself again."

Sara Shaffer was waiting at the entrance when Kim entered the reception area. They drove to the restaurant. Inside, they took a table distant from the congested middle section. Sara waved to someone she knew. Opening the menu, Kim was relieved to see low prices, as she only had a small amount of cash.

"How was Lucy when you saw her?" Sara said.

"In good spirits. She complained about the battery of tests she had had."

Kim took the opportunity to absorb her impressions of Sara Shaffer. She couldn't pinpoint her age more specifically

than to guess the woman was in her late thirties or early forties. She had dark hair and eyes, and wore round glasses. Her
hair was long, and fell in loose natural curls about her shoulders. The face staring across the table at Kim was pleasant fea-
tured if masked by a hint of something cautious.

"It's funny to meet someone new in Montrose," Sara said.
"I get lulled into the belief that I know everyone in town. Do
you mind my asking what brought you here?"

Kim had expected the question. She told the same bare-
bones story she had told half a dozen times before. With each
retelling, it seemed to take on more weight. When she finished,
the other woman surprised her by saying, "So this is more or
less a stopping place for now?"

"Yes, I suppose it is, although I hadn't thought of it that
way."

"No. You have books to finish reading and a commitment
to a softball season."

Kim heard nothing but straightforward assessment in the
statement, and so she agreed that was the term, for now.

"Regardless of how long you stay, you've proved a godsend
to Lucy, that's certain."

They paused from their conversation to order lunch.
Afterward, Kim said, "I'm glad you think so, but I'm afraid
you're giving me too much credit. All I do is read to Lucy. Do
you suppose we could back up? I feel totally lost about what
happened today."

Amusement lingered in Sara's expression. It gradually gave
way to something more serious. "I realize you only have my
word on this, but the fact is that for the second time in the last
several months, Scott has tried to make an end run around
Lucy. He had hoped to have her declared mentally incompetent. Had that happened, he would have gained full power of
attorney over her affairs."

Kim still felt puzzled. "Why would Scott care about getting power of attorney? Are there decisions to be made?"

"Potentially, yes. With unlimited power of attorney, Scott would be free to sell Lucy's land."

"What?"

Sara studied her for a minute. "You don't know about any of this, do you?"

"No."

"Then I suppose I should go back to the beginning. I hope you're not in any hurry."

Kim assured Sara Shaffer she was not.

The dark-haired woman began her tale. "Stories are funny things. That thought's just occurred to me. When I was growing up, I took it for granted that everyone in Montrose knew the story of my grandmother and Lucy Wentworth. Now, as I think of it, I realize it's a story that belongs to another era. My grandfather was a farmer. Originally he had more than a thousand acres of land. Over time, he sold off parcels until he was down to five hundred. He and my grandmother had three children, two sons and a daughter. The tragedy of their lives was that both their boys were killed in the Second World War. Their daughter, my mother, ended up their only child. So with a shrunken family and no sons to inherit, my grandfather didn't need all his land. What he needed was hired help, and he had that up until the time of his death.

"By then, Lucy and Sam Wentworth were established in Montrose. Sam's business was thriving. They weren't terribly wealthy at that time, but they were comfortable. Comfortable enough to purchase my grandmother's farm and to let her go on living there while Lucy took over organizing the help to work the land. And my, what a hand she had for that. Some friendships wither when money enters the fray. That never happened between Gram and Lucy. I won't even pretend to know why. All I know is that up until about ten years ago, Lucy was still running that farm and woe to anyone who tried to tell her differently."

"Is your grandmother still living?"

"No. She passed away some fifteen years ago. Lucy, bless her soul, sold me Gram's house five years ago, and I've been living there since."

Kim smiled. It was a beautiful story. It did speak of another time, another way of life bearing no stigma of greed. "Do you farm the land?" she said, warming unexpectedly to the woman sitting opposite.

"Lord, no. I have ten acres, which is enough pasturage for my horses."

"What kind of work do you do?" Kim said.

Sara laughed. "You don't know, then. I'm a radiologist."

"A doctor," Kim said.

"Yes. I do see patients, though not routinely. My expertise lies in reading X-rays, ultrasounds, that sort of thing."

Kim nodded and sat back. Their waitress was approaching the table with two plates in hand.

They paused to eat.

"How well do you know Scott Wentworth?" Sara said, startling Kim with the question.

"I can't say I know him at all. We've spoken a few times when our paths have crossed at Pine Village." She chose not to mention their ice-cream outing. Then, as if to compensate for the lapse, she added, "I've heard something about him from the women on my softball team. I know people blame him for losing his father's company."

"Scott and I have a history, I'll grant you that," Sara said as she wiped her mouth with a napkin. "He's three years older than I am, but we dated in high school. Thank goodness that reign of insanity closed more than two decades ago. Until five years ago, we had little occasion to see one another, and when we did, our exchanges were cordial. That changed after Lucy sold me the property. Scott resented Lucy's decision to sell off the land, particularly at the price. Her price, not mine. Since then, Scott and I haven't had much to say to each other."

"I suppose Lucy's accident changed that."

"Yes. Her accident changed quite a bit. Pardon me for speaking frankly, but I want to make it clear that I'm concerned about Lucy. That's why I've taken this opportunity, perhaps inappropriately, to confide in you my suspicions that Scott is up to something. That said, I'll leave the next part up to you. If you'd like to hear the rest of what I have to say, just say the word. If not, we'll finish lunch companionably speaking about something of mutual interest."

Kim smiled. For the life of her, she couldn't figure out this woman. But she liked her. Lacking any clue where the conversation was going, she urged Sara to go on.

Sara took a few bites of her sandwich before she spoke. "Lucy owns five hundred and forty acres of prime land just south of town. Do you have any idea what the value of that land is in today's market?"

"I don't. I gather, from the local paper, land prices have sky-rocketed in recent years and farms such as Lucy's are worth far more as development acreage than as farmland."

"That's right. Several days before Lucy's accident, Scott tried to pull a fast one on her. It still boggles my mind when I think what he meant to do. Do you know what a real estate closing is?"

"Yes. It's where buyers and sellers of property meet with lenders and title company officers to sign papers and finalize the details related to the transfer of property ownership."

"Yes. Several months ago, Scott blindsided Lucy. He entered into a deal to sell all of her land without telling her. One morning, he whisked her off to a meeting where she was expected to sign papers parting with her land. She refused to do so. She was having a particularly good day that day. Her mind was sharp. She stood up and walked out of that meeting leaving Scott looking the fool. Afterward, Scott tried to cover his backside by insisting Lucy had agreed to sell. He blamed her faltering mental state for causing her to forget. I doubt his version of events. I rather believe he expected her to cave in under pressure and simply sign where she was told."

Kim felt her face tense in a stark expression of disbelief. "Is it possible he's right and that Lucy had forgotten? Why would he think she'd sell if—"

"Lucy swore she had heard nothing of the plan. I only talked with her about it once. Within a week, she had her accident, and since then, it's been strictly a downhill course for her. Physically, she has stabilized. Mentally, she's been all over the board. At least until lately. I've been mistrustful of Scott, well, for years, but certainly during the last two months. Then he goes and pulls a second stunt in as many months by trying to have Lucy declared incompetent. I have no doubt he intends to sell that land the very instant he gains control over her finances."

"It sounds diabolical."

Sara shrugged and returned her attention to her sandwich.

They finished lunch without probing deeper into what had been said. When Sara removed her wallet to pay for her lunch, she took out a business card. After jotting down her home phone number beneath her name, she slid it across the table. "You see Lucy at times of the day when I don't. All I'm asking, if anything suspicious catches your attention, please give me a call."

CHAPTER 16

The story Sara Shaffer had told weighed heavily on Kim throughout the afternoon. She didn't want to believe Scott Wentworth wasn't a loving son solely concerned with his mother's welfare. Even less did she want to believe she had played any part in the family's saga, and yet, pride washed over her when she recalled Sara's frank appreciation for her having reached Lucy through the one thing the older woman hadn't lost or had taken from her—her love of books.

When Andrea arrived home late in the afternoon laden with grocery bags, a twelve-pack of cold beer, and two large bottles of wine, Kim was glad to see her. Andrea popped open two beer bottles and a bag of chips and, without asking, ordered Kim into the kitchen for instruction on making a perfect chicken marinade. Kim took notes in between retrieving ingredients and returning them to shelves or the refrigerator. Andrea polished off two beers while divulging gossip from work plus a few scintillating details about a softball teammate. "What's new with you?" she asked when the salad was made. A potato dish was in the oven; chicken was marinating in a plastic bag in the refrigerator. The western sky was fading from red to gray.

Kim laughed softly at hearing the forced interest in the question. There was something almost comical in Andrea's sense of superiority over her housemate. But there was also kindness in her—Kim only had to look at the cornucopia of food in the kitchen—and beyond that, something wanting in Andrea. The newly opened wine bottle, sharing counter space with a pair of empty beer bottles, told that story, or part of it.

"Nothing much," Kim started to say, only to be interrupted by Andrea blurting out, "You're a helluva softball player, anybody ever tell you that? That was a great pick you made at third right before the rain came in the other night."

"Thanks. I played in high school."

Andrea said she had played softball and basketball in high school, drawing a raised eyebrow from Kim and the question, "Basketball? You're, what—five six, tops?"

"Hey, I was a great point guard, and I could nail threes when I got in the groove!"

Andrea poured a glass of wine and put the chicken on to grill. By the time they sat down to eat, it was dark outside and their conversation was comfortable. Kim had admitted to having some college coursework under her belt but was undecided about a career. For the sake of something to say, she mentioned a growing interest in criminology.

"What do you want to do, study forensics?" Andrea said.

Kim finished her glass of wine. Feeling light-headed and freer than she had in months, she said, "No. I'm thinking about becoming a private investigator."

"You're serious?" Andrea said after staring at her for a long moment, trying to decide whether she was.

"Yes, I am." With sudden animation, Kim said, "Think of it. You can open your own law practice and I can work for you. I can investigate people who've made false insurance claims, or spouses cheating on one another, or anything that needs investigating in the course of legal action. We'll make a great team."

Andrea hooted with laughter. She spilled a forkful of chicken on herself, cursed, and, still laughing, said, "Damn. I have to change this shirt." She stood up and walked down the hall. Kim heard a door close.

She was smiling to herself, happy with the food and happy with Andrea's company, when a noise at the front of the house startled her. It sounded like something had been knocked over. But there was nothing out there that might have fallen. She went to check on the noise.

She was two steps from the front door when there was the crashing sound of wood splintering. The thin door yielded to a foot kicking through. Another vicious kick, and the door gave way. Two masked men entered, closing what was left of the door behind them. A scream rose and died in Kim's throat when the nearest man grabbed her. He leaned close and whispered, "Hey there, sweet thing." She immediately recognized his voice.

Tyler Haas pushed her against the wall and held her there. "Now you listen to me. We can make this easy or we can make it into somethin' you won't like at all. Where's the car, bitch?"

He tugged violently at her shirt until his hands reached her skin. They moved higher, then lower. Kim struggled but couldn't escape his grasp.

"Just get the car," the other man said coldly. "We didn't come here to mess around."

"What the hell's going on?"

Both men whipped around at the sound of Andrea's voice.

Andrea stood at the threshold of the kitchen. She had a gun in her hand, pointed at the intruders. Kim heard a click as loud as a thunderbolt come from somewhere close by. The second man had a gun, its safety, apparently, released. He pushed

Tyler out of the way and grabbed her, locking one arm around her throat. He pointed his gun at Andrea.

"Let her go," Andrea said.

The man laughed.

"Let's get out of here," Tyler Haas said. He started for the door.

The other man made no move to follow. Kim heard his uneven breath and felt his arm around her twitch. She sensed his indecision.

"Let her go and get the hell out of here," Andrea said.

The man kept his gun leveled on Andrea. When Kim felt him shift his weight to his back leg, she guessed he meant to drag her toward the door, using her body as a shield. Instinctively, she slipped her foot behind his leg. When he moved, he stumbled. The instant he was caught off-balance, she twisted free of his grasp. Shots were fired—three deafening cracks. The gunman sank to his knees, crying out. Blood spurted from his hand. The gun clattered to the floor.

Tyler Haas moved quickly. He grabbed the gun and the man who was still groaning. Haas forced him upright and pushed him to the door. A moment later, they were gone.

"Andrea!" Kim shouted. She raced to her side.

Andrea lay sprawled on the living room floor. Blood pooled at her side. "I got the bastard, didn't I?" she said.

"Yes. Your phone—where's your phone?" Kim said, cursing herself for not owning a cell phone.

"Bedroom."

Kim found the phone and dialed 911. An eternity seemed to pass before she heard sirens in the distance.

—

At three a.m., a nurse took pity on Kim in the waiting room of the local hospital; she allowed her into a private room where

Andrea lay sleeping post-surgery after the removal of a bullet in her stomach. She had lost a great deal of blood but was expected to make a full recovery, in time.

In time for what? Kim wondered, drifting in an interior haze that carried her to places she didn't want to go. It drew her back to the chaos that had erupted in the house with the arrival of two police officers and, within minutes, a team of paramedics. She'd sunk into a corner while all attention was on Andrea. Then more police arrived, and Andrea was taken away on a stretcher, and suddenly too much attention was focused on her. A police officer sat her down on the couch and asked her to tell him what happened. Every light inside the house was on, blazing brightly. She wanted to tell someone to turn them off, all but one, possibly, in the hallway. She wanted to lower her head and tell her tale to the floor. Because she knew she couldn't escape telling it, and she was afraid what someone might see when looking directly into her eyes.

She settled for staring straight ahead. She told the officer about hearing a noise and going to the front door. "Back up," the officer had said, nodding toward the kitchen. "You and Andrea Sampson were having dinner." Kim glanced that way and saw a table littered with plates and serving platters, chicken and potatoes long since grown cold, and a large wine bottle half empty on the counter. Andrea had drunk most of it. Kim had had one glass. It was a wonder Andrea had been able to stand up, never mind shoot straight.

They were having dinner when she'd heard the noise, Kim amended. Andrea had gone into her bedroom to change her shirt. She had spilled something on it.

Police officers were milling through the house as she talked. A forensics guy was kneeling at the front door, taking photographs, measurements, and fingerprints.

Kim described seeing the wood panel on the front door splinter. Two men wearing ski masks entered the house. One grabbed her and pushed her against the wall.

"Hey, Danny," one of the other officers called to a new arrival.

A guy wearing blue jeans and a gray hoodie walked over to where Kim sat on the couch. Introductions were made. His name was Dan Czernak. Detective Dan Czernak, he said. He wanted to conduct this interview at the police station, and in a daze, Kim agreed.

A different officer drove her there. Kim sat for a long time on a plastic hard-shell chair in a bland room vacant of everything except a second identical chair. She was cold. She clutched her arms around each other for the slight warmth they gave. By the time Detective Czernak entered the room, she had had time enough to know what she wanted to say.

Kim surfaced to the sound of a medical machine pulsing. It was monitoring Andrea's blood pressure and heart rate with a rhythmical hissing sound. Andrea lay motionless on the bed in a cotton gown patterned with blue dots. Her long brown hair lay straight on the flat pillow, as if someone had arranged it there, though Kim doubted anyone had. "Are you her—?" the nurse had asked, and Kim had nodded, knowing what the nurse meant and not caring that she'd lied.

Detective Dan Czernak wanted to know exactly what had happened that night, so Kim told him. When she got to the men breaking down the door, the detective asked, "Did you recognize either of the men?" Kim nodded. She said she thought the man who first grabbed her was named Tyler Haas. She'd recognized his voice.

"What did he say to you?"

"'Hey there, sweet thing.'"

"That's all he said?"

"Yes," she answered. "That was all he said."

She gave up Tyler Haas, but she wasn't going to say a word about her car.

When he asked if she had any idea who the other man was, she said no.

The conversation went around and around as he asked follow-up questions about those details, until she admitted to having encountered Tyler Haas in a rooming house and seeing him again on multiple occasions at JT's grocery store, where she worked. Czernak wanted to know more about her. By degrees, she revealed that she volunteered at Pine Village Convalescent Home and played on a softball team. He asked her which one. "The Brazen Hussies," she answered, and he raised his eyebrows. She thought he was surprised by the name.

"You ever hear of a man by the name of Aleksander Voigt?" the detective asked much later.

Kim's pulse quickened. "Yes."

"Any chance either of the men who broke into the house tonight could have been Voigt?"

She told him she didn't know. She had never seen a picture of Aleksander Voigt, the alleged murderer who had walked out of Andrea Sampson's courtroom.

Before the interview ended, Detective Czernak ordered her not to mention either Voigt's or Tyler Haas's name. He urged her to say as little as possible about the home invasion to anyone outside law enforcement. He offered her a ride home, courtesy of a patrolman. Kim insisted on being dropped off at the medical center.

She pulled herself out of her thoughts and returned her attention to Andrea. The machines went on hissing. A nurse popped in and offered her a bottle of water, which Kim gratefully accepted. She opened it, then promptly forgot about it.

It was the guns she couldn't stop seeing. Eyes open or shut, the images stayed there at the front of her mind, so close she could almost touch them. They took her back to a place she never wanted to go again. They took her back to Stephen Bender's office.

Measured in terms of absolute time, it wasn't that long ago that she'd last seen Stephen. A scant two months. But it might as well have been forever. It had been a Monday morning, early. By then, she'd known Michael Leeds had found discrepancies in their inventory files—discrepancies she still hoped might be explained. She was nervous but not unduly afraid when Stephen called her into his office. He met her at the door, an unusual gesture. After she entered, he closed the door, then stood for a long moment looking at her. Not looking—studying.

As if she was a game board and he was deciding his next move.

It came without warning.

He stepped close, reached for her blouse, and in one continuous motion ripped the fabric to expose her chest. He looked for the wire she wasn't wearing.

Satisfied, he laughed.

"Your boy found something he shouldn't have," he said jovially. "Worse for you, he told you about it."

He told her to sit down. He took a new blouse still in its wrapping from a bottom desk drawer and thrust it at her, ordering her to change. She didn't move. He came at her again, leaned close, and whispered dangerously, "I said change your damn shirt."

She did.

The shocking story came out. Michael Leeds, a junior accountant who worked for her, had been murdered the past Saturday night. He was shot dead in the parking lot outside a popular Chicago sports bar.

Days earlier, Michael had come to her saying he'd discovered an error in their inventory database. A pricey item that shouldn't have been there was. Except, it actually wasn't. It was listed in the file but assigned to a warehouse that no longer existed. Michael would never have stumbled upon it but for a customer who had called looking to purchase that particular item—a nearly obsolete turbine compressor.

Michael had known something was wrong. His mistake was failing to guess how much was wrong, and how much this new knowledge would cost him. He dug deeper and uncovered an invoice for the nonexistent compressor showing authorization for the payment and bearing her signature.

Bearing her *forged* signature. She had never seen the document, let alone signed off on it. By her alleged authority, money had been siphoned out of a legitimate corporate account and gone somewhere. Most likely to an offshore account controlled by Stephen Bender.

One day later, Michael was dead.

Andrea made a small sound. She rolled her head before going completely still again. Beyond the window, stars glittered in the night sky. Kim could barely breathe. She wondered how many ways life could go wrong. By the vastness of the heavens above, she thought the answer was infinite.

"Stand up," Stephen had commanded her that morning after cavalierly confessing to having committed fraud and murder. "Well," he'd equivocated. He hadn't been the one to pull the trigger that killed Michael Leeds.

He walked around the desk and stood in front of her. "Close your eyes," he ordered. For reasons she couldn't justify, she did as he'd asked.

Kim longed to reach for Andrea's hand, as if, by touching it, she might cleanse her own of the invisible stain Stephen had inflicted when he'd thrust a gun into her palm and pressed her fingers around the handle.

"Just so you know," he had said afterward, "if you ever try to talk to anyone about this, I will bury you under a mountain of evidence. One thing you need to understand is that there is quite a long trail leading back to you." Demonstrating, he held the gun by a handkerchief around the barrel, grinning trium-phantly. "But no one will ever find anything implicating me."

Night faded imperceptibly into day without Kim closing her eyes to sleep. She hadn't moved when Andrea miraculously opened hers and smiled. "Hey," she said, "are you okay?"

Kim blinked and gave a slight nod.

"I got the bastard, didn't I?" Andrea said.

"You got the bastard," Kim said.

There would be time for the truth later.

CHAPTER 17

Sunday passed in a blur.

Kim left the hospital when Andrea's parents arrived. The landlord was at the house when she returned, taking measurements at the doorframe and inspecting the property for other damage. He didn't have much to say to her, which was just as well, since she didn't feel capable of carrying on a conversation with anyone. She passed the morning dozing in a lawn chair in the backyard, staggered by how much had changed. And how much hadn't. The birds still sang. Lawn mowers roared to life in neighboring yards. No one came to talk to her demanding an explanation for why Tyler Haas had chosen her house to break into.

Because that was the one question she could have answered: Tyler wanted her car.

She didn't think he would be coming back soon.

She didn't think he would be coming back, ever.

It was why she could close her eyes and not feel afraid.

By the end of the day, a new door hung in the place of the old, securely bolted and smelling of fresh wood. Kim went to the hospital in the early evening to find Andrea withdrawn behind a superficial veneer that had something to do with escaping her overbearing mother. A plan was evolving to move Andrea to Pueblo. "You're welcome to stay at the house, assuming you feel comfortable there," Andrea's mother, a trim woman with perfectly coiffed short hair, said. "At least until we decide whether Andrea will be returning here to live."

Kim kept her visit short. She went back the next day, counting on having a private conversation with Andrea, but she was too late. Andrea had been whisked away to a different hospital across the mountains.

Word of the home invasion spread like wildfire through the community, along with Andrea's name and the identity of the suspected culprit—Aleksander Voigt. Voigt was the man who had walked out of Andrea's courtroom, humiliating her, and, as if that wasn't enough, swearing revenge on witnesses and prosecutors alike. He had kept his word. The state's prime witness—who had recanted her original testimony on the stand—was shot dead the night Voigt was released from custody. Andrea was persuaded to take an extended sabbatical, for her own safety as well as for the chance to recover emotionally from the cascading tragedy. Saturday night's events, it was easy to believe, were merely the latest installment.

Kim's involvement was less well known, except among her softball teammates. At the game on Tuesday night, women swarmed around her with questions—questions mostly about Andrea. Kim told what she could and wasn't unhappy when Lois ordered the group to break up and get on with warm-ups. "You okay?" she said after the others moved on.

Kim nodded. "I worry about Andrea."

"Andrea's tough. She'll come through this."

Detective Dan Czernak was the one man in town not satisfied with the popular version of the story going around. Twice that week, he knocked on Kim's new front door. "You want to tell me again why you don't have a cell phone?" he said each time he saw her, echoing the complaint Andrea had made when she'd told Kim she was being transferred to a Pueblo hospital. "Get a damn cell phone," Andrea had insisted. "Call me. Promise."

"I'm working on it," Kim told the detective. The lie beat having to admit the truth—that, other than Andrea, there wasn't a soul in the world she wanted to call.

On Wednesday night, the detective sat in her living room, which had been scrubbed clean of blood, both Andrea's and the man she shot. Who was not Aleksander Voigt, the detective divulged. The DNA didn't match.

"Who was it?" Kim said.

"Unknown assailant."

She let the words sink in while Dan Czernak fingered his trim mustache, watching her. He was a good-looking guy in his midthirties with broad shoulders that made her think he had played football in school.

"Tell me again why you think one of the men was Tyler Haas," he said.

She repeated her previous answer. She thought she'd recognized his voice.

"You and this Tyler fellow, did you ever date?"

"No!"

The single word exploded with more emotion than she wished. It made her sound defensive, which she was. Having offered Tyler's name at the outset, she had no intention of saying more about him than she already had.

"Did he know where you lived?" Czernak said.

Kim shrugged. "I have no idea."

It was the detective's turn to shrug. "I'd say it was pretty obvious he did." He went on to say that not much was known about Tyler Haas. Haas had moved out of the rooming house where Kim met him. He owned a motorcycle, had never been arrested, and had a job history of working in machine shops and convenience stores. His whereabouts were presently unknown.

"Tell me about the other guy, the one with him. Everything you remember," Czernak said.

Kim had already done so. She went through her description again. "He was thin, medium tall, maybe five nine. He wore blue jeans and a dark-colored T-shirt." She tried to remember more. "It all happened so fast. Nothing stands out," she said weakly.

Andrea's shooter had never been arrested. His DNA wasn't in the system. But the police had a sample now.

Czernak asked her to walk him through the events of Saturday night one more time. She did so, not as a rehearsed story but exactly as she remembered. She hadn't seen Andrea when she walked into the room. She'd heard Andrea's voice, and saw her then. She heard gunshots. Next thing she knew, the man whom she believed to be Tyler Haas was bent over the other man, who was holding his arm. Andrea lay sprawled on the floor. The men left. Kim ran to Andrea.

She surfaced from the memories to see the detective watching her, shaking his head and laughing softly. "What?" she demanded.

"Andrea was legally drunk when she shot a gun out of a man's hand. I'd hate to see what she could hit stone-cold sober."

Czernak cautioned Kim not to discuss anything he had revealed that night—namely, that Andrea's shooter was not Aleksander Voigt. He wanted to keep Voigt's name in the press as a suspect as long as possible.

"The man Andrea shot," Kim said. "He would need medical attention, wouldn't he?"

"Yes. He lost a considerable amount of blood."

No one seeking care for an unexplained gunshot wound had shown up in a Colorado hospital or urgent care center. Presumably not in Utah, Wyoming, or New Mexico either, though the detective didn't elaborate on that aspect of the investigation. "You think of anything else, call me," Czernak said on his way out. "Or stop by the station," he added, frowning. He had already told her twice to get a phone.

The house was clean. All of Andrea's fancy cooking gadgets were scrubbed and returned to their rightful storage place after last Saturday's dinner. Kim had filed the recipe—now blood spattered—in a drawer with the other recipe she had from Andrea. She had been through Andrea's bedroom, fingering her clothes for no good reason. Shorts and shirts, her softball mitt, and a clean park ranger uniform. Andrea's bedroom had been left untouched by the parade of law enforcement officers tramping through the house, as was Kim's. Everything had happened so quickly, she had had no time to protect any of her possessions even if she had wanted to. She could have explained her copy of Dr. Abraham Craft's book *The Science of Crime*, but she wouldn't have wanted to try and explain why she had an envelope of photos taken by Emily Riley. Aside from the new door and a constant thrumming of tension in the air—a product of her imagination, she assumed—the house was exactly as she had found it in the weeks before Andrea made a habit of coming home.

CHAPTER 18

All week, Kim stuck to her routine of work, volunteering at Pine Village, and playing softball while guilt for having brought Tyler Haas to Andrea's door ate away at her. Sooner than she expected, she heard from a teammate that Andrea had been released from the Pueblo hospital and was continuing her recovery at her parents' home. Kim bought a long-distance calling card and called Andrea from a pay phone. They spoke briefly, long enough for Andrea to say that if she had to spend much more time around her mother, she was going to start to wish that asshole had killed her. Andrea still believed the shooter—whoever he was—was linked to Aleksander Voigt. She had never heard of Tyler Haas and was of the opinion that even if he was one of the men who'd broken into the house on Saturday night, Haas was there on instructions from Voigt. It was the version of the story she needed to believe.

There was no mention of a possible date for her return to Montrose.

In the immediate aftermath of the shooting, Kim resolved to drop any interest in Emily Riley's murder. Violence had broken through her door—literally. Even though the one had nothing to do with the other, both deeds had something malevolent at their core. She wanted no part of that energy.

She might have stuck to her resolution had she not seen Jeff Nelson one too many times. He had made a habit of stopping by the grocery store when Ashley's shift was nearing an end. Especially if John Trimble wasn't around, Jeff would tease Ashley from a distance, causing her to flush red and giggle when she was supposed to be ringing up groceries. However weak Kim's suspicions were about him being Emily's "phantom lover," his regular presence reminded her she hadn't finished the job she'd set out to do.

Her last conversation with Dottie Goddard came back to her, and with it, the recollection that she had another avenue to pursue in the form of the smiling young woman in Emily Riley's photo collection.

Her name was Jenna Spinelli, and she worked at Countryside Daycare. Kim learned the pertinent details about Jenna the way she learned most things about Emily—from Ashley Crane.

"It's my aunt's house. She hired me for the summer," Jenna said as she and Kim chatted in a backyard busy with brightly colored play structures. A teary-eyed toddler clung to her hand. Nearby, seven or eight preschoolers played in a fort. In the few minutes they had spent talking, Jenna had shared that the childcare job was only for the summer. She planned to attend college in Boulder in the fall.

Pleasantries concluded, Kim said, "I was at the high school recently and spoke to Frank Tattinger. He showed me some of Emily Riley's photography. There were several terrific shots of you and Emily's little brother."

"Oh right, I'd forgotten about those pictures. The ones Emily took of me. I was with her the day she took the photos of Dustin. Actually, now that I think about it, they were all taken on the same day. It was a good day. A really good day."

"Do you remember when it was?"

"March, I think. I'm not sure. Why?"

Kim used the same cover she had used with Deena. "I'm a freelance writer, and I've been toying with the idea of writing an article on Emily. I haven't decided how I want to approach the piece. I've been doing some basic background work waiting to see what focus emerges. I gather Emily was a complicated young woman."

"Yes. She was."

Jenna's short reply forced Kim to jump to several conclusions. Her first impression was that Jenna Spinelli was a teenager with strong feelings. Included among her feelings was a clear fondness for Emily. Kim wondered how inclined Jenna might feel to protect her deceased friend's reputation.

Her second impression gave her greater pause. Jenna seemed made of tougher stuff than Ashley Crane. Kim doubted she would be able to bulldoze her way through to answers with Jenna as she routinely did with Ashley.

"I imagine you've been asked this question before, but I'm curious to know whether Emily ever mentioned any of the guys she was seeing to you."

"Who would have asked?" Jenna said.

"Weren't you interviewed by the police?"

"No. Why would I have been?"

"I had the impression virtually everyone who knew Emily had been interviewed."

Jenna shrugged. "Emily and I weren't really friends. Not until that photography class, anyway. Then we kind of clicked. As for guys she was seeing, she never named names."

Kim rapidly tried to file away the bits and pieces of information. "But you did think she was seeing someone?"

"Kind of. She talked about putting something over on someone. She was vague, and to tell you the truth, I never thought much about it. I didn't beg her to tell me the secrets of her love life, if that's what you're asking."

"Put over what? Do you have any idea what that was about?"

"Money, I thought. I don't remember why."

"Did she ever happen to mention a guy by the name of Cal, or Caleb? I know that was the name of one of her close friends when she was growing up."

"Caleb? No. If it's the guy I'm thinking of, he left town a long time ago."

The cries among the children were escalating. Jenna glanced more frequently in their direction. Kim knew she had to move quickly. But the prospect of asking the next question—the single most important question she had come here to ask—gave her pause. "This may be totally off the wall, but what about Jeff Nelson? Was Emily spending more time than usual with him in late March or early April?"

"Jeff? He's Ashley's boyfriend."

"I know. I just wondered. I know Ashley was worried about flunking some of her classes during the winter and had made schoolwork her priority."

"Well, for that matter, Jeff was close to flunking out too. Now that you mention it, I do remember Emily saying something about that. They had a class together. Economics, I think. After Jeff bombed his first test, Emily started helping him. Tutoring him, kind of. If you want to know more, talk to Mike Lasko. He was in that class."

"Mike?" Kim tried to think where she had heard the name.

"Mike was Emily's boyfriend way back when. He and Jeff are friends. You should probably talk to Mike anyway just 'cause he knew Emily so well when we were all kids."

A minor ruckus was beginning to brew between two of the tots.

"Listen, if there's nothing else, I better get to work," Jenna said. "I do not want to have World War Three on my hands this early in the morning."

"Thanks for your time," Kim said. "Last question. Any idea where I can find Mike Lasko?"

"Sure. He's a waiter at Western Corral out on the edge of town."

Kim worked the rest of the day. The following morning, she went to Pine Village early. Both Christine and Lucy were eager to hear more of the unfolding story of *Howards End*. After leaving Pine Village, Kim went to the library. There, she found a collection of Montrose High School yearbooks. She selected the four most recent editions and sat down to learn about Mike Lasko.

Mike's senior photo showed a young man with clear, wide-set eyes, nice features, and a crooked smile that made him appear instantly likable. He had been captain of both the football and basketball teams. If his academic prowess even slightly mirrored his athletic ability, he looked like a man who would go as far in life as he chose to. Doors would automatically open for him that would never have opened for—Emily, Kim thought. The world still rewarded a guy like Mike Lasko.

She found little of value in the yearbooks other than a series of photographs marking the maturing of Emily, Ashley, Jeff, and Mike from fifteen-year-olds to eighteen-year-olds. When she finished, she sat down at one of the library's computers and went to the website for the *Montrose Daily Press*. She scanned the archives for information on Mike Lasko. His name came up in articles about the high school football and basketball teams, but nowhere else.

She still had ten minutes of computer time when she finished her research. Not expecting to find anything, she typed in the name "Tyler Haas." A variety of results popped up, mainly from websites offering full profiles of men by that name all over the country. For a fee, no doubt. But there was nothing pointing to the man she knew by that name.

Tyler had wanted her car. He had made no secret of wanting it, and he obviously had believed he could simply take it. More troublingly, Tyler had learned something about her that no one else had: that she was linked, through the car, to a woman with a different name. He could only have done that with the help of someone who had access to the Illinois vehicle registration database.

Which meant Tyler had friends in high places. Or, more likely, low places.

On a hunch, she executed a search for recent car thefts in Montrose in the local newspaper. A string of results appeared on the screen. Two imports had been stolen in the last few weeks. One, a Toyota, was stolen from a motel parking lot. The other was a Honda, stolen at Black Canyon of the Gunnison, the national park where Andrea worked. Kim read on. In the past six months, seven other vehicles had been stolen in Montrose County.

Via another search, she found the website for Grand Junction's paper, the *Daily Sentinel*. Seventy miles north of Montrose, Grand Junction was large enough—and near enough to Montrose—to figure into her evolving theory. This time, she took a different tack. She typed the words "chop shop" into the newspaper's search bar and smiled at the results. Grand Junction likewise seemed to be suffering a rash of car thefts, the severity of which had prompted investigators to speculate on the existence of a car-theft ring operating in the area. Ten vehicles had been stolen within the last six months, including two Ford trucks. The article suggested the parts from the stolen vehicles were likely being moved either to Las Vegas or Albuquerque, possibly for eventual transport to Mexico.

Kim sat back. She had learned something, but not enough. She hadn't discovered anything that would let her predict what, if anything, Tyler might do next.

—

On Saturday afternoon, Mike Lasko emerged from the rear door of the Western Corral Steakhouse at five minutes past three. He was striding toward a pickup truck when Kim intercepted him.

"Mike? Mike Lasko, right?"

He stopped. "That's right."

"Hi. I'm Kim Jackson," she said, catching up with him in three steps. She offered her hand, which the young man reluctantly shook. "I'd like to ask you a few questions, if you don't mind."

His eyes were brown; the shock of hair combed to one side of his forehead gave him a dashing look. Mike Lasko was more handsome in person than the grainy yearbook and newspaper photos showed. At the moment, he looked like a man in a hurry. "What's this about?" he said.

"I'm doing basic background research on Emily Riley with the idea of writing an article on her."

He shrugged. "I don't have anything to say. My history with Emily was ancient history."

"I promise I won't take up much of your time."

He had two choices: to be rude and shove off, as he clearly wanted to do, or to endure what a stranger had promised would be a brief interview. Mike chose the latter. "What do you want to know?"

Kim moved in circuitously. "I was wondering if you can tell me anything about Emily's relationship with her mother. Did she like her? Dislike her? Did they argue?"

Mike gave a quick smile. "That's easy. Emily hated her mother. Hated the way she lived, anyway. That string of boyfriends in and out the door—what Emily had to put up with was crap."

"I understand Emily was smart. I'm told she had excellent grades when she first entered high school."

"Oh yeah. Well, that was years back. Things changed. When she started blowing off everything and everyone, I stopped keeping up with her."

"Listen, I really don't want to take up too much of your time. From other people I've talked to, I know Emily was all over the board academically from her junior year up until, well, up until the time she went missing. Sometimes she was on the verge of flunking out of her courses. Other times, she aced every test."

"Yeah, I'd say that sums it up."

"I understand you were in an economics class with her this past winter."

"That's right."

"And she was into it? She did her homework, scored pretty well on tests?"

"Yeah, she definitely knew her stuff."

Kim had planned to ask Mike about Emily's childhood friend Caleb, but she sensed he was losing patience with her questions. Knowing she had at best one shot of getting the information she sought, and that there was no way to ease into the subject, she went for the jugular. "I heard from another student in your class that after Ashley Crane broke up with Jeff Nelson, Jeff and Emily started spending time together. Studying together, supposedly."

"What? That's horseshit," Mike said, clearly reacting to the innuendo. "Jeff bombed his first econ test. Emily did help him afterward, but if you think there was anything else going on between them, you're nuts. Sorry, there's no other way to say it. I don't know what was up between Ashley and Jeff right then. Jeff would never say. Here's the deal. Our final grade in that class was going to be based on cumulative points. Jeff got something like a twenty-eight on that midterm. He was screwed. So, yeah, Emily helped him."

Mike Lasko had a temper. It was information Kim hadn't expected to learn. She acknowledged that she had provoked his outburst. More disturbingly, she wondered at its source—specifically, whether Mike couldn't abide the idea that his best friend and his ex-girlfriend might have had something going on.

"Thanks for your time, Mike. I don't have any other questions."

"What? That's all you wanted to know?" he said, at once seeming relieved and confused by the interview's abrupt end.

Kim nodded, not in the least unhappy to throw the young man off-balance. "I just wanted to know who Emily was spending her free time with in the weeks before she disappeared. Someone else mentioned Jeff to me. I thought I'd double-check with you."

His look became a glare. "It was March when they were putting their heads together prepping for tests. March! Jeff took one dive and came right out of it. By April, he was back on track with his grades."

"Thanks," she repeated. She wondered if the angry young man might blurt out something more, but he didn't. After a pause, he turned and went to his truck. He got in and slammed the door shut.

Kim pretended to walk toward a car parked on the street. She waited to get her bicycle until Mike left the parking lot. Tires squealing, he pulled out and disappeared down the street.

CHAPTER 19

Kim argued with herself for two days over what to do next. She knew what she wanted to do. She also knew that if she whispered a word to anyone about her theory regarding a secret relationship between Jeff Nelson and Emily Riley, she might be opening a door better left closed.

She hadn't settled the argument when she went to the police station on Monday. Even after being escorted into Detective Dan Czernak's office, she told herself she had time to decide what she'd say. She had plenty of reasons for being there.

The detective's manner was reserved when he said hello and invited her to sit down. Nearly a week had passed since she'd last spoken to him. She asked if there were any new developments in the case. The composed, even look on his face should have served as a warning. He said there weren't. "Something you want to tell me?" he said.

She had expected they would find details to talk about at the outset, even if it amounted to rehashing things already said.

She waited too long.

He prompted her again. "Miss Jackson?"

She looked up sharply, mind made up. "This is about Emily Riley."

The detective's glance narrowed. "What about her?"

"I think she might have been seeing a kid named Jeff Nelson either at the time of her death or shortly before."

Kim felt the weight of her mistake instantly. All traces of sympathy faded from Czernak's face. She told herself it didn't matter what he thought. She had come here for Emily. She had come here believing that she and the detective had a sufficiently cordial relationship to sustain the oddity of her message.

"What led you to this conclusion?" Czernak said.

She suppressed a sudden urge to stand up and apologize for wasting his time. Anything else she said was going to back her deeper into an impossible corner. She understood that what she had done was indefensible in anyone's eyes, except perhaps Dottie Goddard's. But right now, Dottie didn't feel like much of an ally.

"I read Emily's personal notebooks. Deena Warren let me borrow them," she said.

"Bear with me for interrupting," Czernak said. "Normally I don't ever interrupt. Tell me again. Exactly what is your connection with Emily's family?"

"None."

"You only knew Emily from working at JT's?"

"No. I never met Emily."

"Then why did you want to read her notebooks?"

Kim swallowed hard. "I wanted to get a sense of who she was. There was so much talk going around about her at the store, and most of it didn't cast Emily in a very good light. Working with Ashley Crane, I got the idea that there was more to Emily than most people ever saw. To make a long story short, Deena let me read the notebooks. In one of her last poems, Emily mentioned a lover. It was someone she referred to as her 'phantom lover.' A line in that poem reminded me of Jeff Nelson."

The lines on Czernak's forehead knitted more deeply. "Go on."

"There isn't much more. I read Emily's poems. I was interested in the one where she mentioned a lover or, more precisely, a phantom lover. Reading it, I believed she was referring to someone real."

"I read her notebooks. Every word. I remember that poem."

That answered one question: someone in law enforcement had read the notebooks. When Czernak didn't say anything else, Kim sensed a psychological shift between them, as though he were ratcheting up the pressure. It seemed a dangerous moment. Strangely, she wasn't daunted. "I have a copy." She removed the page from her back pocket and flattened it on the desk.

Czernak skimmed the lines. "Right. That's what I remember. And you think this refers to an actual lover?"

"Yes."

"I'd appreciate your telling me why."

The single sentence told Kim a great deal. She understood that Dan Czernak never once had considered the possibility that the poem referred to someone real. She didn't think the insight reflected well on him. "Obviously I can't say for sure. As I read it, I hear Emily describing someone in her life who isn't really hers. It's someone whom she is involved with sexually but their relationship is only about sex. They're using each other. They both want something, or maybe someone else. Unable to get that, they take comfort from each other."

Pointing at a different line, she said, "This is where she describes a physical characteristic of her lover: 'a moment's glance into the steely gray glint of your eyes descending.'"

"And you think that seals the deal for Jeff Nelson?" the detective asked incredulously.

Kim flushed. "It's an expression of his. He can't hold eye contact. When he breaks contact, his gray eyes flash down. It's exactly as Emily describes."

"That's not a hell of a lot to go on."

"I never said it was."

Kim grew angry. She wondered at the emotion. By all rights, she ought to turn tail and run. "All I'm suggesting—all I wanted to suggest—is that somebody might want to look at Jeff Nelson to see if there's any chance that he and Emily were more tightly involved during that period than was common knowledge."

"Thanks for the advice. You may not believe this, but I get a lot of that. The hell if I know how I made detective."

Their eyes locked in angry silence.

Other thoughts cascaded through Kim's mind. She regretted the time she had wasted tracking down Jenna Spinelli and Mike Lasko. In light of the detective's patent contempt, she knew she wouldn't mention those conversations. She wondered what Czernak thought of the possibility of a second lover, the elusive "Mr. Money Bags." She was tempted to ask sarcastically whether he had the vaguest clue that he had a chop shop operating somewhere under his nose, but she didn't take that tack, having no cause to totally infuriate the man.

Instead, she came back to a real question. "From reading the notebooks, I know Emily had something over $1,000 in a checking account as of a year ago. I wonder if you can tell me anything about that money, namely, whether it's still there."

Dan Czernak's eyes glinted in surprise. He seemed to debate something. "The money's still there."

Kim hadn't expected a reply. Her jaw dropped as another puzzle piece fell into place. "Then you knew all along she hadn't left town on her own! You had to have known that. Emily would have taken that money if she had left of her own free will."

The accusation stood. The detective flushed.

Sharp rapping at the office door prevented Czernak from the need to reply. The door swung open. A man in plainclothes stood there, one hand on the knob. "Danny, something's come up. You need to see this. Right now."

Czernak was already moving. "I'll get someone to see you out, Miss Jackson."

He passed by without another word.

CHAPTER 20

Montrose, Colorado, may have liked to think of itself as a folksy, small-town kind of place where people knew their neighbors and always thought the best of each other. The townspeople may have prided themselves on living in a place where crime—major crime, murder and the like—didn't happen. Thank goodness, Kim thought, because in the extremely rare instance when it did happen, the hayseed police force proved inept. When it came to violent crime, the local boys were, to put it bluntly, out of their depth.

Such, at least, was her opinion.

It was over. She could let Emily Riley go. The girl in whose path she had walked since her first day in Montrose—finally, she was free of her. The calamitous visit to Detective Czernak gave her that. Back at home, she drank coffee and took solace in the thought.

She fumed until her anger spent itself. Early in the afternoon, she left the house and went to Pine Village. She found Lucy slumped in her wheelchair, sound asleep. Initially, Kim spoke softly, trying to wake her. When that didn't work, she spoke more loudly. The elderly woman was breathing audibly but wouldn't wake.

"She was fine first thing this morning," Christine said acidly.

Kim took the bait. She asked whether something had happened since then.

"Her son was here," Christine said.

Kim drew a heavy breath. She resisted drawing the conclusion that Christine obviously wanted her to reach. "I've heard from the staff that Lucy's condition is still up and down."

"Yes. It's up until her son appears, and it's down after. I'm sorry, Kim. I don't think we should read further without her."

"Then let's go have a cup of tea, shall we?"

Christine sat up straighter, smiled, and said that would be lovely.

—

Sensational news broke the following day. A burned-out car had been discovered in the Dry Creek area west of town, according to an article in the morning paper. The two men who found the car claimed to have seen at least one body inside. At the time the story went to print, the police were unwilling to confirm the presence of human remains in the vehicle.

Working at JT's, Kim's shoulders tensed each time a customer mentioned the stunning news. She thought of the sharp rap on Detective Czernak's door the previous morning, and the urgency in the voice of the officer who summoned the detective. At the time, she was relieved by the interruption. Now she didn't know what to think. All she wanted was for the constant jittery feeling to go away, and unless it was asking too much, she hoped Detective Czernak would forget she had ever been in to see him.

Another day passed. That evening, the detective knocked on her front door. He was frowning when she opened it. "Can I come in?" he said.

She looked up and down the street, saw no sign of a patrol car, and assumed he'd driven there in an unmarked vehicle. There was no unusual activity on the street. She nodded and stepped back, allowing him to enter.

"You ever hear of a man named Clark Adams?" he said.

"I've heard the name." When the detective didn't speak, she said, "Clark Adams lives with Deena Warren. I saw his name in the newspaper."

"You ever meet him?"

"No."

The pieces started falling into place. She kept her expression neutral. She waited for the detective to say it.

"Adams has been missing for a while. He isn't any longer." He broke eye contact, rubbed his hands together, and made a small angry sound before looking up. "Clark Adams was found earlier this week in a burned-out car. I'm sure you've heard about that. He'd been shot twice, once in the hand. Any of this starting to ring a bell?"

It was. She didn't comment.

"He was identified through dental records," Czernak said.

"Where was he shot the second time?"

"In the head."

Kim started shaking. "Not by Andrea, he wasn't. If that's what you're thinking." Unable to stand any longer, she sat down on the couch. She didn't want to know what her brain was trying to tell her: that Clark Adams had been executed. Probably by Tyler Haas—who was a ghost in the wind, the detective had told her a week ago. "Do you think Tyler Haas shot Clark Adams?" she said.

"That's what we're trying to find out. You happen to think of anything else about your pal Tyler you want to tell me?"

She shook her head no. She kept her lips drawn tight. She wasn't going to let him incite her into saying another word about Haas.

Still, there was bound to be fallout from this development. The identity of Andrea's shooter was now known, and it wasn't Aleksander Voigt. The men who had committed the home invasion were local. One had a connection to Kim, which she had revealed by her own admission. She didn't know what Andrea would make of that. She doubted it would give Andrea a warm, fuzzy feeling about her housemate.

On the way out, Detective Czernak said, "Miss Jackson— Kim. A word of advice before I go. Don't go looking for trouble. A person's lucky enough if trouble never comes looking for her."

Through the rest of the evening, Kim's mind spun around the details she had learned. The likely scenario of what happened lit up her mind without any effort on her part to construct it. Clark got shot in the hand by Andrea. There was nowhere to take him for treatment, not without exposing his involvement in the home invasion and as the man who'd shot Andrea. He was a liability. Tyler had shot him. And left the body in a car he'd set on fire miles out of town.

Much later that night, Kim's thoughts turned to Deena Warren. For the second time in a matter of months, Deena had lost someone she loved. Presumably she had loved Adams. They had lived together. Tears trickled down Kim's face when she thought of Dustin.

The next day, she resolved not to think about, or wonder, anything. She worked the early shift at JT's, ignoring every effort by her customers to talk about the revelation that Clark Adams had been identified as the dead man in the burned-out car. She went to Pine Village and spent a delightful hour with Lucy and Christine, came home, ate dinner, and went to the softball game.

On Saturday, she had the day off from work. She stayed around the house in the morning. By early afternoon, wanting to escape the heat of the day, she went to the air-conditioned library. She found a good book and curled up on a chair, reading for several hours. She stayed away from the computers, which were in high demand, regardless.

At home, she wandered from room to room, unable to shake off a troubled feeling of defeat. She had lost her credibility with Detective Czernak. All for what? For a precious theory that, even if true, was worth much less than she had imagined.

With a burst of enthusiasm, she rode her bike to JT's to buy fresh seafood and garden greens. On the way home, she made a second stop for a bottle of wine.

Back at the house, she noticed on the calendar the date was June 21. Summer solstice, she thought, the longest day of the year. It certainly had that feel about it. Well past eight o'clock, it was still bright daylight. Her dinner finished, all the dishes washed and stacked in the drain to dry, she paced until she finally settled down with a book.

It didn't satisfy her. After a few minutes, she tossed it aside and considered going back to the classified ads in the local paper in search of an elusive perfect job. She had been through the listings once and knew there wasn't anything there. Maybe tomorrow, she thought, thinking ahead to the Sunday edition.

She went into the living room and looked out the window. She suffered the feeling she had had lately: a twinge of desire to leave Montrose. More so than before, she felt surrounded by idiots.

"Stop it," she ordered. Lois Hays was no idiot. Neither was Dottie Goddard—or Lucy Wentworth.

April 21 to June 21. Two months had passed since Emily went missing. Kim shrugged off the reminder. Still wandering from room to room, on her next pass through the bedroom, she paused at the chest of drawers and opened the top drawer.

Reaching inside, she found the packet of Emily's photos and took them to the kitchen table.

Her interest flagged quickly. Flipping through the shots, she saw the girl whom she now recognized as Jenna Spinelli. She spared no appreciation for the artistic quality of any shot and thumbed through to the end, ready to be done with the empty exercise.

Then she saw something that piqued her interest.

The nighttime photos taken outside of Dave's Auto Body were at the bottom of the stack. Previously, she hadn't looked closely at them. They were distinctly inferior to the others in quality. Now she inspected them with new interest.

There were several shots of cars in the open doorway of the garage. Alongside one was a man wearing a baseball cap. His face wasn't visible, but by the cap and the long hair showing beneath it, Kim guessed the man was Clark Adams. She squinted, trying to make out the features of another figure deeper in shadow. A magnifying glass might show more, but she didn't have one.

She recalled what Ashley had said about Emily's relationship with Clark Adams. According to her, Emily had wondered where Clark got his money. The guy hadn't been known to hold a steady job.

Connections began to dawn on her. Kim allowed her eyes to linger on the black-and-white image while her thoughts drifted. Clark Adams standing inside an auto body shop. At night. She studied the other figure and wondered whether it might be Tyler Haas. It could be. It was his body type. But she couldn't be sure.

Her eyes were drawn to the vehicle on the flatbed truck. Unable to determine the make and model, she focused on its license plate. Studying the photo more closely, she realized the license plate of the vehicle was squared dead center—and explained why the picture of the man was so far off-center and slightly blurred. She flipped to the next picture and found exactly the same thing. Emily had taken the shots not of the cars but of their license plates.

Kim's mind began racing. Thoughts tripped over each other in their haste to meld into a single theory. Maybe Clark Adams had been responsible for Emily's murder—but not for any reason anyone had yet considered. Kim dropped the last photo, horrified by what she possibly had in her possession. Evidence. Evidence linking Emily to stolen cars. And stolen cars to an auto body shop located in the center of a rural Colorado community.

She pushed the pile of pictures away and stood up. Agitated, she began pacing. She grew angry again, at herself this time. It was absurd. She was making unwarranted leaps, and this time, she was angry about it. She thrust the pictures back in the envelope and replaced the entire collection in the chest drawer.

She poured a second glass of wine and dropped heavily onto the sofa in the living room. It was perfectly clear what she was doing. Anytime she didn't want to deal with her own situation, she skittered away and took a headlong dive into Emily Riley's life.

A shrink would have a field day with that.

She had problems. Yes, she had a mountain of problems, and not any of them had a thing to do with Emily Riley. The simple truth was she couldn't leave Montrose because she was afraid to drive her car. That's what it came to. She was trapped here. No wonder she was beginning to hate the town.

She strode back to her bedroom. She found a pen and notepad and returned to the kitchen table where she jotted down a single date: April 19. It was the day she'd left Chicago. She stared at the otherwise blank sheet.

For weeks she had shied away from the temptation to write down anything about her other life. She had resisted the impulse to draw two columns and fill in the blanks underneath: what she knew had happened inside the walls of Blackwell Industries, and what she had to find out. She already had a short list of questions, starting with: Where had the money gone that looked like an ordinary payment for a turbine compressor? Other questions would follow, of that she was sure. She pressed the pen against the pad. But her fear of writing anything down was too strong. With a sigh, she gave up the task and tossed the pen aside.

She didn't know whether she could ever go back to Chicago. She was no longer sure she had it in her to fight for the truth. She did know she could move to another city or town and start over. She had gained that much from living in Montrose.

She stared at a far wall and watched the sins of her twin lives line up in separate columns. Falsely accused, she wondered what she had really done wrong.

There wasn't a thing she could have done to save Michael Leeds.

In the last two months, this truth had quietly asserted itself until she became able to separate guilt from grief. Whatever wire Michael had tripped on that fateful Friday in March had sealed his fate. It was nothing she could have prevented. Thinking she ought to have known the contents of every single document in every single accounting file may have been laudable, but it was laughable. It was beyond reasonable, and now, more than ever, she needed to stick to reason.

Kim silently repeated the first line of Emily's poem: *I am coming home.* She badly wanted to be able to go home. She wanted to greet with a smile someone whom she had known for ages. She wanted to hear herself called by her real name. For that to happen, she had to tell someone what she knew, and beyond that, she had to trust the evidence to clear her of any wrongdoing.

She stared at faded pink flowers on the dated kitchen wallpaper. She glimpsed the winding path of her future. The road curved and dipped and disappeared into obscurity somewhere at a great distance. But it didn't lead to Chicago.

CHAPTER 21

The light seemed to have gone out of the world. Those were Kim's words for a certain gloominess that had seized her and refused to lift. She felt it at home, in the unsettled quiet of a space that had witnessed violence and now felt sorely the absence of one of its occupants. She felt it at work. Women— why was it always women who did the shopping, she wondered angrily, knowing it wasn't universally true. Women hurried through her checkout lane, rushing to be anywhere but here, while she remained stuck and invisible and seething with frustration. She hated the feel of other people's food in her hands, the inevitable stickiness that resulted from touching meat packets or prepackaged cut-up fruit. Her skin felt dry and abraded from the constant application of sanitizer, and though she never would have said she missed Chicago's oppressive humidity, she longed for the passing glance of moist air on her skin.

Nor was there any escape from the bleakness during the time she spent with Christine and Lucy. Even the pastoral realm of *Howards End* had suffered cruel blows. "Steady on," Lucy had said when Kim bemoaned the world collapsing around the characters she had grown to love.

Nighttime was the worst. At night, she lay awake for hours, listening for sounds that weren't there and trying to fill in the holes of a story she desperately wanted to understand. She wanted to know who had murdered Clark Adams. It could have been Tyler Haas, she conceded. It likely was. But he couldn't have acted alone. The burned-out car Adams's body was found in had been ditched fifteen miles from the nearest major road. Whoever set it on fire and left it there hadn't casually strolled back into town afterward. Someone else had been there. Someone driving a second vehicle.

On Tuesday, Ashley Crane didn't come into work. Kim, in early, watched John Trimble fret for fifteen minutes before he phoned Ashley's cell. Upon getting no answer, he resorted to calling her family's landline. Whomever he spoke to said Ashley wouldn't be in that day.

"You mind working a few extra hours today?" John asked her.

She didn't.

"I'll try and get someone in. Give a holler if lines start to back up," he said.

An hour later, Edie, the store's newest hire, rushed through the entrance. She put on an apron, got her cash drawer from John, and opened the lane where Ashley was supposed to be working. Kim lost hope of getting off work anytime soon. John would never leave Edie alone to handle the store's customers.

The first report of trouble came hours later from a softball teammate. Linda Perez came through Kim's lane and said, "You've heard Jeff Nelson's been picked up, haven't you?"

"What?"

"The police were at his house last night. He's been in custody ever since. The rumor is this has something to do with Emily Riley. You didn't know?"

Kim's heart fell. "No."

Linda said, "I don't know why anyone thinks he's involved. I've been trying to think of a good excuse to call Lois to find out what she knows."

"Why would Lois know anything?" Kim said.

"Her brother's a cop. He's been on the case from the beginning."

"Wait—her brother? What's his name?"

"Dan Czernak."

Kim choked back a small sound. She muffled it with a comment about not believing this latest news. Linda echoed the sentiment. They talked until another customer pulled into the lane and Linda collected her groceries and waved goodbye.

By the time Kim left work, she had heard the story several times. Jeff had been picked up. He was being held for questioning. His family had retained counsel on his behalf. That summed up the known story. Kim walked home, sick at heart. She spent a long evening beset with new worries.

The story broke the next morning. The astounding details were reported in the *Montrose Daily Press*. Kim read the article the moment she arrived at work.

A homeowner from an unincorporated development south of town had made a complaint to the police about a break-in at his property. He and his wife were part-time residents who hadn't been to the house since December. Extended travel abroad in the spring had kept them away until now. They had video proof of two persons who had been in the house in their absence. One was Jeff Nelson. The other allegedly was Emily Riley.

Shock carried Kim through the first part of the day. By afternoon, she felt both raw and numb. Her state mirrored that of most of her customers. People mumbled. They gave the wrong bills for payment, or the wrong credit card. Twice, Kim made a mistake handing back change. She apologized when she shortchanged one woman. The other handed back the ten-dollar bill she had received in error.

Ashley missed her second shift in as many days. No one at JT's assumed she had quit. Neither was anyone guessing when she would be back. Before leaving, Kim promised John she would be in first thing in the morning to cover Ashley's next scheduled shift.

Detective Czernak caught up with her when she was midway down the block. "Miss Jackson! Kim—may I speak with you?"

She turned at the sound of her name. "What is it?" she said.

The detective tapped his watch. "A few minutes of your time, that's all I ask. Mind if we sit in my car? It's the only place around with any privacy."

She assumed he wanted to talk about Jeff Nelson. As far as she was concerned, she had said all she intended to about Jeff. "Really, I don't have much time. I need to get to the bank."

"All I need is five minutes, ten, tops. Are you going to Bank of the West? They stay open 'til five. I promise you'll have plenty of time to get there."

Her expression tightened. Wanting this over with, she followed him to an unmarked sedan.

Once inside, she couldn't help but stare at the dashboard riddled with dozens of switches and knobs. The radio crackled. The detective lowered the volume a notch. Before he spoke, Kim searched his face for a resemblance to Lois. The only one she found was in his intelligent brown eyes. Where Lois's sparkled with laughter, Detective Czernak's were brooding and intense.

"I want to go over some of the things you talked about when you came to the station," he said. "I want you to tell me exactly why you thought Jeff Nelson might have been Emily Riley's boyfriend."

"I never said he was her boyfriend! I thought they might have been lovers. Sleeping together, that's all."

He made a note. "Right. Tell me again where you got that idea."

By now, she'd guessed why he was talking to her. He was covering his backside. He wanted to know what she knew and how she had discovered it. Doubting she had few options other than to answer his questions, she repeated in cursory detail how she thought she'd identified Jeff from the phantom lover poem. This time, Czernak took notes. "I knew my theory was weak," she said when she finished. "The only reason I told you was in the hope of having the possibility of Jeff's involvement with Emily considered."

"Yeah, well, we're considering it now." He thumped his pad. "I'll ask you this one more time. Was there ever anything that happened at the store, something Ashley said, something Jeff might have said, to start you down this road thinking Jeff and Emily had a thing going?"

"No."

The corner of the detective's mouth twisted into a frown. "Obviously I can't tell you what's going on. What I can tell you is that Jeff Nelson is being questioned regarding his relationship with Emily Riley. There's new evidence linking them. You might have heard something about that." He raised his head. "What I think—" He paused. "What I think is that you made a very lucky guess, tracking off that poem the way you did."

"I never thought it was more than that!" Kim said, angry again.

Detective Czernak took no notice. He flipped to another page in his notebook and read something. "I guess that's it."

Kim didn't slam the car door when she got out, though she wanted to. She tried to keep her expression neutral as she walked away. Images flashed through her mind. She imagined Emily, overcome with guilt, wanting to stop seeing Jeff. Maybe she had wanted to confess everything to Ashley. Or maybe she had only been teasing when she suggested coming clean, but Jeff, terrified of losing Ashley, had needed to silence Emily. The house they had broken into was south of town. Had Jeff strangled her there, then driven to Ouray to dispose of her body, managing to do so barely ahead of a snowstorm?

Kim was inside the bank before she realized where she was. With a sharp shake of her head, she cleared the images from her mind. She filled out a slip, then waited in line to deposit her paycheck. Uncharacteristically, she had let herself get down to less than twenty dollars in cash. When she reached the counter, she signed the bottom line on the slip for eighty dollars in cash, hoping that would last her two weeks.

She was putting the bills in her wallet when she came face to face with two men emerging from an office, paying no attention to where they walked. She stopped, unwilling to be run over. The ready scowl on her face disappeared when she recognized Scott Wentworth.

"Scott, hello," she said.

"Kim—didn't expect to see you here," he replied. His heartiness belied the unhappy look on his face a moment before. With the same air of easy bravado, he introduced her to the banker. They exchanged hellos. Scott turned to walk with her toward the exit.

"What brings you here, ordinary bank business?" he said.

"Yes. Just depositing my paycheck." On a whim, she said, "You don't happen to know anyone in town who might be looking to hire an accountant—or bookkeeper—do you?"

"Not that I can think of. Are you tired of working for John?"

"Tired, bored, and fed up. Scott, are you in a hurry? I've had a lousy day, and I could really use something to drink."

His eyes widened. "I'd love to join you for a drink. Are you thinking milkshake? Or something stronger?"

"Do you know any place in town that serves a decent glass of chardonnay?"

They walked to a restaurant on Townsend Avenue, reputed to have the best steaks in town. Bypassing the dining room, Scott ushered her into the dimly lit lounge. They were no sooner seated than Kim felt out of place in the establishment. She was still wearing her work clothes, jeans and a blouse she had picked up in a secondhand store. Her face felt gritty, and her hair—she couldn't imagine what it looked like. She quickly ran her fingers through it, hoping to coax the wayward strands into place. Unable to do more, she reached for the drinks menu. Not surprisingly, prices were high. But she did have a fresh wad of cash in her wallet.

"So tell me about your day," Scott said after they had ordered. "Did you get into fisticuffs with some woman over the price of lettuce?"

"Not today," she said, rankled by the tease. "It does happen, though."

"I've no doubt. I've been behind some of those women."

Assuming Scott only meant to keep the conversation light, she ignored his sexist quip. She said, "Today was hard for other reasons. You know—or maybe you don't know—Emily Riley used to work at JT's. Her best friend, Ashley, still does. The talk never stops all day long."

"Right. I hadn't thought about that. Lord knows I've heard enough of it myself, and I've been cooped up in an office most of the day."

There was an interlude of silence. Kim thought to say something about Lucy. Some censor stopped her. She remembered the last time she'd seen Scott—the day he'd left the nursing home after meeting with Lucy's lawyer and doctor. And Sara Shaffer.

She pushed the reminder away. "I'm irritated about something else," she said, testing the waters with a tentative glance.

A smile creased his handsome features. "Do tell."

"It's stupid."

"I can cope with that. Maybe we can have a good laugh together. Come on, you've got me curious now."

"Promise you won't laugh?"

"Oh well. Now you're asking too much."

Kim drew in a long breath. "I'm totally pissed off at a guy named Dan Czernak. He's a detective—"

"Danny Czernak? What's this about?"

She blinked in confusion. "You know him?"

"We grew up together. Course, he was a lot younger than me in those days," Scott said, grinning at his own weak joke. "I knew his sister better. So what did Danny do to you?"

His sister—Lois, Kim thought, thrown once again by the lifelong connections of Montrose residents. "He blew me off," she said.

Thinking she would only tell the bare-bones version of her first encounter with Detective Czernak, Kim launched into her story. Pent-up emotion got the better of her. Without directly admitting she had gone to Deena Warren to get Emily's notebooks, she mentioned having read one of Emily's poems and her eventual conclusion that the lover referred to was Jeff Nelson. To her pleasure, Scott listened intently.

"After essentially telling me I was an idiot when I talked to him at the police station, the guy comes crawling back this afternoon, wanting to know exactly what led to my idea about Jeff and Emily having some relationship. He's such a jerk."

"Whoa," Scott said, pretending to be jolted backward. "You're not afraid to mix it up with anyone, are you?"

"I don't know about that."

Kim fingered the stem of her nearly empty wineglass. It had been much too long since she had had a real conversation with anyone. The desire to talk nearly overwhelmed her. "I know Czernak didn't have any reason to take me seriously. But he could have behaved more decently. I'll be the first to admit I wouldn't want some amateur telling me how to do my job. Not when I'm working a real job," she added with emphasis. She hoped Scott would take the cue and ask her to clarify. For once, she wanted to allude to her professional accomplishments.

He didn't press the subject.

Uncomfortable, she went on. "The truth is, I probably did get carried away by thinking I could figure out something about Emily's case. The police weren't getting anywhere. People in town seemed to think Emily got what she deserved. I don't know." She shrugged off the unfinished sentence.

"You don't know what?"

His question nearly caused her to swoon. She couldn't remember the last time anyone had listened so closely to her. She shook her head and was about to beg off. Instead, she decided to trust him. "You have to keep your promise not to laugh."

With a quiet chuckle, he assured her that was a promise he assuredly could not make. "How about if I promise not to laugh too hard?"

She agreed that would be satisfactory. "Anyway, as I said, I got tired of hearing everyone's opinions about Emily. That's what made me decide to try and learn something about who the real Emily Riley was."

"And?"

"Emily was a complicated young woman, there's no question. Smart. Beautiful. And frightened too. Frightened that her life would turn out to be a carbon copy of her mother's. All she wanted was to get away from Montrose. It's hard to believe, but I suppose there's a good chance Jeff Nelson actually killed her."

"The police will determine that. Hopefully."

"Right. Hopefully."

It was the outcome she had scripted several weeks ago, when she'd first linked Jeff to Emily. Kim mulled over the scenario, unaccountably disturbed. There was a problem with it now. She laughed softly, trying to sort out the loose ends.

"What?" Scott said.

"Nothing. Everything. I don't know."

Scott cupped one hand around his drink. Without saying anything, he invited her confidence. When she didn't speak, he said, "As if you haven't noticed, you've got me on the edge of my seat."

Their waitress sidled up to the table and asked whether they needed anything.

"Another of each," Scott said, pointing at the empty glasses.

Kim started to object. Scott's grin stopped her. "What were you about to say?" he said.

She shook her head, feigning irritation at his presumption in ordering a second round of drinks. But the light buzz from the wine felt good. Almost as good as it felt to be sitting here with him. "You'll think I've gone off the deep end. I've been playing with this other theory. I don't know how or where Jeff Nelson fits into it."

"And this theory states—what?"

"I'm such an idiot," she muttered, regretting having started down this path. The waitress returned to exchange full glasses for the empties. Kim waited until the woman walked away. "My other theory has it that Emily was killed for a completely different reason, something no one has investigated so far. It has a lot to do with her connection to her mother's boyfriend. Former boyfriend. Deena Warren was involved with Clark Adams." She stopped abruptly, uncomfortable saying Adams's name out loud.

Scott showed no such discomfort. His eyebrows knitted together in a question. "You've lost me."

"Sometime last winter, while Emily was excited about a photography course she was taking at school, she started following Adams to find out where he went at night. She wanted to know how he was making money. And I think"—she paused to take a sip of wine—"I think Emily discovered Adams was part of a car-theft ring operating in town. She took nighttime photos of a place called Dave's Auto Body. Who is Dave? Do you know?"

Kim glanced over, waiting for Scott to answer. Meanwhile, a separate thought occurred to her. Discovering whether or not the cars Emily had photos of were stolen would be easy enough. She had the license plate numbers to check.

"Dave Kresten. Sure, I know him. He's a good guy, a really good guy. Sorry—what was your point?"

"Oh, probably nothing. I had this idea that Emily found out that stolen cars were going in and out of Dave's shop and maybe that had something to do with why she was killed."

"Good Lord, you never quit, do you?" Scott said, shaking his head in either mock or genuine amazement. "Dave Kresten is a pillar of the community. I've never heard him accused of—" He broke off in a laugh.

Kim blushed. "God, I am such an idiot. I'm sorry, Scott. Tell me you'll forget everything I just said. I can't believe how stupid it must have sounded."

"No, no. It's completely entertaining. I just—can't imagine where you came up with such an idea."

"Please, write it off to my overactive imagination. I guess it's painfully obvious I need a life."

"How do you know Emily took photos of Dave's place?"

The flush in her neck and face deepened further. Kim took slim solace from knowing Scott wouldn't notice her color in the room's low lighting. Admitting the truth was out of the question. So she soft-pedaled the details. "Deena told me Emily was running around at night taking pictures. I talked to Emily's photography instructor. He showed me some of her work. His theory was that she had taken the pictures of the auto body shop to contrast blue-collar guys with white-collar guys for an assignment."

"But you came up with a different theory."

"I did, but for no good reason. I thought I could make out Clark Adams in one of the photos. I had a wild idea that he might be involved in some of the local car thefts." She paused to give a long look at the man sitting opposite. "Listen, Scott, I'm really sorry. I've completely humiliated myself. Can we please talk about something else?"

"Sure. Only—" He broke off to look at his watch. "Kim, I'm sorry. I have a meeting tonight. I'm working up an idea to run TV ads for my business, and I'm supposed to meet with some people from the station. I'm sorry. I didn't realize how late it is."

A wan smile masked her crushed feeling. She had blown it by talking too much. Or by talking about the wrong things. Or maybe Scott had a date planned all along and was looking for an opening to cut short this dull interlude.

"Sorry. I should be going anyway," she said, hating it that her words sounded pained. She reached for her wallet and put a twenty-dollar bill on the table, hoping it would cover the cost of her wine.

He took a moment to glower at her. "Now listen to me, Miss Jackson. If you know what's good for you, you will kindly put that bill back in your wallet. In addition, I hope you will accept my invitation to have dinner before the end of the week."

Appeased, she retrieved the twenty.

"Now if I might have your phone number," he said, reaching inside his pocket for a card to jot the number on.

"I don't have a phone, Scott."

"And no car yet either?"

She recalled the story she had told him weeks earlier of having loaned her car to a friend in Denver. "No car yet."

"Then I suppose I'll have to find you at JT's."

She smiled. "Thank you. I'd love to have dinner with you. And I promise I won't—"

"No promises necessary," he said. He left a couple of bills on the table to cover their drinks. "May I say, the conversations I have with you continually surprise me, in all the best ways. Shall we go?"

CHAPTER 22

Kim worked another long shift the next day, putting in an extra hour past what she was scheduled to work. Finally off work, she emerged from the air-conditioned building into intense heat shimmering from the sidewalk. She couldn't remember when she had last felt so tired. It wasn't just the long hours. It was the cloud of grief hanging over the town. Ashley Crane still hadn't been back to work. Today, John had broached the subject of hiring a replacement for her.

Glad to reach the quiet blocks north of Main, Kim thought ahead to the rest of the week as she walked home. She had another full day of work tomorrow, a day off on Saturday. A softball game was scheduled for that night. She planned to go to Pine Village on Saturday morning. Unless—she dreaded the thought—John asked her to work for a seventh straight day.

Jeff Nelson was the talk of the town. He hadn't yet been formally charged in Emily Riley's murder. Everyone seemed to think it was only a matter of time until he would be. All week, Kim had listened to the editorials of patrons passing through her checkout lane. Opinions spanned the full range of human expression. She doubted anything could surprise her any longer. She had long since tired of hearing what a good boy Jeff was and how that wanton girl Emily must have done something plain evil to seduce him. Only rarely did she see sadness cross someone's eyes and hear a sympathetic thought spoken for two futures lost—Emily's and Jeff's.

Kim reached her block. She was nearly home when she was startled to see someone get out of a car and hurriedly approach from the opposite direction. It was Scott Wentworth. "Scott, what on earth are you doing here?" she said.

"Kim, I am so sorry to bother you. It's Mother. She's terribly upset, disturbed, I can't think how to describe it. She keeps asking for you. It's something to do with that book you've been reading to her. If it's not too inconvenient, could I beg fifteen minutes of your time? Would you mind running out to Pine Village? Please, Kim, I'm at my wits' end trying to calm her down."

"Scott, wait. Slow down. Of course, I'll go with you. Only, I can't imagine what help I'll be. What exactly did your mother say?"

He shook his head. "She keeps saying, 'Kim knows. Where's Kim? I need to ask Kim.' To be honest, I think she just wants to see you."

Kim recalled the past week. Normally she saw Lucy every two or three days. Her hectic schedule at the grocery store had made visiting impossible. Worse, she hadn't considered what her absence might mean to Lucy and Christine.

It wasn't until she was inside Scott's car that the oddity of him appearing at her house sunk in. She had never told him where she lived. "How did you find me?" she said as she buckled in.

"I went to JT's hoping to catch you before you left work. John said I'd just missed you. He wouldn't give me your address, but he seemed certain that if I headed north on Nevada, I'd catch up with you. Which is exactly what I did." Scott was speeding down backstreets, barely slowing for stop signs.

"When did your mother's condition change?"

"After dinner. She hardly ate a thing, and was more distracted than usual. A couple of the nurses were in and out, including one who seemed especially concerned. Next thing any of us knew, she was talking pure nonsense. When a few bits started to fall into place, I realized she was talking about the book you've been reading to her."

"I haven't been able to visit this week. Work has been insane. I'm sorry, Scott. But I'm sure everything will be okay."

At the highway, he turned left, heading in the direction opposite of Pine Village. Kim, unaccustomed to traveling by car, didn't realize his mistake until they crossed the main intersection at the center of town. "Why are we going this way?" she said.

"I have to pick up something for Mother at her house. It's only five minutes out of our way. Sorry, I thought I'd said. I'll be quick." He looked over and smiled—or rather, forced a smile. "On the bright side, you'll get to see the house. I'm sure you've heard Mom talk about it."

Kim noticed that he suddenly seemed uncomfortable. He hadn't mentioned the detour; she was certain of that. Irritated, she told herself it was no big deal.

Just past a strip mall, Scott turned right onto a county road. Some distance farther, he pulled into a long driveway. A house stood at the end. Heedless of the bumps, he drove fast. Kim was about to tell him to slow down, she wasn't in that much of a hurry, when he hit the brakes and slammed to a stop.

"Come on," he said. "I'll give you the thirty-second tour."

She got out of the car. "Oh my," she said, of no mind to go inside. Now that she was here, all she wanted was to take in the view. The house was set on a rise. A wide, lush lawn flowed down to a creek, partially obscured by brush. She saved the best view for last. She raised her eyes and gazed south at the jagged line of the San Juan Mountains.

Her breath caught. The place was quiet, remote. It spoke of peace.

But the backdrop of peace was shattered when Scott came around the car and grabbed her arm. "This way," he said.

"Scott, stop it. What are you doing?"

He didn't answer. He dragged her to the unlocked back door, opened it, and thrust her inside.

They stood facing each other in the kitchen. Kim knew then what he had done, though not why. He had lured her here under false pretenses, using her feelings for Lucy against her. His eyes bore a crazed look. They were full of latent danger, and somehow served as a warning. Too late, she remembered everything she had heard about Scott Wentworth. Her softball teammates had warned her to stay away from him. Sara Shaffer had made it clear she didn't trust him. Kim had ignored them all.

She was sure he meant to rape her. His eyes grew cold. The beginning of movement at his mouth frightened her as much as his voice when he finally spoke. "I have a problem. And you must help me solve it."

"What problem?"

"Money. Isn't it always about money?"

She didn't answer.

"I need money," he said, as if that explained everything.

He had crossed the line into violence. Now that he was there, he had no reason to go back. "Come on," he said. He grabbed her arm. She stumbled when he pulled her toward another room. "Move!" he bellowed.

Kim heard something in his voice that made her stop. She looked at him, all but daring him to reveal how far across that line he meant to go. "What does any of this have to do with me?" she said.

He swung the back of his hand and landed a clean blow to her face. She cried out and fell against the wall. She tasted blood on her lip.

"Shut up," he said. He grabbed her and a chair and dragged them both through the doorway into the next room.

They were in a family room. The front wall was a line of windows facing the mountains. Fleetingly, Kim remembered Lucy had said that she and Sam had built this house. This room was obviously the showcase. The interior was simple—a stone fireplace, pine-board walls, a multihued wool carpet. Dazzling sunlight poured into the room, the last of the light still illuminating the distant mountaintops.

At that moment, she hated Scott and pitied him—pitied him for being the flawed son of exceptional parents.

"Are you going to kill me?" she said.

"I don't know. Don't talk about it."

She guessed that meant yes.

He thrust the chair forward and pushed her onto it. He pulled her arms through the chair's woven slats. Before she knew what was happening, he'd turned her wrists outward and bound them. The cord, pulled taut, sliced into her skin. He mumbled as he worked. "I don't know why you came here. You ruined everything. Unbelievable how you could ruin everything."

He spoke low and fast. Kim thought he was speaking to himself. When her arms were bound, he stood back. He rubbed his hands together as though finished. She held her breath. Her legs were still free. Maybe he was just crazy enough to forget what he had left undone. Watching him, she saw his eyes clear. When he spoke next, he had regained his focus. He knelt down to secure her ankles.

"Mom and I are going to make a deal," he said. "You are part of that deal. Her doctor has stated that Lucy is mentally competent. Perfect. She'll have no trouble comprehending my terms. She is going to sign over papers giving me power of attorney over her finances and, in exchange—" He paused to cinch the cord tighter, causing Kim to cry out. He laughed. "In exchange, she gets to guarantee your release. Or so she'll believe." Working quickly, he bound one leg to the chair. Tying off the knot, he moved to the other. "Is she incompetent or is she mentally sound?" he said in a singsong voice. "We'll know soon. She's been playing the fool all these months. Acting dumb so no one would know. Meanwhile, she's got it all perfectly together." He stood up when he finished. "And now she gets to make a choice. Her precious land. Or her precious Kim. And everyone knows how much she cares for you."

"What are you going to do, Scott?"

Scott surveyed his handiwork. Confident that she couldn't escape, he relaxed. "What does she need all this land for?" he said, gesturing at the scene beyond the windows. "She's stuck in that nursing home. She's going to live there the rest of her life, however long that is. All she has to do is let me sell her land and borrow against my future inheritance. I am not going down again." His voice hardened. "I will not go through that."

Kim began to understand. "Your business is in trouble," she said.

"Shut up," he roared. He slapped her harder than before, nearly knocking her over. "It's not her money. It was my father's money. And I have a right to it."

Kim didn't agree. Nor did she argue. She waited, unable to do anything but glare at him.

"Mom cares for you. We'll see how much she cares." He crossed the room and took out his smartphone. "Mother has her wits, so she gets to choose. Her land or you," he repeated, beginning to snap pictures. The shots were of Kim bound with the view of the mountains as the backdrop. "I shall put it to her directly. And if she should tell anyone what I've done, who's to believe her? What a story it would make," he said, laughing, snapping one picture after another. "A senile old woman or her successful son—who would you believe?" He laughed cruelly, moving from one position to the next, mimicking the movements of a professional photographer.

Kim knew her mistake then. In Montrose, she had as little status as Lucy Wentworth—a feeble woman who experienced mental lapses. Kim had given Scott all he needed. She had passed herself off as a drifter, a no-account person in the community. Who would believe her wild story of having been kidnapped—even if she managed to escape? Who would give more than passing notice if she went missing? If she had harbored any doubt about Scott's designs, it had now faded. His plan suddenly seemed terribly cunning.

"Mom will sign, I'm sure of that," he said. "She's a bit afraid of me anyway, haven't you noticed? Tomorrow I'll process the papers. We'll schedule the closing to sell the land next week. My buyer hasn't gone anywhere. Why would he, when I've promised to deliver? And by Independence Day, I will be a free man." Without prompting, Scott said, "Chances are excellent Mother won't recall any of this anyway. She'll drink her milkshake. Of course, I'll take her a milkshake when I see her tonight. She'll sleep it off and in the morning will be no wiser."

"And what about me?" Kim said in a cold voice.

"Oh, Kim, Kim, Kim. I just don't know about you." The crazy way he laughed made her think he did know. "Who are you? It's a funny thing. No one seems to know much about you. Not that I've probed too deeply. Wouldn't want anyone thinking I'm too interested. But you've no friends, no family. Not even a car for anyone to trace. Fond as I've become of you," he said, stepping closer and laying the palm of his hand against her cheek. When she jerked her head away, he laughed. "Well, we'll just have to see what happens when I come back. It could be a terrible thing. You could end up over the side of a mountain in Ouray, the circumstances of your death bearing an uncanny resemblance to the death of another young woman. Now wouldn't that just fuel the fears of Montrose citizens? The possibility of a serial killer living in their midst?"

"I doubt it. The police already know who killed Emily Riley."

"So they think. Innocent until proven guilty," Scott said, wagging his finger. "The discovery of a second body would throw great confusion into the case against Jeff Nelson. I certainly wouldn't mind doing my part to help clear that innocent boy's name." Scott paused to check the photos. Apparently satisfied, he said, "All of that is for us to discuss later. Maybe after we've had a chance to get to know each other better. Despite everything, I really do find you attractive, Kim. But just now, I need to finish up. Not that I'm expecting any company, but I'm going to lower these blinds."

He did so, blocking view of her from anyone who might wander by. Not that anyone would. The property was remote. Kim didn't have any idea how close the nearest neighbor lived. She hadn't seen another house on the drive in.

"Now here's a little something for you," he said, returning to her side and producing a white pill and a glass of water. He used both hands to jam the pill into her mouth. She was certain it was a sleeping pill. The knowledge dawned on her then that he had likely been drugging Lucy's milkshakes with the same pills for weeks. When he reached for the water glass, she spit the pill out, praying he would never notice it on the carpet. "That should keep you nice and relaxed until I get back," he said as he forced her to take a swallow.

Using duct tape, he covered her mouth, wrapping the band around her head. "Sorry about this," he said. "That's probably going to hurt like hell when I pull it off. I'll try to be gentle," he said in an ugly voice, and laughed.

Stony-eyed, Kim watched him leave. She heard the back door slam. Seconds later, the car engine roared to life. Tires spun on the gravel.

Silence engulfed the house.

She tried to shake herself out of the nightmare. Scott had kidnapped her. He was holding her prisoner. The first rush of adrenaline gave out, and she felt a sick sensation in the pit of her stomach. She couldn't have known, she told herself. She couldn't have known Scott would resort to this. She had to believe that no one who had ever warned her about Scott Wentworth had believed him capable of this.

And perhaps no one would ever know what he had done.

A wave of dizziness swept over her. Kim recognized it. She could not—she dared not—let herself black out now. She strained against the ropes, trying to force them to slacken. The strands only bit deeper into her wrists. But the pain was welcome. It steadied her. Strangely, it calmed her.

She whipped her head in both directions, looking for anything she could use to free herself. All she saw was a comfortably furnished den. There was a leather sofa against the long wall, a teak coffee table in front of it, several chairs, a pair of end tables, and a painting hanging above the sofa. An empty vase hinted that flowers had once accented the room with a splash of color.

In front of her, there was only glass. Large panels filled most of the wall. Along the floor, a line of small rectangular windows extended the length of the room. Each one was screened and had a handle for opening. An idea came to her. She moved without thinking. She chose the shortest path to the window and lunged left. She tipped over, as she had hoped to. Her head struck the floor—there was no helping that. Stretching, she could nearly touch the pane of glass with her right leg. In one blind motion, she lurched forward, counting on raw momentum to propel her toward the glass. She gained a few inches. She repeated the motion. Three times, she shot forward, indifferent to the rope burning her skin. On the fourth lunge, she put her foot through the window. Glass shattered. The sound exploded in her ears, so loudly, she wondered that no one else could hear it. But the house quickly settled back to quiet. She felt the first throb of pain on her cut ankle. She gritted her teeth. There would be more pain.

She started with one leg.

She was wearing long pants, socks, and sneakers. On her feet all day at the grocery store, she depended on the shoes for comfort. She had to find the rope's edge and pin it against the protruding shard of glass. Working carefully—blindly—she moved her leg back and forth, trying to cut the braid. She cut herself too. She gasped each time she scraped the open wound.

Long minutes passed. She concentrated fiercely, fighting the pain. Finally the rope broke. Giddy with relief, she shook her right leg clear. She debated pivoting and trying to cut the rope binding her wrist. But she knew she had to get her left leg free first. She worked her way into position and started sawing. She flinched when she felt the first fresh cut.

She sawed back and forth, not sure whether she was chewing up more rope or skin. As before, she couldn't tell what was happening. It seemed to be taking too long. She resisted a sense of fury and the temptation to push harder in a desperate bid for freedom.

At long last, the rope began to give. It took more minutes of sawing before her foot broke free. Once it did, she had a new problem. If she were still upright, she could have hobbled to the kitchen and looked for a knife to cut the rope binding her hands. Stuck on the floor, she had no leverage. All she could do was shuffle around and aim for a position to bring her wrists to the glass.

It wasn't going to work. Her hopes for freedom sank when she realized she couldn't push her hands far enough clear of the chair to place them against the protruding shard of glass.

Another idea came to her. Swiveling around again like a turtle stuck on its back, she returned to her original position.

From there, she put her foot through the open window. She lodged her shoe against the far side of the glass and pulled in, breaking off a wedge. It rattled onto the floor. In one quick motion, she swiveled around again. She groped to locate the glass, then picked it up with her right hand. Twisting it inward, she immediately nicked her palm and the skin on her left wrist. But she found the cords and began cutting.

There was no avoiding new wounds. Her fingers became sticky with blood. She felt the stabs when the glass missed the rope and found her wrist. But she worked quickly, certain now of success. When the first loop broke, she felt a surge of relief. A minute later, her left hand was free.

She stood up and pivoted around in the chair to get better access to her right wrist. For the first time, she could see what she was doing. There may have been a faster, better method for freeing her right hand, but she stuck to what worked. Holding the shard of glass in her left hand, she cut the rope binding her right wrist.

The instant her hand was free, she pulled the tape off of her mouth, then more gingerly, removed it from her hair.

However much she wanted to run, she didn't. Cold awareness settled over her and, with it, the knowledge that she needed to do this right. She went upstairs, found a bathroom, and left the tape with strands of her hair inside a drawer, leaving evidence. She washed her cuts and applied Band-Aids. She left fingerprints everywhere. She washed her face one last time, then left the house.

Outside, she grew terrified that she had taken too long. Scott could come back any minute, and if he did—

She didn't let herself think about it.

She began jogging.

At the end of the long driveway, she turned right on the county road. When she glimpsed a car approaching, she ducked behind a thick growth of shrubs. After it passed, she resumed jogging.

Nothing looked familiar. She searched her memory for landmarks she'd seen on the drive in, but saw nothing. She stopped to get her bearings and was instantly sorry she had done so. Both directions looked identical. She had no idea which way to go. In a panic, she started running. Sprinting furiously, she was winded within seconds. She gasped for air with large, wracking sobs but didn't slow down.

Still running, she felt something creeping from behind. Forsworn to escape it, she forced her legs to pump harder.

But the thing chasing her caught her. And then everything went black.

CHAPTER 23

Kim didn't know what awakened her. She heard a voice. Light filtered into a room where she lay on a bed—a strange bed, not her own. She had no idea where she was.

Terror coursed through her veins. She dared not move.

In the shadowy light, all she could make out was the shape of the double bed and a pair of windows on the near wall. There was a chest of drawers and a nightstand on the opposite wall. Nothing looked familiar.

From beyond the open door, she heard a woman's voice. The voice grew louder. Kim braced for a face-to-face meeting. When the voice went quiet, she heard only footsteps. "Who's there?" she demanded.

The door to the bedroom opened wider. A woman stood there. "You're awake," she said. It was Sara Shaffer.

Kim said nothing. She sat bolt upright when Sara entered the room. Lying flat, she felt much too vulnerable.

"How are you feeling?" Sara said.

Kim watched her warily. The question was far too complicated. Rather than answer, she said, "Where am I? How did I get here?"

Sara smiled. She drew a chair close to the bed and sat down. "That's a bit of a long story. Do you know who I am, Kim?"

Kim nodded.

"You're in my house. You're safe here."

Kim closed her eyes. It was a perfectly ludicrous thing to say. Mustering energy, she sat up straighter and said, "I'll go now. I'm sorry if I've been any trouble."

Sara laughed warmly. "Hold on. Slow down. It's one o'clock in the morning, and just for the record, you aren't going anywhere tonight." Her look was studied. "What can you tell me about tonight?" Kim didn't answer. After a pregnant pause, Sara said, "All right, I'll tell you what I know. Sometime past eight o'clock, I received one of the strangest phone calls I've ever had. The caller was the night manager at a self-storage business out on Highway 550. He's just a kid, nineteen or twenty. His girlfriend was with him in the office when you showed up. You were obviously frantic, but you weren't making a lot of sense. You kept insisting you wanted your car."

Kim closed her eyes and drew in a quiet breath. With extreme effort, she kept her face empty of expression.

Sara said, "They tried persuading you that their place of business was not a garage. Credit goes to the young woman, I think, who thought to ask for someone they might call for you. It was clear something was amiss. The wonder is they didn't call the police. Who knows? They may have had their own reasons for not wanting to draw attention to themselves. In any case, the young woman found my business card in your wallet and phoned me. I came and picked you up and brought you here."

Silence fell between them. Kim kept her glance averted.

"How long have you suffered from these sorts of episodes, Kim?"

Kim's head shot up. "I don't know what you're talking about."

"In case you don't remember, I'm a doctor. I'm not a psychiatrist, but I know enough about altered psychotic states to know something about what I saw tonight. And so I repeat, how often do you suffer from these episodes?"

With extreme effort, and speaking softly, Kim said, "Not often."

"I take that to mean you've had them before?"

Kim wanted to shrug but nodded instead.

"Can you describe what happens?"

Kim didn't want to get into it. There were more important questions to answer, namely, she still couldn't piece together what had happened that night. After a long moment of silence, she said, "It's nothing I want to talk about."

"I'm sorry, but that is not one of your options. When I brought you back to the house and had a chance to see the condition you were in, I seriously debated taking you to the emergency room."

Kim glanced up sharply. "No."

Sara reached for Kim's wrist, which was freshly bandaged. She said, "If this was a suicide attempt, it ranks as a weak one, fortunately. All of the cuts are on the outside of your limbs."

"It wasn't a suicide attempt."

Kim was certain of that much. Puzzled by the bandages, she took a quick assessment of the rest of her body in hopes of sorting out what had happened to her. She felt an achiness from head to toe. Her wrists and ankles were sore; the side of her head throbbed. And the cuts? All at once, it came to her what Scott Wentworth had done that night. Not trusting her own memory, she said nothing about it.

Sara said, "Let's start over. What happens to you when you experience one of these episodes?"

"I black out. That's what I call it," Kim said, resigned to answer. "I lose awareness of myself and my surroundings, but I don't lose consciousness."

"Is it something you've had treatment for in the past?"

"Yes."

"Are you on any medications?"

Kim felt roaring in her ears. She couldn't have this conversation. The top was being ripped off, and she couldn't bear to suffer exposure. So she spoke brusquely, meaning to get it over with. "Yes, I've had treatment. No, I'm not on anything. No prescription drugs. No drugs, period. Ordinarily I don't have any problems with this. It only happens when I feel too much stress."

"I'm glad to know that. Are you hungry? I don't know whether you had dinner tonight."

The abrupt shift startled her. Kim made an instantaneous decision. She would do whatever necessary to get through this night. First thing in the morning, she would leave Montrose. For good. "I'm very hungry," she said.

"Good. Then before we go downstairs, I want to tell you more about what happened when we got back here tonight. As I said, I debated taking you to the ER. Instead, I put you in my bathtub and let you soak off the sweat and blood. I have to tell you I checked for bruising on your legs but saw no sign that you had been violated. Afterward, I dressed your wounds and kept my fingers crossed you would come around before long. Instead, you fell sound asleep."

"Did I say anything?"

"Nothing I could make heads or tails of. When I pressed you with questions, you closed up completely."

Kim winced when she tried to swing her legs out from under the covers. Sara waited until she was standing before handing her a cotton robe. Kim noticed the nightgown she was wearing. It was plain and soft and clean, and still, it felt like an indignity hanging on her shoulders. Downstairs, in the kitchen of the old farmhouse, Sara put on a kettle of water. She opened the refrigerator and removed a package of cheese. She sliced an apple and a peach and arranged them on a plate along with hunks of cheese. By the time she finished cutting slices from a loaf of French bread, the water had boiled. She poured two cups of tea. Kim watched her. All the while, fragments and images from earlier that night floated like so many jigsaw pieces in her head, waiting for her to mold them into one coherent whole.

She reached for a slice of apple.

"I've told you my version of tonight's events," Sara said. "Now I really do need to know about those wounds on your wrists and ankles."

The reality that Scott had kidnapped her and held her hostage had sunk in. Kim knew she couldn't keep secret what had happened. Nor did she want to. She lowered her head and began to talk. "This won't make any sense, but I swear to you it's the truth. I cut myself on glass trying to escape from Lucy Wentworth's house. Scott tricked me into going there. Once there, he tied me up and held me hostage."

Sara's sharp intake of breath stopped her from saying more. "Good Lord, Kim. Wait, please wait. Back up. Is there a way to start at the beginning?"

Dulled by shock, Kim told the story of how Scott had approached her earlier in the evening, entreating her to go with him to Pine Village, for Lucy's sake. "I didn't have any reason not to believe him," she said, feeling defensive. "So I agreed to go. But instead, he drove to Lucy's house. He said there was something he needed to pick up for her. It didn't seem like a huge deal, at least not until we were there and it became clear he had tricked me."

"What happened next?"

"He tied me to a chair and took pictures—me, with Lucy's land in the background. He said Lucy was going to have to choose between her land and me. Scott is in some kind of financial trouble. Terrible trouble. I don't know what it is, only that he needs Lucy's signature so he can sell her land. He thought he could bully her into signing by threatening to harm me."

"Okay, please, go on."

"I don't know what he intended to do with me. He threatened to kill me. He said no one would even notice if I disappeared, which is probably true. He took the pictures and then he tried to force me to swallow a pill. A sleeping pill, I think. I spit it out before he put duct tape around my mouth. Then he left." Kim took a swallow of tea. "I escaped by breaking a window with my foot and cutting the rope with the glass shards. That's why my palm is cut. When I was free, I went upstairs to a bathroom and washed off the blood and bandaged the cuts, best I could. Then I left the house and started running. That's the last thing I remember."

"Well done, Kim," Sara said approvingly. "That bastard," she muttered. She stood up. "I need to call the nursing home. I had a call from them earlier. Lucy was terribly upset. I need to make sure they don't let Scott anywhere near her." She went to a wall phone, dialed the number, and spoke to someone who took her message. When she returned to the table, she said, "I have to call the police. This needs to be reported."

Kim shot her a wild look. "Please, not yet. I can't talk to anyone. Not like this." Her voice faded, and she knew she meant, *Not when I'm like this.*

"You're not the only one who's at risk from Scott. Lucy is. Maybe others are too. I'm sorry, Kim. This has to be done."

Sara picked up the phone and made the call.

CHAPTER 24

The call to the police resulted in a summary order to take Kim to the emergency room. They would be met there by a Montrose police officer.

"I promise, nothing will happen to you," Sara said when she saw Kim's ashen face. "Someone other than me needs to examine you—your cuts and abrasions. It supports your story. It's evidence against Scott, and it must go on the record."

Kim stared blankly. She could barely manage to change into the clothes Sara produced for her: shorts, T-shirt, and a pair of sandals. Sara bundled her other clothes into a plastic bag in case they were needed as evidence.

As they left the house, Sara said, "The important thing is to make this initial report and to document your injuries. Tougher, more complicated questions will likely come later. The hardest question tonight will be why I delayed calling this in, and I intend to answer honestly—that I didn't know what had happened. I will describe your condition in the early evening as traumatized. Once you tell what happened—exactly as you told it to me—it will be enough for you to say you panicked. No one can argue with that."

"What if I black out again?" Kim said hoarsely.

"You must try very hard not to let that happen. I will be with you. And trust me, I will do everything in my power to keep this session as brief as possible."

Two police officers were waiting at the entrance to the ER when they arrived. Contrary to Sara's promise to stay with her, Kim was whisked into an exam room while Sara was detained by the officers for questioning. A nurse assisted her into a flimsy gown. The middle-aged woman proceeded to gingerly remove the set of four bandages from her wrists and ankles. Kim felt nauseous and dizzy, and under no obligation to answer any of the questions the doctor asked when he came in. She pressed her head into the padded surface of the table, grateful for the stabs of pain radiating from the bruise there. It was all that steadied her. Meanwhile, the doctor examined her wounds, dabbing them with something damp and painful. It was taking too long. He commented on her racing pulse and elevated blood pressure. Finally he left, telling the nurse he had a question for Dr. Shaffer and would return in a minute.

He didn't return. As time passed, Kim's mind started spinning the way it sometimes did before a blackout. She clenched her fists tight, concentrating on the feel of her fingernails pressing into her palms. Finally, when she feared she could hold on no longer, Sara entered the room and dismissed the nurse.

"Bunch of asses," she muttered. "Here, drink some water. How are you holding up?"

Kim shook her head numbly. "I don't think I can—"

"Of course, you can. Come on. We'll get you through this, then get the hell out of here."

As Sara had predicted, the sticking point for the police officers was Kim's behavior after her escape. It was completely irrational. She should have run to the nearest house for help, or stopped the first car she saw. Instead, she had done what?

Gone to a self-storage business looking for her car? That made no sense.

Kim didn't deny it. After one of the officers asked the same question five different ways, Sara blew up. "Kim has answered all of your questions. Unless you have something else to ask her, we're leaving."

The lead officer said, "I guess that's all for tonight."

Back at Sara's house, Kim collapsed in the double bed where she had awakened hours earlier. Without expecting to, she sank into deep sleep.

Soft tapping at the bedroom door awakened her the next morning. She hadn't fully roused herself when she heard the click of the latch. The door swung inward.

"Good. You did sleep, then," Sara said.

Kim made a feeble attempt to reply through a yawn.

"I wish I could let you sleep as long as you like. Unfortunately, there's a great deal to be done this morning."

"Okay."

"I have a pot of coffee made. Come downstairs when you're ready. There's a toothbrush and toothpaste on the bathroom counter."

Kim rose and stretched stiffly. Soreness radiated through her, especially near her wounds. She went through the motions of a morning ritual, feeling out of place wearing Sara's clothes, waking in her house. A bedside clock showed it was eight o'clock. And the day was—Friday. A workday. In a panic, she rushed downstairs.

"I've already called John Trimble," Sara said calmly. "And I've called my office as well. Neither one of us is going to work today."

While Kim sipped coffee and tried to eat a piece of toast, Sara said she had made several other phone calls. One was to Lucy's doctor, another was to her attorney. She warned them both to be on the lookout for Scott. Then she said, "The other thing is, I've already had a call from the police. They're sending someone out to take a detailed report. I held them off for as long as possible. Someone will be here within the hour."

Too soon, Kim heard the telltale sound of tires crunching on the gravel drive. She was trying to brace herself to get through this interview when she saw the man standing on the other side of the screen door. Her heart fell. It was Detective Czernak.

"Morning, Sara," he said. "Miss Jackson."

Kim nodded.

Sara started to introduce the two. She stopped when she realized they weren't strangers. "You know each other?"

"We do," the detective said. "I understand there was some trouble last night."

The three sat down at the kitchen table. Detective Czernak accepted a cup of coffee.

Kim told her story. "Last night, Scott Wentworth lured me to his mother's house under false pretenses. He said he needed me to go to Pine Village to see Lucy. I've been volunteering there and reading to Lucy Wentworth for the last several months. Scott claimed his mother was badly disturbed, and was asking for me. So I went with him. While we were driving, he said he needed to pick up something at Lucy's house. That's how we ended up there. Once we'd arrived, it became clear— he'd tricked me."

"Go on," Czernak said.

"Scott is in financial trouble," Kim said. "Last night, he meant to coerce his mother's signature on papers by threatening to hurt me. He said Lucy was going to have to choose between her land and me. I think he thought he could bully his mother into signing."

Czernak maintained a reserved attitude while Kim told her story. After she finished, Sara told her part, providing the name of the self-storage business where she had found Kim following the call from the night manager. This piece of information, more than any other, troubled the detective. "I know that place," he said. "Between the Wentworth house and there, you had to pass several homes and at least three other businesses, including the twenty-four-hour mini-mart. Why didn't you go there for help?"

Sara said, "Kim wasn't looking for help. She was looking for her car. She made a mistake and assumed she was at a garage."

"Is your car in the garage?"

"No," Kim said. "I no longer have a car. I was badly confused."

Sara spoke again. "Kim was in a state of shock when I reached her. She wasn't making sense. I'm sure when you speak to the night manager, he'll confirm this. It was several hours before I learned exactly what had happened. By then, it was the middle of the night. I phoned in the report when I heard what Scott had done."

Detective Czernak did not seem satisfied. He tugged at the hairs of his neatly trimmed mustache. He kept his glance averted. "The medical report says your wounds are consistent with glass cuts. The abrasions are consistent with rope burns. My problem is with the five or six hours it took you to make up your mind to tell someone what happened. Now, if you and Scott got into something you later decided you didn't want to be part of, sure, I could understand your reluctance to report."

"Shut the hell up, Dan," Sara yelled. "How dare you! Kim collapsed when she got here. She fell asleep, totally spent from the adrenaline rush that may well have saved her life. The minute she woke up, she told me everything. Find Scott. Get a forensics team over to that house and let the evidence tell you what happened. But do not presume to sit in my kitchen and pretend to know what Kim should or shouldn't have done after having suffered such a vicious attack!"

Czernak bristled.

Sara wasn't finished. "One other thing. When you find Scott, you can be damned sure he'll have one sweet story to tell explaining the whole thing. You know as well as I do he's been talking his way out of trouble his whole life. If you do anything besides lock him up, I swear I will scream bloody murder."

"Thanks for the advice, Sara. I hope you'll return the favor one day and let me tell you how to do your job."

"Do your job, Dan. That's all I'm asking."

The detective stood up. He didn't look happy. To Kim, he said, "Where will I be able to reach you?"

"She'll be here," Sara said. "Until this thing gets settled."

Kim nodded her assent.

CHAPTER 25

"How are you feeling this morning?" Sara asked Kim after Detective Czernak left the house.

"Sore. Beat up," Kim said.

"Which you were." Sara came closer and inspected the swollen bruise on her face. "Is this where Scott hit you?"

"Yes. The bump at my hairline is where I hit my head when I fell over trying to get to the window."

"I pray that was the first and last time a man ever hits you."

"It was the first."

In a brighter voice, Sara said, "I don't have a clue what this day is going to bring. We have time now. Would you like to go to your place to pick up some clothes?" She caught herself. "I'm sorry, Kim. I don't mean to be running roughshod over you. I just thought it might be best if you stay here for another day or two."

"I don't know. I don't know what I should do."

"Then humor me. Agree to stay one more night. We'll see where things stand tomorrow."

A few minutes later, they left the house and went out into a bright summer day. Driving down the county road, Kim wondered why the surroundings seemed familiar. Then she knew. She recognized Lucy's house in the distance.

"What is it?" Sara said. Then, realizing, she said, "Oh. It hadn't occurred to me we'd drive by here."

Sara sped up until they were past the house. Kim tried not to see anything. She specifically did not want to see anything that reminded her of the blind run she had made last night. She didn't speak again until they were in town. When Sara asked her address, she gave it.

At the house, she gathered a few items, shirts and a pair of shorts, underwear and socks, her toothbrush and comb. Driving back, Sara chatted easily. By contrast, Kim felt undone. When they were at the house, Sara suggested a meal. Kim deferred to her, as she had been doing since regaining consciousness ten hours earlier. Sara heated soup and cut slices of bread and fruit. After they finished eating, she said, "Come with me. I want to show you my horses."

They followed the gravel drive down an embankment to a red barn at the end of the lane. Looking back, Kim saw Sara's house set on the rise. A wide lawn fronted the house and, beyond that, on the right, lay an open meadow. Lucy's house was somewhere in the distance, not visible. Ten acres, Sara had said. Ten acres of her grandparents' original five hundred acres. All of it had been farmed once. Lucy had farmed it. And now Scott wanted to sell it for development.

"I have a young guy who works for me," Sara said. "He's still in high school, a 4-H'er. He takes care of the horses. Right now, with my schedule as it is, I can't do all the work for the girls myself."

"The girls?"

"Brody and Shane."

The two horses were in a grassy corral, nibbling hay. One was a beautiful bay, the other, a sleek brown mare. Sara handed Kim slices of apple and showed her how to feed the horses.

After a few minutes, they left the corral. Sara led the way to the creek and urged Kim to share a blanket she had brought from the barn.

Minutes passed; neither woman spoke. Then Sara said in a voice of quiet authority, "I need to ask you a few more questions about the episode you suffered last night. What you called a blackout."

Kim tensed. She had sensed the visit to the horses was a prelude to something, but hadn't anticipated this. "I'm sorry. It isn't something I'm comfortable talking about."

"I'm sure you're not. All the same, it's something we need to go over. I don't think the police have finished with their questions. So, please. Do your best to answer mine. I'll try to make this as brief as possible. Have you always had these blackouts?"

"No."

"Do you know when they began?"

"Yes."

"Was there a specific event that triggered their start?"

Kim stared at the blanket. "Yes."

"I want you to tell me what that event was."

Had Sara's approach been indirect, had her questions been more convoluted, Kim might have been able to decline to answer. As it was, she couldn't refuse. Later, she would have to wonder whether she had wanted to. "It's complicated," she said, hedging.

"Start anywhere you like."

Kim studied the weave of thread in the blanket until her eyes blurred at the mesh of color and fabric. She raised her head and looked straight ahead. The words, when she spoke, erupted of their own volition. "I killed my father." Startled by the confession, she added, "What I mean is, I was responsible for his death. I didn't intentionally kill him."

"Okay," Sara said in a different voice, more serious, maybe a shade less warm. "What happened?"

"It was a car accident. I'd taken my father to a doctor's appointment. He was being treated for prostate cancer. On our way home from the medical center, we were driving in Chicago traffic." The city name was out before she could call it back. She couldn't believe she had said it. The admission violated every precept she had lived by for more than two months. Since there was nothing she could do about it, and not wanting to draw unnecessary attention to the detail, she went on. "Approaching an intersection, I heard police sirens in the distance. I slowed down and looked for flashing lights. I saw them to my right, far down the block. Traffic around me was moving. I had a green light. So I moved with the traffic through the intersection." She paused. "I had a green light, so I went. Other cars, in both directions, were moving too. That's all I remember. An instant later, we were hit. A car hit mine broadside. It wasn't a police car. It was the car they were chasing. I never saw it. My father died instantly."

"It sounds like a terrible accident. Were you badly hurt?"

Not badly enough, Kim thought. *Not as badly as I wished I had been.*

"No. The airbag released. I guess that saved me. I had cuts and bruises. And a minor concussion."

"Did you need to be hospitalized?"

"Yes. For one day."

Sara waited a long moment. "I suspect many people have already told you this. You didn't kill your father. He died in a car accident. There's a world of difference." After another pause, she said, "Was that when you experienced your first blackout?"

"No." Kim drew in a deeper breath. "That came later. I tried to believe the accident wasn't my fault. When two police officers came to the hospital, they told me the same thing. I had to give a statement. It was an important case. It was the second time in a month that someone had died in a high-speed chase.

There was an investigation. The police told me that both cars to my left had proceeded through the intersection. Those drivers made the same decision I did." She closed her eyes. "If I had stopped, the car to my left would have been hit. Somebody else would have died. That's what the police said. It was just a tragic accident."

"Did their words help you find peace?"

"I thought so. There were children in that car. A young mother. Not that you can balance these things, but that's how it was."

"What happened next? What triggered your break?"

Kim stared ahead at the dark water burbling in the creek. Leaves stirred in the light wind. For all the time that had passed since her father's death, it may as well have been no time at all. Except it was worse than if no time had passed. Even worse things had happened since then.

"It was after the funeral. The funeral was held a week after the accident. I got through the service. Everyone was very kind. Most everyone. Thad, my brother, Thad—" Kim gave up. There was so much she hadn't yet said, so much more that required explanation.

"Tell me about Thad."

"Thad is older than me. By twelve years. We didn't grow up together. I was a late child for my parents. My mother was in her early forties when she had me, my father was older than that. Thad's a horrible person. He's an obnoxious, arrogant know-it-all who would have been happier if I had never been born."

"Okay. What did he do after the funeral?"

"We were at my father's house. My mother had already died. That happened years before. I never knew what set Thad off. I was sitting in a chair. My aunt was there. He came up to me and started screaming, 'It's your fault! It's all your fault. Why the hell didn't you stop?' Once he started screaming, he never stopped. Or that's what it seemed like. He said out loud, in front of everyone, all the things I'd been saying to myself and trying not to believe. So many people had made sure I knew it wasn't my fault. But I couldn't stand up to Thad. That's when I blacked out. I woke up in the hospital. On a psych ward."

She heard Sara's soft intake of breath.

"That was kind of it," Kim said.

That was it, and so much more. The beginning of her end—only she wouldn't know it until a year later when the full fruit of that terrible harvest came to bear.

"How old were you when this happened?"

"Twenty-eight." The truth, Kim reckoned. Every word she had spoken thus far was the honest truth of her life.

"Kim, I am so terribly sorry for what happened to you. How long were you in the hospital?"

"Two days in the first hospital. Then I was moved somewhere else."

"Was it a psychiatric hospital?"

"Yes."

"And how long were you there?"

"Three weeks."

"I see."

Kim wondered whether Sara did see. And what she saw. And what she thought about what she saw. In a burst, she said, "The final diagnosis was some fusion of post-traumatic stress, depression, and a dash of anxiety disorder thrown in, mostly, I think, so they could justify experimenting with drugs."

"I wondered about medication. Did any of the drugs help?"

"No. Therapy helped. Later, after I was released. The drugs—I never wanted the drugs."

"And the blackouts?"

"I had a few in the hospital. When I surfaced from them, I assumed I'd been unconscious the whole time. But that wasn't true. I learned I'd been awake, functioning on some level, and that was far more disturbing than the episodes themselves."

"Have you had others recently, besides the one last night?"

Kim closed her eyes. She wanted to lie and deny it. But it was too late. Sara already knew. "One other time. I'd been feeling a great deal of stress. That's what the doctors concluded, that the episodes were caused by stress. Their implication was that I could prevent them by dealing with the stress and not letting it build up to the point where I—gave up. That's what they thought I was doing. They thought I'd discovered a way of opting out of a situation I didn't want to be in. Clever, they seemed to think it. I didn't agree. It felt too much like loss of control."

Kim was surprised by what happened next. She had managed to tell her story in a state of preternatural calm. Now that she had finished, she waited for the familiar surge of anxiety. It didn't come. More curiously, she felt relieved. Justified or not, she trusted Sara Shaffer, maybe more than she had trusted Jennifer, the therapist she had seen until six months ago. In their weekly sessions, Kim had always felt an eye of criticism on her, as if Jennifer were waiting for her to be or become someone else. Frustrated, she had terminated the sessions despite Jennifer's insistence that Kim wasn't ready to stop therapy.

"Were you able to reestablish a relationship with your brother?" Sara said.

"No. He visited me once in the hospital when I first went in. That led to another blackout. The doctors suggested he stay away until I was ready to see him. It turned out I never was."

"And you haven't seen him since?"

"No. I used to see his wife, my sister-in-law, occasionally. But even that became too hard."

"What about other family and friends? Did you get support from them?"

Kim turned an imploring look on the other woman. "Do you have any idea what it's like to live only revealing this much of yourself?" She held up a thumb and forefinger, only a sliver of space showing in between. "It was exhausting, pretending. Pretending to be okay. I was so sure everyone was always watching, waiting for the next time I would crack."

"So no matter how long your streak of good days lasted, it almost didn't matter. Is that what you're telling me?"

Kim nodded. "I always felt like I was waiting. Waiting for my life to start. When I couldn't wait any longer, I walked away. However hard it is, I have to work things out for myself going forward."

Sara laughed softly. "All things considered, I'd say you're doing a good job of that."

Kim looked up in surprise. "Oh, I'm doing great. I nearly got myself killed by trusting Scott when everyone tried to tell me to stay away from him."

"Kim, you were caught off guard. Scott took advantage of your feelings for Lucy. Never mind Scott. Look at the rest of it. You have me now. And you have Lucy, and Christine, and the women on your softball team."

Sara's kind words offering friendship felt like a blow. Kim endured the feeling, waiting to see what new brand of pain it would cause. But the moment passed.

"Thank you for telling me, Kim. I'm sorry for everything you've been through. I think you must have something very solid inside that's enabled you to go on."

Kim nodded. She couldn't say anything more. She couldn't bring herself to tell Sara how wrong she was.

CHAPTER 26

The phone was ringing when they returned to the house. Sara answered. Scott's name came up several times during the conversation. After hanging up, she said, "Scott was picked up this morning. He was at his house, packing, when a sheriff's deputy found him. He's under arrest."

Kim released the breath she didn't know she'd been holding.

"The evidence at Lucy's house bears out your version of events. Besides a boarded-up baseboard window, the police found blood traces on the carpet near the window and on the stairs. They also found duct tape in a bathroom drawer with a multitude of dark strands attached, presumably yours."

"I forgot about that."

"Scott claims you and he had a date and that things got out of hand. He tried to sell some story about kinky sex. The police aren't buying it. To top it off, he did show up at Lucy's bank this morning with a slew of documents, ready to take control of her accounts. Except there was a problem—the papers were dated wrong. Lucy must have dated them incorrectly when she signed, maybe on purpose, and Scott never noticed."

"Thank goodness," Kim said.

"In the confusion of everything that happened last night, I never told you about the call I had from a nurse at Pine Village. Lucy went on a rampage sometime after midnight. She had been sound asleep before then. When she awoke, she charged into the room of her neighbor, whose name I can't recall—"

"Christine."

"Yes. She went to Christine and insisted they had to summon help for you. Christine didn't know what she was talking about. No one did. Lucy refused to be quieted, and only exclaimed more loudly when someone offered to try and find Scott. In the end, they phoned me. I spoke to Lucy. I told her you were here and that you were fine. That seemed to help."

"I should go and see her."

"We both should. But I wonder whether you shouldn't lie down first. We both had less than a full night's sleep."

An hour later, rested, if not entirely refreshed, Kim hobbled down the stairs and accompanied Sara to her Jeep. At Pine Village, Sara spoke to the head nurse and learned that Lucy had been in a subdued state all day after not sleeping well last night.

Kim's first stop was Christine's room.

"Kim! I'm so glad to see you. Have you seen Lucy? Have you heard about our excitement last night?"

"I did hear about it. I'm on my way to see Lucy now."

"What a terrible dream she must have had. I've never seen her so determined. She was dead set on rounding up a posse to rescue you. There wasn't anything to it, was there?" Christine said.

"Yes—and no. There was some confusion last night. But I'm fine. I'll tell you the whole story after the dust settles. Hopefully I'll be able to come back tomorrow and we can continue reading *Howards End*."

Awareness dawned on Christine that perhaps Lucy's nightmare hadn't been the stuff of dark fantasy. "But you're perfectly safe now?"

"Yes. I am."

Lucy was sitting with her back to the door when Kim and Sara entered the room. Kim called her name softly.

Lucy whirled around. A look mixed of shock and joy lit her face. She opened her mouth to speak but only managed a small cry. Kim rushed to her side.

For several minutes, Lucy remained caught in silence. Her eyes showed her relief at seeing Kim, at perhaps knowing she was safe. Still, she either couldn't, or didn't want to, try to articulate what was going on inside her mind. Sara eventually managed to connect with her by talking in a slow, warm voice, describing the progress of her vegetable garden and the problems she was having with tomato plants, which were turning brown at the edges.

"Yes, they'll do that," Lucy said. "The soil is too acidic. You'll need to add a base compound. Ground eggshells work best."

Sara smiled. "Of course. You've told me that before. I'll do it as soon as I get home."

They didn't visit long. Both women left with the promise to return soon.

The rest of the afternoon passed without further developments. Kim would have raised the subject of going home had Sara not gone to some trouble to prepare dinner. Through the evening, she waited to feel a backlash of regret for the story she had told about her psychiatric history. She had confided more secrets to the curly-haired physician than she had ever shared with anyone. But the backlash never came.

In the morning, Kim broached the subject of going home. She said she wanted to go to Pine Village to visit Lucy and Christine but needed a ride to her house to get her bicycle and book. Sara said, "I have a better idea. Why don't you take my car? You do drive, don't you?"

Kim studied the other woman's face, looking for any hint that it was a trick question. If it was, she didn't see it. "Yes."

"Then unless you have a reason for not wanting to drive—" Sara ended the sentence with a toss of her keys. "I'm going to be here anyway. It's my day to take care of the girls."

At Pine Village, Kim found Lucy alert and anxious to resume their reading. In all the most important ways, it was an ordinary Saturday morning. Kim read twice as many chapters as usual. When she finished, she was surprised to see a woman standing at the door of Christine's room, listening in. Apparently she had been there for some time.

Kim pushed Lucy's wheelchair toward her. "Hello, Mother," the woman greeted. To Kim, she said, "I'm Eliza Danning." She extended her hand and offered a smile.

Eliza had dark-blond hair and an open expression. In her eyes, Kim saw a resemblance to Scott, which troubled her. But Lucy's delight in seeing her daughter negated any concern that the likeness provoked.

They walked next door where Kim said goodbye to mother and daughter.

"I imagine I'll see you later today at Sara's house, won't I?" Eliza said.

"I expect I'll be there."

"Good. I'll see you then."

Kim drove back to the farmhouse. After lunch, she felt restless. She felt weary but not sleepy. Most of all, she longed for time alone; so while Sara was busy at the house, Kim went for a walk. In the last two days, she had been pushed and pulled in all directions at constantly changing speeds. Even if she was no longer moving at warp speed, her life was far from being restored to anything resembling normal.

Normal life. She didn't even know what that meant any longer.

She stopped at the corral to watch the horses. They paced, sometimes breaking into a trot for no reason she could see; they lowered their heads to nibble at hay, then threw their heads back, shaking and whinnying. They stared at her with large brown eyes seeming at once to look at her and see through her. In the same way, she looked at them and beyond them to the mountains hovering in the distance. The legacy of love for this land moved her deeply. She lowered her chin onto a fence post, ignoring the rough grains of wood biting into her skin. Hollowness swelled inside her. It would never be her privilege to live in one place long enough to nurture a bond of attachment as Lucy and Sara had for this land. Wherever she went, however long she stayed, her bond with any place was destined to remain superficial.

She backed away from the corral. At the creek, she found a place to sit.

The past lingered in her thoughts. Subjects she ordinarily didn't let herself think about were suddenly there. Her apartment—she saw it the way she had left it: a couple of pieces of fine furniture in the living room, the two paintings she had debated purchasing for weeks hanging on the walls. She felt a twinge of loss for her mother's pair of Chinese vases and carved jade tiger. She wondered what had happened to her possessions. She assumed, because it was what she wanted to believe, that Julia, her sister-in-law, would have seen to the packing up of her belongings and transferred them to safe storage. Too many times to count, she had wanted to call Julia, to reassure her that she was safe and not a victim of a random crime or of her own deplorable mental fragility. She'd had a breakdown— that's what Kim expected people would be saying about her. That she'd gone off the deep end and was either living on the streets or in some anonymous mental ward.

Stephen Bender alone would know what she had done. It was perfectly clear now what *he* had done, beginning a year ago with the car accident and her subsequent "lapse"—the sterile word he used to describe her breakdown. For all she knew, he had merely shortened the word "collapse" into one a bit more palatable. She had no doubt he had used her vulnerability against her under the guise of being a patient mentor, steering her rise through the corporate ranks. Then, while she wasn't looking, he had manipulated data under her supervision, faking entries and making real payments that went to accounts controlled by him.

She couldn't fathom why he had taken the risk.

She couldn't imagine which he had wanted more—the money or the thrill of getting away with the crime.

The water flowing in the creek sparkled and splashed as it made its way downstream. Kim envied it its untroubled journey. Long before today, she had understood that it would never be hers to measure bounty in terms commonly used by other people. She would never be able to sink her roots into a single place and stay there as long as she liked. Something would inevitably chase her away. Nor would it be hers to share her deepest secrets with someone she loved. Love—it was the one thing she had become persuaded she could live without.

By the ache in her heart, she realized a new truth. The price of her estrangement had grown sharply higher.

CHAPTER 27

There was an unfamiliar car parked in the driveway when Kim returned to Sara's house. As she approached the back porch, she heard voices from inside the kitchen. Two women were talking, Sara Shaffer and Eliza Danning.

Eliza's voice was strident. Kim sat on a step to listen.

"All I can tell you is Scott insists they were on a date. According to him, they were playing a game. It got out of hand."

"And you believe him?" Sara said.

"I'm not sure what to believe. Do I believe what he says is possible? Yes, I do."

"The evidence supports Kim's version of events."

Eliza made a small dismissive sound. "You know as well as I do that evidence can tell a story more than one way. I'm not saying Scott didn't exercise bad judgment. He's at least guilty of that. He left her alone in the house, tied up, that's clear. He says he went out to buy alcohol. Leaving her alone was supposed to heighten the thrill. According to him, Kim panicked and it all fell apart. He claims he was terrified not knowing what happened to her when he returned."

It was Sara's turn to make a disdainful sound. "If that's true, why were they at your mother's house, not at his place?"

Eliza didn't have an answer to that. In the same strident voice, she said, "Okay, so bondage games aren't my thing, and presumably they're not yours either, Sara. For all his past mistakes, Scott's never been violent before. Grant me that much."

Kim didn't hear a reply.

Eliza said, "How well do you know this woman—Kim?"

Kim closed her eyes and felt her stomach sink.

"Not terribly well. I'm getting to know her better. But I believe her, Eliza. What about the power of attorney papers Scott tried to exercise yesterday morning? That fits in with what Kim said he was going to do."

"It's likely he mentioned something about that to her."

"And your mother's agitated state on Thursday night? Can you explain that?"

Neither woman spoke for a full minute.

"The papers bother you too, don't they?" Sara said.

"Yes."

"And it bothers you that Scott apparently is flat broke? He can't even raise money for his own bail."

Kim was blown away by the revelation.

"Yes, that bothers me. He says Charlene took all their money when she and the kids left."

"An answer for everything," Sara muttered.

"Believe me, Sara, in my whole life, I've never wanted to be in the position of having to defend Scott! All I'm saying is that, in general, I prefer simple to complicated explanations. In this case, Scott's account rings truer for me than the fanciful story Kim has told."

Kim had heard enough. She tiptoed away and headed to the corral. This time, she wasn't consoled by the peaceful setting. Her only thoughts now were of leaving Montrose.

Her time here was at an end. It would be her word against Scott's. She saw that now, and saw also that, whatever else happened, she would be tried in the court of public opinion and found wanting. Until hearing Eliza, it hadn't occurred to her that the story of her kidnapping could be told any other way. Lucy wasn't a credible witness. No one else could back up her version of events. Even her own actions testified against her—the patently bizarre act of running to a self-storage business and demanding access to her car.

There was nothing to choose between. Scott's lawyer would make mincemeat of her in a courtroom. If it came to that.

Sometime later, Sara found her at the corral. "You've been out here a long time," she said.

When Kim turned, she couldn't hide the pain in her eyes.

"What is it? What's wrong?"

"I haven't been out here the whole time. I came up to the house. I heard you and Eliza talking. I didn't mean to—listen. But what Eliza said, I—"

"Oh, Kim, I'm sorry."

"No, really, it's all right. I should know what people are going to say."

Sara frowned. "I'm not going to say there won't be some who don't hold with Scott. Most won't, though. You'll be believed. Trust me on this."

Kim turned away. She looked beyond the corral to the view of the mountains, white clouds hanging above them. She took a deep breath and fought to speak calmly. "I know you and Eliza are friends. I'm sure she must be a good person if you say she is. But I can't pretend to feel comfortable being around her right now. Would you please drive me back to my house? My team is playing a softball game tonight. I'd like to go."

Sara had a different idea. For the second time that day, she offered to lend Kim her car. Kim gratefully took the keys to the Jeep and left.

She spent a couple of quiet hours at home before arriving at the field early. Lois and Linda drove up together. They were talking excitedly when Linda saw her, and called out, "Kim, hello. Have you heard the news?"

"What news?"

"Scott Wentworth was arrested yesterday. Word is he attacked a woman."

Kim went deathly cold. "It was me," she said.

There was no use denying it. They were going to find out anyway. Everyone was going to know. Nervously, she fingered her bandages.

Lois reached her first. Lois, who had been her guardian practically from the first day she arrived in Montrose, wrapped her in a fierce hug and let loose a string of curses.

Kim told an abbreviated version of the events. When she reached the part about Scott's rumored financial troubles, Linda spoke savagely. "I'd rather get caught between a rattlesnake and a mama bear than between Scott Wentworth and his money. Shit, girl, are you okay?"

"A little banged up. But I'm okay."

Lois touched her face. "You don't look okay. You look like you were somebody's punching bag. Are you sure you want to be here tonight?"

Kim's glance flickered away before returning to settle on Lois's firm countenance. "It doesn't really matter, does it? I have to get through this. I just hope—do you think we could keep it from being a big deal?"

"Leave it to us," Linda said. "We'll figure out some way to keep it quiet."

Soon the others began to arrive. Linda shepherded Kim to a distant part of the outfield to warm up. Before the game started, she said, "You need anything, you just yell at me, okay?"

Kim nodded.

She had brought her glove without expecting to play. Now she desperately wanted to be in the game. Lois moved her from third base to right field in the hope she would be involved in fewer plays. During the game, especially when the team was on the bench, Kim heard the talk about Scott. She sat apart, flanked by Lois or Linda. When a teammate noticed her face and asked about the bruise, Lois said, "She crashed that damn bike of hers. I've been telling her for months to wear a helmet."

Kim didn't think about the injury to her hands until the first time she came to bat. When she made contact with the ball, pain tore through both hands and along her arms. Worse pain came in the third inning, when she fielded a ball and made a strong throw to second base. She suspected the wound on her right palm had opened. When no blood seeped beneath the bandage, she ignored it.

In the fifth inning, she came in from the field to find Sara sitting on the bench.

"Eliza dropped me off on her way back to see Lucy," she said. "I decided to come and watch. It never occurred to me you meant to play tonight."

Kim shrugged off the tease. She kept her hand hidden from view in case any blood had begun to show.

When the game was over, she said to Sara, "I want to stay at my own house tonight. I'm scheduled to work tomorrow. I think it's time for me to be on my own."

"I don't mind if you stay another night or two with me. I think you know I prefer it."

Kim nodded. She did know.

"Then let's go to your house—under one condition."

"What is it?"

"That you'll let me clean and rewrap those filthy bandages. By now, I'm sure you've broken open every cut on both hands."

Kim opened her mouth to deny it. Then she laughed.

Their eyes met. The contact lasted long enough for Kim to grasp the enormity of the trust she had placed in Sara Shaffer. At some point during the day, she realized she had given Sara more than enough information to discover her true identity. She had described a well-documented traffic fatality in Chicago. She had mentioned having spent time in a psychiatric hospital. She had shared her brother's first name, though not his last, and although she didn't think it had occurred to Sara that her real name might not be Kim Jackson—the fact remained: if Sara ever had cause to check her background, she would rapidly discover a lengthy list of deceptions.

CHAPTER 28

On Sunday morning, Kim returned to work. The rapidly healing cut on her left wrist was covered by flesh-colored tape. The more troubling cut on the palm of her right hand was protected by a thin bandage and more tape. She didn't think her injuries were likely to draw attention. And, as her name so far had been kept out of any media reports, she didn't think anyone would connect her with Scott. Just the same, she braced for a long day.

She couldn't have been more shocked when Ashley Crane came into work.

"Sorry I'm late," she said breezily to Kim. "John told me this was my last chance to keep my job."

Through the first hour, Kim wondered whether she imagined that the store's regular customers shied away from Ashley's lane. "I heard they dropped their case against that boy," one woman said in a whisper, surreptitiously nodding at Ashley.

"What?" Kim said.

"It doesn't look like Jeff Nelson's going to be charged. They couldn't shake his alibi."

In retrospect, Kim thought she had heard rumblings of the same last night at the softball game. She hadn't paid enough attention to grasp the full story.

Late in the afternoon, she closed out her register and walked home.

It was probably only the latest chapter in a familiar story, she thought, thinking of the bungled police investigation into Emily Riley's murder. Except she couldn't make herself believe that. She trusted that Jeff Nelson had been thoroughly investigated as a suspect, and if he'd been released, it had to be because authorities couldn't connect him to Emily's murder.

She resisted dwelling on the implication. It slipped past her mental barriers anyway. If Jeff hadn't committed the murder, obviously someone else had.

She quickened her pace as she neared her house and all but ran up the steps and locked herself inside.

Monday morning, she was at Pine Village early for a visit with Christine and Lucy. They were approaching the conclusion of *Howards End*. As Kim also felt her time in Montrose was coming to an end, she wanted to finish the book. She stalwartly refused to think about what her departure would mean for her two elderly friends. When she left the nursing home, she went to the library where she waited ten minutes for a computer.

She searched the Montrose newspaper archives for the articles reporting recent car thefts. Before leaving home, she had jotted down license plate numbers from Emily's nighttime photos of the cars on a flatbed truck arriving at Dave's Auto Body. Within minutes, her hunch was verified. The license plate numbers in the photos matched the stolen cars reported in the newspaper. Emily Riley had nailed a car-theft ring. Kim allowed herself one hollow breath of victory. Then she logged off the computer. She went to a quiet corner of the library and took out a blank sheet of paper. She wrote a timeline of events, beginning with her visits to Montrose High School photography teacher, Frank Tattinger. She noted how she had come into possession of Emily's photos and her eventual conclusion regarding what they showed. At the bottom of the page, she scrawled a final note: "I know you'll have other questions. You know where to find me."

She put the note and the photos in an envelope, sealed it, and penciled Detective Czernak's name on the front. She returned to the front desk and asked to see Lois.

"She's not in today," another librarian told her. "She takes Mondays and Fridays off during summer. Otherwise she loses vacation time. Can I help you with something?"

Kim started to shake her head. Then she thought better of leaving without completing her mission. "Can I drop off something for her? It's actually for her brother, but I hoped she could pass it on to him."

She put the envelope meant for Detective Czernak inside a larger envelope with Lois's name on it. As she walked away, she knew there would be consequences. There would be harder questions to answer. She would deal with them when the time came.

Officer Mickey Burke came into the grocery store late on Monday afternoon. He spoke briefly to John, then told Kim he was there to see her. "This is just a formality," he said once they were outside. They stood on the sidewalk a short distance away from the door. The concrete radiated heat from the ninety-plus afternoon temperature. "I wanted to let you know Scott Wentworth posted bail this morning. He's been released. Don't worry. Nothing changes for you. Scott's been warned not to come near you. I don't think he'll try. He seems pretty darn confident he's going to beat these charges. But just to be on the safe side, we'll have a patrol car swinging by your place for the next day or two, longer if necessary."

Stricken by the news, Kim said, "Who bailed him out?"

"I think his sister. But I'm not sure, and as I said, it makes no difference to you. Scott will stay away."

Kim wondered how the young officer could be so certain. She decided he probably wasn't that certain. Those were just easy words to say.

When she left the store several hours later, she dreaded going home. She thought about calling Sara but didn't. Instead, she talked herself around to Officer Mickey Burke's point of view: obviously it was in Scott's best interests to avoid her.

At home, she opened the refrigerator and stared at the shelves. She wished Andrea were home bustling in the kitchen, drinking wine, and chattering about anything. Kim felt hungry but couldn't decide what to eat. Leftover chicken or pasta? She chose neither and went into the living room. Slouched on the sofa, she thought about the groceries she'd rung up that day. Hamburgers and hot dogs, baked beans and corn on the cob. Strawberries and ice cream, paper plates and plastic utensils. Everyone who came into the store was stocking up for a Fourth of July barbecue.

Independence Day. The phrase rattled around in her mind, teasing her with what was missing in her life: independence. She wondered whether she would ever celebrate her own independence day.

A ripple of fear trickled from her belly to her chest. At first, she couldn't account for it. Then she knew. It was fear for Lucy. Last week Scott had gloated he would have his independence day. Kim closed her eyes and wanted to scream. Scott was a free man. What if he tried to hurt Lucy?

"Damn it," she said.

Eliza had done this. She had arranged Scott's release from jail. Her mother's safety should be her responsibility.

Kim glanced at the clock. It was after seven o'clock. Pine Village visiting hours ended at nine. She didn't finish the thought. She didn't listen to another argument telling her what she could or should do. She was already on her feet, preparing to leave.

The summer night was warm as she pedaled through familiar streets to the nursing home. Once there, she rode around back and locked her bicycle to a bench. The parking lot was nearly empty. She encountered only a few residents on her way to Lucy's room.

"Kim!" Lucy exclaimed in delight. "I never see you this late. Did you come to read?"

"Not tonight, Lucy. I came to sit with you for a bit. I hope that's all right."

"Oh yes."

Guiltily, Kim hoped Christine wouldn't hear her voice. Since Lucy had joined their reading sessions, she had never visited one friend without making time to see the other. Lucy's focus shifted to a TV program. Kim sat down on a sofa. She had no sooner settled there than her stomach growled, reminding her she had missed dinner. She stood up and poured a glass of water. On the counter, she found an open package of crackers and ate a few. She tried to get interested in the TV program.

It was a sitcom. Another time, it might have held her interest, but not tonight. When it ended at eight thirty, she debated leaving. She felt calmer now, and certain she had overreacted. She was already thinking about eating both the chicken and the pasta once she was home.

A commercial came on between TV programs.

Kim's heart caught when she recognized the local business. It was Dave's Auto Body. Handsome, blond-haired Dave Kresten was announcing some special deal. She must have made some sound because Lucy looked over. "That Dave is the nicest man. Very good family."

"You know him?" Kim managed to say.

"Oh yes."

"How do you know him?"

"He and Scott are friends. Although Scott owns the business, I'm sure Dave is responsible for its success."

The commercial ended. The TV went momentarily quiet. In the heartbeat of silence, Kim's world stopped.

"What?" she said.

Lucy looked at her blankly.

Kim made the leap. "I didn't know Scott owns Dave's Auto Body. I thought he had the oil change shops."

"Oh yes. He has those too."

The next program started. Lucy's attention went to it.

Kim forced herself to think. Scott and Dave. Dave and a chop shop. She knew she had a new piece of the puzzle but couldn't think fast enough to know what to do with it. She looked around for a telephone. She found it but didn't make a move toward it. She couldn't think who to call.

Meanwhile, connections tumbled into place. Emily had found evidence of a car-theft ring. Jenna Spinelli had said Emily was trying to put something over on someone. On Dave Kresten, Kim wondered, forcing herself to slow down.

No.

If Emily knew Scott owned the business—she would have gone after him.

Kim closed her eyes. Finally it fit. Scott was Mr. Money Bags.

She tried to figure out the whole story.

Last winter, Emily must have established some relationship with Scott—after she discovered stolen cars going into a business he owned. Kim recalled from reading Emily's journals that the teen had mentioned a Saint Paddy's Day toast with the man she'd christened "Mr. Money Bags." Would she have gone so far as to try blackmailing him? Scott had money. Everyone in town knew about Scott's family money. Emily no doubt wanted some of it.

Instead, Scott had killed her.

Kim's mind raced. She tried to recall what Scott said the night he'd abducted her. He had meant to kill her. Now she knew why.

She thought back further—to the night they had a drink together. Sitting in that dimly lit bar, reveling in his attention, she had laid out her elaborate version of Emily's discovery of the stolen cars moving through Dave's garage. Kim choked in disbelief. What had Scott thought sitting there, listening?

Killing her had been his real aim when he had manipulated her into going with him last week. But he'd become greedy. He had used the threat of violence against her to extort Lucy's signature on legal documents. Which meant he still had a reason to kill her.

Kim glanced at the phone again. For the second time, she wondered who to call.

"Do you watch this program?" Lucy said.

Kim shook her head, trying to clear away the cobwebs. "No. I don't have a TV."

"It's a good one. I enjoy it."

She needed to leave without upsetting Lucy. She decided she would leave in twenty minutes, when visiting hours ended.

She ran through her theory of the crime again. She remembered Scott calling Jeff Nelson an innocent boy. It was information only the real killer could know.

She was trying to force herself to remember what else he had said when she heard voices in the hallway, and recognized Scott's. Terrified, she leapt to her feet. She looked at Lucy and pressed one finger to her lips, begging her elderly friend to be silent, and slipped inside the adjacent bedroom. Seconds later, Scott entered the room.

"Hello, Mother. You must be wondering where I've been. I had a business trip to Denver for a few days. But Eliza came to see you, didn't she? She promised me she would."

Lies and more lies, Kim thought. How easy it was to confuse Lucy.

"Oh, here's your milkshake. You didn't think I'd forget, did you?"

Kim's worst fears crystallized into one terrible fear for Lucy. Milkshakes—she had forgotten Scott's admission about doping his mother with sleeping pills crushed up in milkshakes. Kim moved. In one silent, fluid motion, she burst out of the bedroom, startling Scott, as she had expected to. She seized the cup from Lucy's hands and, in the same move, hurled it at the wall. Scott was on her in an instant.

"You bitch!" he roared. He dragged her into the bedroom.

"You killed her," Kim screamed. "You killed Emily!"

Scott flung her at the wall. Kim tripped over a stool and fell backward. As if she were no more than a rag doll, Scott reached down, picked her up, and threw her a second time. Her head caught the sharp edge of a dresser.

Scott fell on top of her. "I did not kill her, but I will kill you!" he said through clenched teeth. His hands throttled her throat and he began squeezing. "I should have killed you before. If not for you," he said, tightening his grip. "If not for you," he repeated, and then the words trailed off. All Kim knew before she lost consciousness was the rage in his eyes and the sound of despair in his voice.

—

There was pain through the fog. Pain in her head and at her throat. She coughed and the pain got worse.

Sara was there. Kim assumed she was waking up from a bad dream. She thought she must have cried out and alerted Sara. Only this pain was worse than anything she had ever felt in a nightmare.

"Thank God," Sara said.

"The milkshake," Kim tried to say. Her voice was broken. The words crackled. They were hardly words at all.

"Shh, don't try to talk. An ambulance is coming."

"The milkshake," Kim said. "Test the milkshake."

"Okay. Yes, we'll get the milkshake tested. Shh, don't try to talk."

Kim didn't. The rest happened in a blur. Paramedics arrived. They checked her vital signs. A long time seemed to pass before they lifted her onto a stretcher. After that, all the rest was lights and voices and people probing her body, but she no longer cared.

She had done everything she could.

CHAPTER 29

There are many ways by which one person can save another's life. In the hours following Scott Wentworth's brutal attack, Kim understood that Sara Shaffer had saved her life. Sara did it with her quiet presence in the hospital room where Kim lay recovering from the assault. Sara did it by staying near yet allowing Kim space for silence. If the curly-haired physician with the round eyeglasses was acting on instinct, her instinct was true. Everything she did was exactly right, even the precious few questions she allowed herself to ask when she must have been ready to burst wanting to know answers to a dozen more.

Kim's list of physical injuries was blessedly short. The worst were to her head: a mild concussion from the battering Scott had inflicted, and a gash where she had struck the edge of the dresser in Lucy's bedroom. Her throat was badly bruised from Scott's aborted attempt to strangle her. Both swallowing and talking promised to be painful for days, and while Sara insisted she engage in the former, sipping water at the very least, she absolved her from the effort of the latter. They managed their communication in other ways.

On Tuesday morning, Sara told Kim her version of what happened in Lucy's room the night before. "When Scott screamed at you—I assume it was when you intercepted the milkshake—he inadvertently summoned a trio of rescuers. A man and his sons were just leaving. They were near enough in the hall to hear Scott and to know that something was wrong. They reached Lucy's bedroom in time to pull Scott away from you. In light of your injuries, I suspect they arrived moments before he would have crushed your windpipe."

Kim, pale and remote, sat upright in the hospital bed.

"I was minutes behind them," Sara said. "I got home from work late and heard the voice mail from the police saying Scott had made bail." Her eyes softened. "My first thought was to jump in my car and come and find you. I overruled that impulse, presuming it wasn't what you wanted. My third thought overruled the second. I went to your house. When you weren't there, I called Lois to see if you had a softball game. I can't believe it took so long for me to think of going to Pine Village."

Sara had reached Lucy's room to find Scott subdued by two brawny teenage boys and their father bent over Kim. The police and an ambulance already had been summoned. Sara told Kim she had regained consciousness before help arrived, but that memory was gone.

"Have you thought of anyone—" Sara began, but didn't finish the question.

Kim knew what she wanted to know.

Last night, Sara had asked for her brother Thad's phone number. Kim wouldn't give it. Insisting it was only a formality, a contact name and number to add to her medical chart, Sara subsequently asked for the name of another relative. She promised the person wouldn't be called. Still, Kim had refused.

Now, as before, Kim barricaded herself behind a wall of silence.

Sara was due at work. She soon left, promising to stop back later.

Detective Dan Czernak came to visit that afternoon. Serendipitously—or perhaps not—he arrived when Sara was away from the room.

"Miss Jackson. Kim," he said in a softer voice. "How are you doing?"

She shrugged.

"You've been busy."

By his dry tone, she guessed he was trying to tease her. Another time, she might have been interested in this side of the man but not today.

"I received the packet of photos from Lois. I'm going to have a hell of a time establishing a chain of evidence with them. But I guess that's my job."

"Did you talk to Frank Tattinger?" Kim said.

"I did. Your story checks out. The guy's kind of funny. He rattled off a list of every single one of the pictures in that packet without me saying a word to prompt him. Didn't miss a one."

"He thought highly of—" She broke off to cough.

"Yeah, I get that. Look, I just wanted to tell you a couple of things. And to ask one question."

She narrowed her eyes.

"Here's the update. We executed a search warrant at Dave's Auto Body this morning, and although we're still counting all the parts, we definitely found pieces of chopped-up stolen cars. You were right about that."

"Emily was," she corrected.

"Right. Emily was. Scott talked his fool head off when we took him into custody last night. He swears it was Dave who killed Emily, not him. He stopped blabbing the second his lawyer showed up. We're a long way from sorting this thing out, but I think we have the right players in our sights now."

She nodded.

"The second thing I want to tell you is I have the lab report on the milkshake Scott brought his mother last night. We've notified the district attorney to amend the indictment against Scott to include attempted murder of Lucy in addition to the pending charges regarding the assault and attempted murder of you. That milkshake was laced with barbiturates. Our lab guy said that had Lucy Wentworth swallowed half of it, she would have gone to sleep for good."

Kim closed her eyes.

"Do you have any idea why Scott wanted to kill his mother?"

"Money," she said bluntly.

"Isn't it always about money," Scott had said mockingly the night he'd abducted her.

"But I don't know why he needed money," Kim added.

"Okay, last question. Is there anything else you know that I need to know?" He leveled a long look at her.

"Not that I can think of."

"You'll call me if you think of anything?"

She couldn't help smiling at his earnest expression. It gave him a boyish look. For the first time, she saw in his sparkling eyes a strong resemblance to his outgoing sister. "I'll call you," she said.

Tuesday evening, she was released from the hospital. Sara drove her back to her farmhouse where Kim settled on a chaise longue on the back porch and promptly fell asleep.

Everything was out now—almost everything. Sara and the local police knew exactly what Kim had done in her pursuit of answers about Emily Riley's murder. It was only a matter of time before word reached the general public. But there were deeper secrets Kim still needed to protect. So she clung to the state of shocked numbness that she'd felt since she awoke in the hospital.

The next morning Sara announced she had arranged to take a half day off. She didn't need to be at work until noon.

After breakfast, she went to Kim's house to pick up clothes and toiletries. The hard questions started when she returned.

"Here's what I think," Sara opened without preamble as they sat outside in the morning sun. "You can shake your head if I'm wrong or nod if I'm right. Or do neither." Kim eyed her steadily. "I collected your belongings the other night when you were admitted to the hospital. It was only your clothes, shoes, and keys. But I couldn't help noticing the distinctive key on your key ring. It's a beautiful key, as those things go. Embossed with a gold letter *L*, I believe it's the logo for a rather exceptional line of cars." She paused.

Then she said, "I think you do own a car, but there is a reason why you can't drive it. I suspect that car is parked somewhere in Montrose. Possibly it's inside a bay at the self-storage business where I picked you up the other night!" she said in an exaggerated tone, as if she were suggesting a perfectly ludicrous idea. "It may be that you don't have insurance on it. It may be that it belongs to a friend and you simply don't feel comfortable driving it." In a quieter voice, she said, "It may be something else altogether."

Kim glanced away. Sara knew about her car. There was no point denying that truth.

She waited to see which direction Sara would turn with the knowledge. But the interrogation ended there.

When noontime came, Sara went to work.

Visitors arrived in the afternoon. Lois Hays and Linda Perez stopped by. Kim sat with them on Sara's back porch. She told them she was fine, or would be soon. She tried to laugh when she said she should have listened to them both and stayed away from Scott Wentworth. "You might have been better off," Lois said. "I can't imagine what would have happened to Lucy."

Her teammates promised to return for another visit, and sent the best wishes of others on the softball team.

Kim dozed on the chaise longue after they left.

She was still there when Sara came home from work. Sara was inside, rummaging around in the kitchen, when Kim heard the sound of a car approaching on the gravel drive. A minute later, Eliza Danning came up the porch steps. Apparently she had been invited for dinner.

Eliza's attractive features twisted in sheer apology the moment her eyes met Kim's. She said, "There's nothing I can say to tell you how sorry I am. Or how grateful."

Kim glanced away. "How is Lucy?"

"She's calmed down since Monday night. She knows Scott is in jail and that you were in the hospital. She's anxious to see you."

Kim nodded.

Eliza left Kim sitting on the porch and went inside to help Sara with dinner. Kim slipped into the state most comfortable to her—staring, not even trying to listen to the conversation in progress behind the screen door.

The following morning, more of the story broke. At the end of business on Wednesday, Scott Wentworth was in default on a $250,000 loan from a Grand Junction bank. More troubling than his bankruptcy, investigators learned he had fraudulently taken out the loan. He'd used his business as collateral, claiming to be the sole owner. Unbeknownst to anyone in Montrose, he had taken on a business partner sometime back, a man from Delta. Both the man and the bank had filed criminal charges against Scott. They were merely the latest in a growing list.

For Scott, old habits died hard. He had continued to play the stock market even after the debacle of losing his father's company. A decade ago, he had netted a windfall on a dozen savvy investments. Even after paying back an enormous loan, he was ahead by several hundred thousand dollars. Everyone in town knew he had used the money to build a grand new house.

It hadn't been enough. That money was long since spent.

When the itch struck again to play the market, Scott had finagled a new loan. This time, his timing was all wrong. He bought high, then watched as the value of his positions steadily eroded. Scott hadn't been able to recoup his original investment in time to pay back the loan.

Details into the investigation into the chop shop operated out of Dave's Auto Body were sketchier. Dave Kresten had been arrested and was being held without bail. By his service records, a link was established between stolen cars and parts he had used on customer repairs. Meanwhile, Emily Riley's fingerprints had been found at Scott Wentworth's house. Faced with the evidence, Scott had admitted to a relationship. He also admitted she had tried to blackmail him about the stolen cars. He claimed to have panicked under the threat and turned to Dave for help. "Dave handled it," he told investigators. No one yet had been charged in Emily's murder. That investigation was open and active.

Kim barely listened as Sara regaled her with the details of each new bit of Scott's wrongdoing. She didn't try to disguise her lack of interest.

Either Sara's patience had been exhausted or she deemed Kim sufficiently well enough to face tougher questions. After dinner that night, without giving so much as a hint of warning, she demanded, "Are you in trouble with the law, Kim?"

Startled, Kim's eyes shot up. "No."

Not that I know of, she added silently.

Sara paced across the living room. It was the first time Kim had seen her even slightly unsure of herself. Sara spoke in a clipped voice. "Last week, when all of this started, when I first began to get to know you—" She broke off. "I thought you were protecting yourself about your past. Specifically, about your psychiatric history. Now I think you're protecting yourself for some other reason."

The evening air was soft beyond the open windows of the house. Inside, it shimmered with Sara's intensity. "Can you tell me what kind of work you did before you moved to Montrose?" she said. She laughed unhappily. "I can't believe I've never asked you."

Kim kept her expression neutral. "No."

Undaunted, Sara continued. "When I was at your house this week, I saw several suits hanging in your closet. God knows I don't know the first thing about clothing brands. But I know quality when I see it. You've graduated from college, haven't you?"

Kim nodded.

"Another degree too? Wherever you worked in the past, you were at a high level, weren't you?"

Kim didn't move.

Sara said it. "Who are you running from, Kim? Please, tell me who you are so terribly afraid of that you won't tell me one single thing about the life you had before you came here!"

Kim closed her eyes. She felt more than heard roaring in her ears. Dimly, she recalled something Sara said to her days ago when she was still in the hospital. "You didn't black out last night. You do know that, don't you? Maybe it's something to think about, for later."

Kim was terrified she would black out now.

Meanwhile, Sara waited.

Speaking slowly, indifferent to the pain in her throat, Kim forced the words out. "Just because a question can be asked, that doesn't mean it can be answered."

She had neither conceded the truth—that she was running from someone—nor denied it, yet she was certain Sara knew. It wasn't possible a path led forward from this point.

Sara went to the windows at the far wall. She stood there, gazing out. Kim grew terrified at a prospect she hadn't considered. That Sara perhaps knew far more about her than she had admitted. She wondered if Sara already knew her real name.

Abruptly, Sara laughed. "I know what you mean." Her tone of voice had shifted 180 degrees. She turned around and came back to sit next to Kim on the sofa. "There's a question I'd give anything to be able to ask Lucy, if it wasn't potentially so upsetting."

Kim didn't understand. Incredibly—Sara had backed off.

"The question I want to ask is whether Scott pushed her down those stairs last spring."

Kim gasped.

"Scott was at the house at the time. We know that. Had it not been for Lucy's friend driving up with a tray of plants to give her for the start of her spring planting, I don't know what Lucy's fate would have been. Scott insisted that Lucy had just fallen and that he had phoned for help. It all seemed— suspicious. But not nearly as suspicious as Lucy's X-rays, which I saw a few days later. I'm a radiologist. Reading X-rays is my specialty. What I saw on film didn't suggest a slip and fall. Her collarbone was broken; her shoulder was badly bruised. Both indicated a forward tumble. Her right hip was broken at the front. Had she fallen backward, the fractures would have presented differently."

"Do you think Lucy knows what happened?" Kim said.

"I don't know. I wouldn't be surprised if it's something she's blocked out. If it happened."

"But it made you that much more suspicious of Scott."

"Yes, it did."

After a moment, Kim reached for Sara's hand. With the slight pressure in her grip, she tried to convey what she couldn't say: her gratitude for everything Sara had done for her. She tried, by gently squeezing, to answer every question Sara still wanted to ask.

"I'm going to be okay," she said, a promise.

EPILOGUE

Rounding the steep curve, Kim signaled well ahead of her turn into the overlook's parking area. She found a space, pulled in, and sat for a moment. When she left the car, she walked several steps, then stopped to cast an admiring gaze back at the baby-blue sedan. She laughed. It was a Cadillac.

Until a few days ago, the car's owner was Lucy Wentworth. Eliza Danning had pleaded with Kim to accept the vehicle as thanks for all she had done for Lucy, who would never drive again. Kim saw Sara's hand all over this burst of generosity but had been too humbled by Eliza's kindness to do more than accept the gift. Eliza further had insisted on paying the first insurance premium despite Kim's objections that she had plenty of money for insurance. And so the car became hers.

Lucy was living at home again. Eliza had made the arrangements. She had hired a full-time aide and approved the renovations that would allow Lucy to live on one floor of the rambling house. Kim had visited Lucy there. They had shared the view of the land: the stand of trees in the foreground and the cathedral of mountain peaks descending from clouds in the distance. Kim had left Lucy still lost to the view, and thought she would always picture her that way. Content to be in her own house. Gazing out on her land.

In the two weeks since Scott had attacked her, a great deal of new information had come to light. Most of it came from Scott himself. Under questioning, he had admitted to knowing about the chop shop operating out of Dave's Auto Body. He had also admitted to having a personal relationship with Emily Riley. What he wouldn't admit to was killing her. Crime scene techs had scoured his home and found evidence that Emily had spent time there—but none that she had died there. Scott told investigators that Dave Kresten was responsible for her death.

According to Scott's tale, Emily appeared in his office one day with a request to interview him. She said it was for a school project. He had readily agreed. They met a few times. He admitted to enjoying the young woman's company though refused to say whether they were ever intimate. He said he freaked out when she dropped the bombshell—that she knew about the chop shop operating out of Dave's Auto Body.

She demanded $7,000 in exchange for her silence.

Scott said he laughed and told her she was wrong about the chop shop. She told him she had proof—she had photos on her phone. He demanded to see them. She said she'd show him the photos when he gave her the money. She would delete them then and there, and he would never hear from her again. She promised him she was leaving Montrose the day she graduated from high school, and she was never coming back.

Buying time, and her silence, Scott told her it would take him a day to get the cash.

Scott met her the next day on a quiet side street a few blocks from her house. He wasn't alone. Dave Kresten was hiding in the footwell behind the passenger seat of the SUV. It was snowing. Emily got in the car to make the exchange. Dave Kresten strangled her. The date was April 21.

Scott said he drove back to Dave's shop. Dave moved Emily's body to his tow truck and drove away.

According to Detective Czernak, only one solid piece of evidence linked Dave Kresten to Emily's disappearance. The day she disappeared—the day of the snowstorm—Dave used his tow truck to pull a car out of a ditch on Highway 550 near Ridgway. He had towed the damaged car to a garage in the small town. In his meticulously kept records, investigators found receipt of payment for the towing service. What they didn't find was any reason for Dave to be on that road. He claimed to have been dropping off parts in Ouray, but that story couldn't be confirmed. Worse for him, everyone who knew him swore he hated leaving his shop in the middle of the afternoon. He said there was always too much work to do. Still, with only a shred of circumstantial evidence against him, and on the word of a man charged with a string of other crimes, Dave Kresten had been arrested on suspicion of murder.

No real progress had been made in the investigation into Clark Adams's murder. Police had revealed that Adams had been shot with his own gun—the same weapon used to shoot Andrea. It was further revealed that the burned-out car in which his body was found had been stolen. Privately, Kim wondered whether Dave Kresten had shot Adams and, along with Tyler Haas's help, disposed of the body. Tyler Haas was still in the wind. Kim wondered whether he was dead. Dave Kresten, she had concluded, was not a man who tolerated loose ends.

Scott Wentworth wanted a deal. He had no desire to face the public humiliation of a trial. Prosecutors intended to oblige him, but not until after Dave Kresten's murder trial. No one in the criminal justice system wanted to hear insinuations of a deal, sweet or otherwise, trotted out before the jury.

In their last conversation, Detective Czernak had told Kim that Scott still didn't get it. He seemed unable to comprehend the seriousness of the charges against him for his involvement in the car-theft ring and in Emily's death. His ego was built entirely around his self-image as a white-collar guy. His sense of guilt and remorse—to the extent he felt any—began and ended there.

With the final puzzle pieces settling into place, as much as they would in the short run, Kim had decided to leave Montrose. She had promised Detective Czernak she would send him her new address.

And so, with a full and aching heart, she had said goodbye to Christine. She had said goodbye to Lois and her other softball teammates, and also to Dottie Goddard. She and Andrea had spoken a few times, conversations mainly involving the house, which Andrea intended to return to once she was fully recovered. She suggested the possibility that Kim might come back to Montrose at that time. "I still have a helluva lot to teach you. You get that, don't you?" Andrea said during their last call. Kim laughed and said she did.

Hardest of all, she had said goodbye to Sara. Before leaving, Kim had promised she would call—for any reason. She had likewise promised that she would come back. The last was a promise she was bound to keep, if only for the reason Sara already had guessed. Her maroon Lexus waited for her, locked behind a nondescript beige door in a self-storage bay.

Kim took the flowers from the back seat and walked to the edge of the overlook. She ignored the curious stares shot at her by strangers mingling in the parking area. The last time she had stood here, flowers were strewn everywhere. Now there were none. She placed the roses on top of the wall and gazed into the chasm. Not given to prayer, she was unsure what to do next. She needed to mark the moment.

"I am coming home," she said softly. It was the opening line of one of Emily's poems. She knew then what she needed to do.

She silently recited the lines she had memorized, heedless of the tears streaming down her face. In the end, she did pray. She prayed Emily had found her way home.

When she finished, she turned and gazed up the canyon, at the mountain that she could barely see from this vantage point, standing at its base. Then she went to her car and drove up the mountain.

ACKNOWLEDGMENTS

I would like to extend special thanks to everyone at Girl Friday Productions who has been involved with this book. It wouldn't have happened without you! Thanks also to Carol Martin, Pauline Casey, Georgiann Sanborn, Kelley O'Reilly, Shari Dagg, Chris Lehnertz, Kate Shea, and Sue Cobb, for all the shared escapades and for being willing readers; to Sue Lenski and Katherine Powell, for your insights and encouragement; to Barbara Gallivan and Eleanor McDuffie, for always being in my corner; and finally, simple heartfelt thanks to the Lewises: Pam, Jim, and Sharon.

AN EXCERPT FROM THE
NEXT BOOK IN THE
COLORADO SKIES SERIES

HALF-TOLD TRUTHS

PROLOGUE

How silly it had been to worry.

She could admit it now, no longer afraid. Her daughter didn't hate her. Her little girl didn't hate this cabin, built in the shadow of the San Juan Mountains. Her ex-husband had fought this visit to the point where she hadn't been sure he would put their child on the plane this morning. But Jesse was here now, and nothing else mattered.

Late in the afternoon, the girl's chatter mixed with sunshine spilling in through the cabin's screen door. "Mom, tell me again. How big is the swimming pool at Glenwood Springs? Is it the biggest swimming pool in Colorado?"

"I think so, honey. We'll ask a lifeguard when we're there tomorrow."

The aroma of grilled toast and melted cheese lingered in the air. Only cutoff bread crusts and a few asparagus spears remained on the child's plate. The woman's dinner of vegetables and rice lay untouched. Her stomach knots had untied since she picked up her daughter at Durango's airport earlier that day, but not enough for her to feel ready to eat. All she wanted was to gaze in wonder at this beautiful child. Six months was too much of Jesse's life to have slipped by without having seen her. Eight years old now, her tiny girl face still showed through leaner, more mature features. The woman ached for the days she had missed, days that, nearly seamlessly, had left their mark. She wanted to spin the wheel of time back and undo choices she had made years earlier. Though, what could she have done differently? When their marriage ended, her ex had wielded his father's money and power to yank Jesse away to what he laughably called a "richer, more stable" life in LA.

"Mom, where did you and Dad live when I was little?"

"Paonia. Paonia, Colorado."

"Right. Maybe we could go back there, and Dad could come too."

"Sweetie, your dad's married to Chloe now."

"I know. But Chloe says she's going to be very busy when the baby comes. I think she's going to be too busy for me *and* Dad."

The little girl with straight blond hair and her mother's unmistakable gray eyes prattled on, leaping across subjects. She talked about her best friend, Wanda, and the five puppies born to a neighbor's dog. One puppy never stayed on the blanket and was always getting lost. Jesse said she could find it every time. The woman drifted into a daydream of Jesse growing up in Colorado, an adventuresome dog at her side. The bucolic image was cracked by the piercing ring of the phone.

A chill ran down her spine. She didn't move.

A second jingle followed.

"Aren't you going to get that?" Jesse said.

By the third ring, the woman was on her feet. She collected plates and scraped food scraps into the garbage pail.

"It could be Dad," Jesse said.

"We'll call him later. I don't want to talk to anyone right now."

She turned on the tap and frantically scrubbed plates. She told herself the caller could be anyone, a wrong number, even. But she didn't believe it. By the time she set the pair of dishes in the plastic drain to dry, the ringing had stopped.

"Sometimes Chloe doesn't answer her phone. But she turns it off. It never makes a racket," Jesse said.

The woman wanted to put her head down. She wanted to weep and scream at the same time. She loved this place, but right now, she wanted to be anywhere but here, a thousand miles in any direction with her only daughter at her side. "What do you say we go for a walk?" she said, mustering a cheery voice.

"I don't want to," the girl said, abruptly turning stubborn.

"I've told you about the doe and fawn I sometimes see, haven't I?"

"I said I don't want to go!"

The air crackled with heat after the child's shout faded away.

"I want to watch TV," Jesse said. "How can you possibly not have a TV?"

The woman counted to five while she drew a calming breath. The cabin housed a small library of middle-grade books and several board games. There was ice cream in the freezer for hot fudge sundaes later. She saw her yoga mat rolled up in the corner and the sketch pad she had nearly filled, and understood she had chosen to make this her home but there was no reason on earth why she ought to expect Jesse to make the same choice. She hadn't yet found the words to woo her daughter back to her when she heard the low throttle of a truck engine.

"Sweetie, come with me," she said urgently.

"What's wrong, Mom?"

The woman grabbed the child's hand and hurried her into a back bedroom. She sat her on the bed and looked deeply into her daughter's eyes. "Listen to me. Everything's going to be all right. I have to go out for a little while. I won't be long, I promise."

"But, Mom! I can't stay by myself."

The mother pressed a finger to Jesse's lips. "Please, do this for me. I'll be right back. Don't say a word. Just don't say a word."

Tears formed in the girl's eyes, but she nodded.

—

The woman came streaking out of the cabin before he pulled the truck to a stop. There was something wild about the way she looked, something frightened. It told him exactly what he wanted to know. She had heard the phone ringing and ignored it.

"Get in," he said through the lowered window.

She scurried around to the passenger door.

He cast a long look at the cabin and wondered if there was someone inside. It was a violation of their arrangement for her to have visitors. Lucky for her, he was in too much of a hurry to bother searching the place.

He put the truck in reverse and slammed the accelerator.

"So you've stopped taking my calls now?" he said.

"I was outside. I didn't get to the phone in time. Besides, I thought you were leaving for Salt Lake today."

He kept his eyes fixed straight ahead, to where the dirt road began to rise. They were in the middle of nowhere, on ranchland that had been in his family for generations. His land. His rules. "You're a lousy liar. Anyone ever tell you that?"

The truck bounced over ruts. Once they cleared the rise, the big house came into view. He parked at the back. She got out when he did. They went inside through the patio door.

He paused in the den to pour himself a Scotch. She stood nearby, waiting. Ordinarily he offered her a glass of wine. Tonight he'd given her goddamned chauffeur service instead.

"Let's go," he said, finishing the whiskey.

He strode down the long hallway. She followed. Once inside the bedroom, he flipped on the overhead light and loosened his belt. She moved toward the bed with an air of resignation that said she only wanted to get this over with.

"Stop!" he said.

She did, standing a few paces away. Her absent gaze infuriated him. She needed a lesson.

"Stand underneath the light," he said.

"What?"

"You heard me."

Brow furrowed, she moved to the spot.

"Take off your clothes. Do it slowly."

"You want me to strip?"

"Just do as I say," he said, enjoying this new twist.

She stared at him without blinking. He knew he was a good-looking guy and that this arrangement, including the sex, suited her too. He didn't know what the hell her problem was tonight. He was on the verge of becoming seriously annoyed when she reached for the bottom of her shirt. In one motion, she pulled it over her head. One look at her taut belly and full breasts, and his breath caught. This was some kind of new fun.

She started to undo her jeans. She had the zipper halfway down before she yanked it up again. "This is bullshit," she said. "I've done everything you've asked. But not this." She picked up her shirt. Before he could react, she was out the door.

He staggered after her. "You little—"

Bitch, he would have said. By the time he caught up with her, he'd lost interest in saying anything. He grabbed her and tried dragging her back to the bedroom. She wrenched away, stumbling toward the den. He bulldozed past her. Once in front, he seized her by the shoulders and shook her violently, causing her to trip and fall. He dropped on top of her.

"It's just like all the other times," he said as he pinned her arms with his knees. "Just like all the other times."

He didn't know his hands were around her neck until much later, when he moved and she didn't.

CHAPTER 1

The face in the crowd shouldn't have been there.

Kim Jackson wasted time she didn't have riveted to the sight of a man whose clean-shaven, angular face looked familiar. Too late, she caught him looking at her.

His eyes widened. He opened his mouth and shouted at the same time as a train whistle blew, obliterating the sound of his voice. Betraying nothing, she turned and walked away. The image of a tall Anglo man dressed casually in shorts and a T-shirt, framed by the wooden facade of the Durango & Silverton Railway depot, stuck with her. A pretty brunette teen stood next to him. Father and daughter were surrounded by a sea of disembarking passengers, flocking into town.

Kim Jackson hurried along Durango's main street. She weaved around tourists slowing to window-shop at a Western hat store and at the Rocky Mountain Chocolate Factory next door. Beyond the row of shops, a crowd congregated at the curb. She joined the throng and kept moving, edging in front of a tall couple, counting on their hefty bodies to shield her slender one from view. Furtively, she glanced back. Anthony Yeager was closing the distance.

The light changed, and she started running.

A voice she once knew called her name. She told herself not to look back, but she did anyway. Anthony Yeager, at something over six feet, had his arms stretched above his head, holding his phone. He was taking a picture. Of her.

She stuck close to doorways in hopes of making herself a smaller target. Pedestrians obstructed her path, along with bicycles chained to trees and dogs at the end of leashes. Main Avenue was the heart of Durango's tourist center. On a summer afternoon, the art galleries and shops drew a constant crowd. Kim raced past a kiosk advertising white-water adventures. Down the street, she passed tents hanging in the window of an outdoor equipment store. She ran as if her life depended on it, because it did, even though Anthony Yeager would never dream of harming her.

But Durango was her town, and she knew things about it he didn't. At a brewpub, she veered in from the sidewalk. With a terse apology to the hostess and a claim to be late meeting friends, she cut through the dining room to the garden patio at the rear. From there, she beat a hasty exit to the alley, turned left, and kept running.

At the end of the block, she darted right. She took her chances that he wasn't there, because if he was, there was no hope of evading him now. The commercial district lay behind her. A quiet neighborhood lay ahead. Breathing hard, she kept running. In the stillness of the summer day, she strained to hear his voice, the name on his lips. All she heard was her own ragged breathing. When she reached the next corner, she doubled over, hands on her knees, shirt drenched with perspiration in the arid air.

She hadn't yet caught her breath when she pulled herself upright, furious. Twenty-nine years old, born and bred in Chicago, she had never done a thing wrong in her life, and here she was, running like a common thief down the street.

Her parents were dead. She didn't know why she was thinking of them now, especially since she had cut off all ties with her past, including giving up the name they gave her. The move had been working brilliantly until a few minutes ago. Then a man she knew in another life got off a train ride into the San Juan Mountains and threatened to destroy everything she had worked to create.

She turned and looked behind her. A banged-up Jeep was approaching at a snail's pace. An SUV loaded with kayaks followed it. Otherwise, the street was deserted. She took little consolation in having eluded Yeager. Worse things could still happen, she reminded herself. The phrase had become her motto, unfortunately not soon enough. Too many worse things already had happened by the time she'd properly learned the lesson.

She crossed the street and walked to a blue bungalow, the second house in from the corner. The door hadn't latched behind her when a different door swung wide on the left wall. Lena Fallon wheeled out from her private quarters into what had once been the home's living room. No living to speak of went on there any longer.

"What are you doing here? Can't you remember anything? You're supposed to use the back door," Lena said.

Kim smiled, relieved on one count. House rules no longer applied. "Hello, Lena. How are you this afternoon?"

"How am I—what?" Lena's voice rose with the question. She demanded, and ordinarily received, complete subservience from her staff of one. In the brief time Kim had been in the thirty-nine-year-old paraplegic's employ, this marked the first time she had spoken to her as a peer.

"I thought you were working at the bakery. Did you get fired?" Lena said.

Kim felt no compunction to answer. The part-time book-keeping job, for which she was grossly overqualified, was a breeze. Lena didn't know that, and never would.

As she stood there, not speaking, their eyes met by mistake. For one eerie instant, Kim felt hypnotized by the other woman. Lena's gaunt face was rigid, absent of a speck of human kindness. Her stony torso was sculpted beneath a black turtleneck, her skinny legs appendages, welded to a chair. She was an unrelenting dark storm of anger locked in a broken body and broken soul.

Kim sighed. Lena, a pain-in-the-ass ex-cop, was one of the "worse things" that could still happen to her. "I haven't been fired, Lena. I forgot something. I'm in a hurry, that's why I used the front door."

She started toward the stairs. Lena shot forward to block her path. The abrupt movement caused the folder on the woman's lap to fall. White pages scattered fanlike on the wood floor. Kim bent over to gather the loose sheets.

"Get the hell away! I'll get them," Lena said.

Kim, quicker, scooped them up. Curious, she started reading the top page. "Sensory impressions of crime victims are notoriously unreliable. Studies show . . ."

"Did you write this?" she said.

Lena snatched the pages away from her. "That's none of your damn business."

"Right." Kim sidestepped the wheelchair and continued upstairs.

"Get back here! I'm not finished with you," Lena said.

Kim ignored her employer and landlady. Coming off the top step, she grabbed the newel post and flung herself around the corner. In the bedroom, she fell on the bed, wondering why she had lied about forgetting something. She had come here with a short list of things to do: pack and leave. Now she reveled in the knowledge that she was in one of the few places in the world where no one could reach her. Only Lena knew where she was, and she couldn't climb the stairs.

Kim inhaled the musty air clinging to the bedspread. Eyes closed, she saw Anthony Yeager where she usually did: seated in the corner conference room at Blackwell Industries in Chicago. Their gang of seven division managers used to meet regularly on Monday mornings. On clear days, Lake Michigan's choppy gray surface rippled, seemingly forever, across the eastern horizon.

Only four months had passed since she had walked out of that job and out of her life. Anthony Yeager wasn't a man she had known well. His field was marketing; hers, accounting. She remembered listening to him joke with his buddies about weekend golf games and brag about his daughter's heroics on the high school track team before their meetings began. Meanwhile, she had sat by quietly, immersed in numbers, waiting for a different man to arrive, her and Anthony's boss, Stephen Bender.

The past glistened as though she were viewing it through an icy-clear prism. It might as well have been someone else's life she was looking at. In a way, it was. Stephen Bender had been her mentor, and she, his protégé. Or so she had thought, up until the day he'd laughed in her face and told her one thing she already knew, that he had committed corporate fraud—and one thing she didn't, that he was responsible for the murder of a junior accountant who worked for her, the man who'd discovered the fraud. That should have been the worst, but it wasn't. He went on to tell her that he'd framed her for both crimes.

Kim rolled over. Bright sunlight filtered in through pale-yellow curtains fluttering at the open window. Her cheek brushed the satin bedspread patterned in swirls of beige, green, and pink, meant to resemble something floral. The bedspread bridged the color of the carpet, green, and the single chair in the room, pink. Besides the bed and chair, she had a chest of drawers, a closet, and a tiny bathroom. The accommodations, however sufficient, were a far cry from the modern one-bedroom apartment she had left behind in Chicago.

Seconds ticked by. "Go," she whispered. Meaning to her car parked in the garage and to another town to start over. Not a tourist town, a place where no one from her past would ever step foot. She tried to imagine it. All she saw were tumbleweeds and boarded-up buildings. A ghost town. A perfect place for a woman who had become a ghost.

Inertia held her there, and something else—a pang of grief. With the clock still ticking, she realized the grief was for more than what she had lost. It was for what she was about to lose. If she left now, there would be no coming back. She weighed her choices and realized she didn't need to leave Durango immediately. There would be time to make that decision later. Anthony Yeager did not know exactly where she was. He wasn't, at this moment, rallying troops to assist in her capture as though he were a bounty hunter and she his elusive prey. She drew the first deep breath she had taken since laying eyes on Yeager and stood up.

She changed out of her white shirt into a green blouse. She grabbed a backpack, thrust her cap and sunglasses inside, and bounded down the stairs. "Found what I needed," she said to Lena, who remained parked in the center of the room, emanating silent fury.

"You're lying!"

Yes, she was, Kim thought, escaping into a sunny afternoon through the same off-limits front door.

CPSIA information can be obtained
at www.ICGtesting.com
Printed in the USA
BVHW030216150921
616785BV00014B/143

9 781737 297703